RETURN TO YOU

JENNIFER MILLIKIN
LEIA STONE

To our readers.

Trigger Warning

This book has themes/thoughts of abortion. Nothing graphic.

Chapter 1

Autumn

I JUDGE airplane flights on a drink scale. The drinks being alcoholic beverages, and the scale being how many I should have to get me through the terrifying experience of hurtling through the sky in a metal tube.

I've checked the weather and I know what the skies have in store for me on my trip from New York City to Phoenix. If only I could use radar to see what's in store for me once I land. Going back home to the small town of Sedona that I left ten years ago doesn't exactly fill me with excitement.

The flight-attendant on this flight has a kind, lopsided smile, and the second my backside is firmly planted in my first-class seat, I request a glass of wine from her. So far, it's a one wine glass kinda flight.

That's bound to change though, especially with the shitstorm of a day I've had.

I smile gratefully when she hands me the dark red liquid. I inhale before taking a sip. I'm not one of *those* people, the wine connoisseur with the discerning palate. It's just I find the scent of the wine comforting. It's my airplane ritual, a signal to my brain that it's time to relax. Wine and I are old friends.

My shoulders are the first to relax, inching down from my ears, followed by the unraveling of the muscles in my upper back. Passengers board as I unwind, and I watch them casually, my gaze flickering away if our eyes happen to meet. I've always feared prolonged eye contact with strangers. Or … maybe not *always*. Just since *then*. I fear that someday a person sensitive to the sins of others will look at me and *know*. The way an animal senses an earthquake before it happens, they will see in my soul the dark stain of shame.

Shame stains all of us, but not everybody nurtures it the way I do. I could let it go, but it would take with it more than just its smudge. It would take *him*, and I'm not sure I can do that.

I chug the rest of my glass, but promise myself to wait until we're in the air to order another. I can't show up and be drunk in front of my poor sick mother. Her life is hard enough as it is. There's no way I'm going to pile my troubles onto her. She needs a doting, thoughtful daughter, and that's exactly what she's going to get.

I'm so busy thinking of my mother that I barely register the woman who's had one too many facelifts until she nestles in across from me. She clutches her tiny Pomeranian like a life raft, her fingers decorated with a diamond ring on each finger. We share a quick glance before I turn away.

I don't belong up here in first-class. I make good money, but spending it on a fancy ride from the east coast to the desert feels wasteful. I've made this same trek a dozen times since I moved to Manhattan, but I've always flown coach. Until now … until my mom called and asked me to move home. Then I dropped everything: my job, my apartment, and two grand on a last-minute airplane ticket.

My gaze stays firmly fixed out the window. The sky darkens, but the night steadily lights up. It's mostly white-yellow, the light from apartments, but there are neons too. And tonight, the top of the Empire State Building is purple.

I shift forward in my seat as the plane backs away from the gate. We taxi to the runway, join the line of other planes waiting their turn, then pick up speed. Nerves claw at my gut as I think of what I'm leaving behind, what I'm going home to—the unknowns that hide in every corner of my old town like hidden shadows waiting to pull me under.

Fuck this day.

My fingers press into the cold window, the heat from my skin leaving behind slick marks, as I whisper goodbye to the city I spent six years calling home.

The plane lifts off and the feeling of weightlessness makes me gasp. The sprawling city twinkles at an awkward angle as we ascend. When I first came here, twenty-two years old and eager, this place smelled like hope and possibility. Now I know better. No matter how good something seems in the beginning, it cannot possibly maintain its luster. Eventually, everything fades.

"FOLKS, we have touched down in Phoenix. Current temperature is eighty-six degrees, and unfortunately, it's only five A.M. So, you can expect that number to increase."

The pilot continues to thank us for choosing the airline, but it's drowned out by the collective moan of passengers after hearing the early morning temperature.

The heat doesn't bother me. Where I'm headed, two hours north of the valley, it'll be twenty degrees cooler. But, considering what's waiting for me there, it's not an even tradeoff.

I gather my purse and slip from the plush seat when

it's my turn, leaving behind the complimentary blanket and headphones.

Not gonna lie, first class was amazing, but my wallet can't afford to make a habit out of it. Now that I'm jobless, I'll need to go on a budget until I can find something else.

As I slip past sluggish travelers wheeling heavy carry-ons, I notice their zombie-like appearance. I've always been a morning person, trained to function on little sleep, so the early hour isn't a problem for me. A few hours of sleep on the plane is enough to carry me through until I can grab a nap later. The energy zinging through me now has nothing to do with sleep. Despite the reason I've come back, I'm excited to see my mom.

The thought has me moving faster, propelling me around a family wearing brightly-colored Hawaiian shirts. I sneak a peek at them as I pass, and they all look tired, mildly sunburned, and a little depressed.

I see my mom as soon as I round the corner. She stands only a few feet beyond security. Any closer and the TSA employee would probably ask her to take a few steps back.

A grin stretches my face. She looks good. Skinnier than I imagined, but healthy. Bits of silvery gray weave through her shoulder-length brown hair, showing me what I will one day look like. I don't even allow the other half of my DNA into the equation. I think of my dad as a donor, and that's it. He walked out on my mom before my first birthday, so he doesn't deserve more than a fleeting thought.

The closer I get to her, the more I take in. I see it now … the way her t-shirt hangs limply on her body, and then I realize she's in a long-sleeve and it's hot out. There are deep dark bruises on her legs and my mouth goes dry. I don't mean for my smile to falter, but it does, and like a reflection in a mirror, her grin falls a fraction too.

The cancer has returned. It has hit her not once, not twice, but three fucking times.

Who the hell gets cancer three times? It's not fair, but I can't go down that road right now or I'll end up cursing God in the middle of this airport.

The odds aren't good for her … but I am here now and I'll be damned if cancer is going to take my mother from me.

Maybe my presence will be the difference. During her first two diagnoses, she'd told me to stay in New York and keep working. I'd argued, but my mom is stubborn and firm. I'd have better luck arguing with a brick wall. So, I listened. I also knew she needed my help financially, even though she didn't say it. The best way for me to help was to stay at my job and keep climbing, making sure those paychecks came in and got bigger along the way. I sent her a chunk of money each month and she accepted it gratefully.

But this time, when she called to tell me about the current diagnosis, she asked me to come home. She didn't tell me to stay put like she had before. She just told me she'd pick me up at the airport.

That's how I knew it was bad.

I won't let her see my fear now. I won't make her console me, not when her energy is needed so badly on the inside. I'm here now, and I will add all my strength to this fight.

Walking the last few feet past the TSA employee standing like a sentry, I pass the sign that reads *No re-entry beyond this point* and straight into my mother's open arms.

She is smaller, and it feels like a role reversal. I am, for the very first time, bigger than her.

But she still smells like my mom. Her lemon and lavender scent sinks into me, silently providing me comfort. My throat clenches with emotion but I clear it and keep my shit together.

She pulls back, searching my face. Concern pulls at her eyes, deepening the lines. "Did you get any sleep on the plane?"

"A little."

"How many wines?"

A smile tugs up one corner of my mouth. "It was a two-wine flight."

"No turbulence, then?"

Other than the turbulence of leaving my career behind to go and care for my sick mother?

I shake my head. "Not really." I'd been grateful for the smooth skies during the flight, but I had the second glass of wine because I couldn't shake my thoughts of *him*.

No matter how hard I try, memories of Owen Miller are on a tether, connected to me, and the slightest tug brings them bounding back.

I want to avoid him. It shouldn't be too hard, not in a town like Sedona. There are enough tourists, enough vacationers, and as long as I avoid the places frequented by locals, I won't be likely to run into him.

None of that will work though. He broke my heart, I broke his, and we walked away from the mangled remains of a love that had burned so bright it was blinding.

After what we went through, I should avoid him at all costs.

Too bad he's my mother's fucking oncologist.

That was karma giving me a big old kick in the ass.

Thanks, universe.

My mom knows I'm thinking about him. She can see it in my eyes, and I can see it in the pitying look on her face

Reaching out, she wraps an arm around my shoulder and steers me toward the elevator bank. "It'll be okay, sweetheart."

I'm not sure if she's referring to her cancer, or me being forced to have Owen Miller in my life again.

"Sure, Mom," I agree quickly, slipping my arm around her waist and dragging my bag behind me. My palm rests on her hipbone and I swallow the lump in my throat.

"Baggage claim?" she asks when we reach the elevators, even though she has already pressed the button.

I nod, letting my head tip to the side so I can lay it on her shoulder. My mom has different plans though. She lets go of my shoulders and takes a big step away from me. Her eyes light up, mischievous.

"Guess," she says, raising her eyebrows up and down twice.

Despite my anxiety, my fear and my sadness, I grin. Quickly I glance around at the numbers above the elevator doors. "Six," I say.

"One," she counters, her eyes on the small white number.

We've played this game as long as I can remember. Whoever guesses which elevator will open, or the number closest to it, gets a prize. When I was little, it was a stop for a donut before starting the long drive home from the airport. After I turned sixteen, it was who had to be the driver.

We wait, expectant, and then a *ding* fills the air. Our eyes swing toward the sound. Elevator five.

Mom makes a face. "I lost. I'll drive."

"No, I'll drive. I miss driving," I tell her, stepping on first and sticking out my hand to ensure the doors don't start to close before she can get on. I can't believe she has even made the two-hour drive from Sedona to Phoenix in the first place.

She frowns. "You didn't get much sleep on the plane."

"I got enough," I argue. "A stop for some strong coffee and I'll be good to go."

She looks tired. There is no way I am making her drive.

Mom relents, and instead of relief I feel sadness. The mom I've known my whole life would insist on being the driver. She'd dig in her heels and order me to get in the car.

Not anymore.

After we collect my bags, I wheel them to her car and get in the driver seat. I turn on the air conditioning, but after fifteen minutes my mom reaches into the backseat and grabs a sweatshirt. When she pulls it on, I turn down the air with a frown.

"Nonsense," she argues, "that's why I'm putting this on."

"I was getting cold too," I lie. Does she not have enough fat on her bones to keep her warm? The thought completely freaks me out and my knuckles go white on the steering wheel.

I stop for coffee, ordering a double espresso for me, a tall morning blend for mom, and two breakfast sandwiches. The two-hour drive isn't bad, but I want to get on the road before rush hour traffic, so I shoot the espresso as if it's tequila and we keep going. In between chatting, we eat our breakfast sandwiches as I point the car north. For the next ninety minutes, I stay on the same interstate, watching the scenery switch from bustling city, to suburbs, to saguaros, to scrubby brush. Beside me, my sweet mom sleeps against the glass window.

I alternate between driving and glancing at her. My mom. My protector, encourager, and teacher. I cannot live without her.

Owen has to save her.

Chapter 2

Owen

I NEVER KNEW what tired meant until I became a doctor. I imagine it's like having two newborns on opposite sleep schedules. Not that I would know from experience.

It's not really the hours I spend at the hospital that exhaust me. I'm fine on my feet for extended periods of time. It's the emotional exhaustion I'm referring to.

Working in oncology will do that to you. Having patients die regularly hardens your soul.

Especially this morning. I wish with all my strength that my ten o'clock appointment wasn't with Faith Cummings.

In med school, I'd heard of patients who became like family. But what about people who were like family and then became patients? Med school didn't have a chapter on that one.

I was an intern the first time Faith was diagnosed. The second time, I was a resident. This time, I'm her doctor. As my career developed, so did Faith's cancer. The maudlin parallel isn't lost on me.

I'm not stopping at oncologist though. I'm in a surgical fellowship, and when it's over I'll be a surgical oncologist.

Which basically means I can remove tumors from patients here in Sedona instead of sending them down to Phoenix. Tumors have always fascinated me. When you resect the pink healthy tissue, there it is, like a wadded piece of gum, so clearly alien to its surroundings.

Before I can head into Faith's exam room, I need food and coffee. I have to fuel up before I see her, because each appointment with her leaves me emotionally drained. It's not the fact that she looks so much like her daughter, a daughter who was simultaneously the great love and complete destroyer of my life—okay, it's a bit that—but mostly it's the fact that Faith is like a second mother to me and the pressure to save her life is so heavy … at times it crushes me.

"Hey, Theresa." I stop in front of the stout brown-haired woman sitting behind the nurses' desk. She looks up slowly from the computer, her chin leading the way and her eyes the last part of her face to rise.

"What's up, Doc?"

I want to make a joke about Bugs Bunny, but I don't dare. Theresa is no-nonsense. To be honest, she scares me a little. But what she lacks in warmth, she makes up for in ability. Nothing shakes her. If I needed medical care, I'd request Theresa as my nurse any day.

My gaze shoots down the hall, then back to Theresa's cool expression. "I'm mentally preparing for Faith Cummings' appointment."

At the mention of Faith, warmth trickles into Theresa's chocolate-brown eyes. Theresa loves her work, but she especially loves Faith. After all the years Faith has been coming here, they've formed a friendship.

She leans forward, her floral printed scrub top crinkling against the edge of the desk. "Don't tell anybody, but, about ten minutes ago, I put homemade cinnamon rolls in the staff room." Her tone is hushed when she says the words *homemade cinnamon rolls*. My palms meet in front of my chest, pushing together as if in prayer while I try to contain my drool. "Thank you," I mouth. Theresa is an amazing nurse but an even better baker.

She sits back in her chair and focuses on whatever she was doing at the computer, as if I never stopped by.

I leave, my steps quickened by the smell and taste of sweet cinnamon even though I'm not there yet. Funny how taste and smell can be burned into your memory. There's a certain someone living in Manhattan whose fault it is that I can still smell cucumber melon scented lotion without needing to be anywhere near it. But I don't think about that. About her. Those thoughts aren't allowed anywhere near me, because if I let them in, they won't stop. Like an angry mob at the closed gates of a kingdom, they will pound at my walls until they break in. Focusing on the taste of cinnamon rolls is much, much safer for the well-being of my heart.

I'm the third person to help myself to the pastry. There are only twelve in total, and the remaining nine will be gone in minutes. Thank God Theresa likes me. If she hadn't, she wouldn't have said a word to me.

If I were Ace, for example, Theresa would've kept her mouth shut. She doesn't like my best friend. She thinks he's a player, and, to be fair, she's right. It took getting his heart smashed just one time for Ace Drakos to become a self-titled bachelor for life. It's made for some drama around the hospital, but he makes it clear from the outset what he's about. Still, it doesn't seem to stop some of the women from giving him dirty looks. Or keeping delicious homemade pastries a secret from him.

I'm the nice guy, the good cop, the one you give secret pastries to.

As I finish my roll, I down the contents of a too-hot cup of coffee and leave the staff room with a sweet yet slightly burnt taste on my tongue.

Time to see Faith.

"HOW'S MY FAVORITE PATIENT?" I beam as I step into

the room. I say that to everyone, but she's the only one I mean it with.

"Hey there." Faith smiles as she speaks. For someone so sick, Faith never stops appearing happy. Once, during her second battle, I'd complimented her upbeat attitude. She told me joy is a choice and she'd choose it any chance she got.

I think of her words frequently, but I haven't fully followed her advice. In my job, even if there is more good than bad, the losses are so heavy, they often outweigh the wins. Sometimes I regret my choice to go into oncology. It's a constant balance beam of saving people and watching them die.

"Good morning, Faith." I return her smile and close the door behind me. "How are you feeling?"

"Good as new," she responds, cheerful.

To be honest, she *does* look peppier than the last time I saw her. Her eyes are twinkling. Her legs, dangling from the examination table, softly bump against it.

She's excited about something.

It makes me happy to know something has excited her. The current state of Faith's world is anything but happy. I find myself wondering what it could be, but try to keep a distance emotionally during our appointments.

"Let's get this exam underway." It will be quick. A cursory exam before chemo can begin in a few days. I check her lymph nodes and glance for the tenth time at her bloodwork. "Everything looks good to start chemo, Faith."

She's a veteran to what some of my patients call "the poison drip;" she simply nods her head, fearless.

I'm busy checking her blood pressure when she says, "I have a question for you. A hypothetical question."

With my feet firmly planted on the ground, I push back, and the stool I'm sitting on rolls a foot away. "What's up?" I ask, looking up at her.

Please don't ask me what percentage chance I think she has to go into remission this time. I hated the question, and I couldn't do it with her. It made me feel like I was playing God. Even a skilled doctor and mathematician can never get that question one hundred percent right. The fact that her cancer is back again for a third time is not good.

"If a person knew something that might make another person feel a certain way, should they tell them about that something?" Faith raises an eyebrow.

My insides tighten. It's ridiculous. We haven't talked about Autumn in a long time, and yet I know it's about her. Faith is being sneaky, which isn't her normal demeanor. I swallow hard, readying myself to hear bad news. *Autumn's getting married. Autumn's pregnant. Autumn anything.* The ever-present pain stabs at my heart as I imagine what Faith is about to say. My memory kicks in, the angry mob bangs on the gate, and I see Autumn in my mind.

There she is, the girl who owns every piece of my younger self.

The girl who haunts my nights, my days, and every relationship I've tried to have since her.

The girl who massacred my heart and left me for dead.

I push past the turmoil inside and ask, "This *something* you refer to ... will it make the person feel bad? Or good?"

Faith purses her lips and tucks her hair behind her ear. "Definitely bad. But also, maybe good?"

"Maybe good?" I ask, my eyebrows raised. Maybe it's not about Autumn after all. I can't imagine there's anything Faith would know about Autumn that would make me feel *maybe good*. "I suppose those are pretty decent odds. I'd want to know. Hypothetically speaking, of course." I wink at Faith, the vise-like grip on my stomach loosening.

"Autumn's home."

No tightening in my core now. Just a feeling like my bones have turned to jelly and they're undulating inside me like ribbons in the wind. Those two words send me over the edge.

"Owen?" Faith's forehead leans closer, urging me to speak.

My throat is dry but I find words. "For how long?"

Faith looks away. She shrugs. "I don't know. She's moved back for now. Someone took over her lease on her apartment in the city. I suppose it depends on how all this"—she gestures to the room around us —"goes."

Holy fucking shit. Autumn Cummings was back home. And not like in the past when she came back just for a weekend, in which case I could hole up inside to make sure I didn't run into her. She was *back*. I realize that she's come back to care for her mother, which means Faith must be thinking this is her last fight.

"It's going to work, Faith," I assure her, remembering that I'm the doctor here and need to comfort my patient. I don't know that, of course. I don't have a crystal ball, or a magic wand. All I have is an ardent desire for a favorable outcome.

Faith extends a hand between us, and I catch it.

"Of course it will," she says, squeezing my hand gently before she lets me go.

The curiosity is killing me. I have to ask. "How is she?"

I regret it the second I say it. I shouldn't show interest, it will only encourage Faith. We made a pact ten years ago: we don't talk about Autumn. Now that pact is broken and I want to know everything.

"She flew in on a redeye early this morning. So, right now she's tired. But I bet she'd be up for a visitor later this afternoon." Faith's face looks hopeful.

Is this woman trying to kill me? I can't see Autumn. No way. She should know better than to encourage us to get together … but of course she doesn't. She doesn't know the hell I walked through with her daughter. Neither of us made it out of that fully alive.

My head shakes back and forth. An automatic response. "She doesn't want to see me, Faith."

I don't want to see her either, but because Faith doesn't know why we broke up, only that it was ugly, so I am trying to play it cool.

Faith lowers herself from the exam table and reaches for her purse, winding it over her shoulder. "Perhaps before I die one of you will finally tell me what happened between you two." There's an undercurrent of irritation in her tone.

My only response is a nervous chuckle. If Autumn hasn't told her mother yet, it means she doesn't want her to know. And after everything that happened, I can at least respect that.

"That's what I figured you'd do," Faith says tartly, and the laugh dies in my throat.

Through my lab coat I feel the warmth of her palm, and I turn toward it. Since I was fifteen Faith has been like a mother to me. My own mom left me and my dad when I was five, and when Autumn and I became friends, Faith welcomed me into her home. Soon I became Autumn's boyfriend. Faith treated me like a member of the family. We had family meals together, she listened to me gripe about the guys on the soccer team, and I knew I could go to her with anything. I don't know what would've happened to me without Faith's love and guidance. I was a flailing teenager, a good kid at my core, but my heart had been broken by the rejection of my own mother. Faith's presence and inherent mothering filled in the cracks in my heart.

Autumn may be in pain, knowing this is her mother's third dance with the devil that is cancer, but she doesn't have the market cornered. I'm hurting too.

Faith looks at me, hope plain on her face. "So, will you come by for dinner?"

Fuck no. Willingly walk into the lion's den and see the woman who owned the scars on my heart?

No way.

"Tonight?" I ask nervously. Shit, it's hard to deny this sweet woman.

She nods. Dinner on Monday has become a ritual of ours, and I don't have anything planned tonight because I assume I will be eating at her place. It started when she beat cancer the first time. I took her out for a celebratory dinner, and while we were at the restaurant, she'd commented on how nice it was to spend time with me away from her health issues. We'd decided then that we'd make it a weekly occurrence, and aside from illness and the odd vacation, we haven't missed a Monday. Last month I started mowing her lawns on Sunday. It was safe to say that if Autumn was living at her mom's, I wouldn't be able to avoid her without being rude to Faith, and that I would never do.

I sigh. "I don't know, Faith. I've got a lot of work to catch up on."

Please, God, let me stay away. Let me resist the hold that Autumn has over my life.

A disappointed look creeps into her eyes, but she's quick to tuck it back.

Her upset makes me feel the need to amend my statement. "For now, at least. Give me a few days to catch up on work and I'll see if I can stop by."

A few days to think up an excuse on why I could never go over to her house again was more like it. I could avoid Autumn forever, right? I'd just hire a private investigator to map her schedule and favorite stores and then I'd steer clear of them...

The strap on Faith's purse slips down her arm and she hoists it back up into place. "You're going to see her sooner or later. Might as well rip the Band-Aid off." She winks at me as she says it.

Busted. Faith always has a way of reading my thoughts. She knows this isn't about work.

My head tips back in silent laughter. "I'll keep that in mind." I watch her walk to the door. "See you soon," I say with a wave.

"*Soon* being the operative word, Owen." She gives me a motherly look, the kind with affection and warning rolled into one.

"Yes, ma'am." I couldn't deny that woman her happiness, especially since the cancer was back. I'd eventually have to force myself to see the girl who demolished my heart and then go home and lick my wounds like any respectable man.

She slips through the door and I watch it slide into place, closing with a blunted thunk.

A deep breath escapes my chest. My fingers press into my eyes as images of Autumn parade through my mind.

Young, innocent Autumn the day I met her. Only fifteen.

Not-so-innocent Autumn the day I held her in my arms and we passed the point of no return.

Autumn, tears staining her face, as I said things I can't take back, no matter how much I regret them.

What would it be like to see her now? I have to admit, the idea is exhilarating and terrifying.

Would she turn me away? Invite me in? Throw her arms around me? Smack me across the face?

Excitement presses into the corners of my body. *I could see Autumn again*. Tonight, if I wanted to. In just a few short hours, I can have the reunion I've spent too much time envisioning. For years I thought of what I would say if I ran into her in town, what she would look like…

I pull my phone from my pocket and pull up Autumn's name.

All these years, I've kept the same number. I wanted to make sure she always had a way to reach me in case she needed me. I was a schmuck like that. I liked the pain apparently.

If I kept my number, maybe she has too.

My thumb hovers over the screen, then it drops down. I press her name. It's dialing.

Holy shit.

I actually did it. I was calling her.

I stare at the screen until I hear a faint "Hello" float into the air.

"Uh, hello," I say, bringing the phone to my ear.

What are you doing you idiot? She tore your heart in two and then popped it into the blender. She ghosted you on an epic level after three years together. HANG UP!

The excitement and trepidation bounding through my chest deflates like a popped balloon as I hear the voice say hello again. It's not Autumn. Even after all this time, her voice is burned into my soul.

I push on, because I don't want to hang up on this woman and I don't know what else to do. "May I speak to Autumn please?"

"No Autumn here," the woman answers, then hangs up.

My chin rests on the edge of my phone and I look out at the rest of the room.

She changed her number. She knew we were over. She fully let go.

I was the idiot who kept hope alive.

Chapter 3

Autumn

I'M WOKEN from my nap by a smell that's as odd as it is comforting. Following my nose into the kitchen, I find onions sizzling in a pan. I rarely cook in the city, and now that I'm smelling something so typical of my mom's cooking, I feel homesick despite the fact that I am already home.

My mom stands beside a cutting board, using what looks like all her strength to squeeze a clove of garlic through a press.

"Mom, let me," I say, hurrying forward when she grabs another clove.

She shoots a look of irritation at me but relinquishes the tool. "Two more after that one, then put it all in the pan."

I do as she says, stirring the mixture after I've

followed her instructions. My mouth waters, and I realize I haven't eaten since the breakfast sandwich this morning. My redeye caught up with me and I slept through lunch.

Across the counter, I see two pounds of chicken and more vegetables. "You don't need to make a big dinner for me, Mom. I usually just eat a sandwich or some take-out noodles."

She makes a face. "They don't eat real meals in the big city?"

I stifle a sigh. "They do. You would've seen it first-hand had you accepted my invitations to visit." My words sound harsh, but they are delivered in a soft tone. I didn't come here to expose unhealed wounds.

"I had some things going on, Autumn. You know that."

I nod, staring down at the contents of the pan. But even when she got better, she never visited. Part of me thought it was her way of saying she didn't agree with my decision to move across the entire country even though she begged me to follow my dreams.

"Turn that down, sweetie, or the garlic will burn."

I do as she says. The air in the kitchen is thick with hurt feelings. And my guilt. So much guilt. I should have moved back years ago, after her first diagnosis. What kind of asshole daughter just sends money to their sick mom and thinks that will fix things?

My head hangs with shame as my throat tightens

with emotion. "I should have come back years ago," I say almost to myself.

Mom's arms wrap around me from behind, resting her head on my shoulder. "Stop, honey. Don't beat yourself up. I'm the one who told you not to come home—"

I shake my head. "I shouldn't have listened to you."

"I'm your mother. I raised you to listen to me." She gives me her no-nonsense tone and I can't help but grin.

"But you're not always right."

She pulls me spinning me around to face her. Her eyes are wide, surprised. "What? That's not true. Who told you that?"

I laugh and she pulls me closer, until my cheek is pressed to hers. "I should've come to visit you. I was wrong," she whispers.

I raise one eyebrow. "Can I get that in writing?"

I feel her chuckle, and when she pulls back, she keeps me in her arms. "No, you may not. And you'll never get me to admit to saying it, not even in a court of law."

I smile at her playfulness, and try not to show my surprise. Since when is my mom this lighthearted? Cancer has changed her.

"How was your appointment?" I ask, and at the same time the doorbell rings. "Are you expecting someone?"

Her eyebrows pull together. "Normally, yes. But not

tonight. He told me he couldn't make it."

He?

I follow her out of the kitchen. "Mom, are you dating someone?"

Hell yeah, Mama, get some.

She ignores me, and I steel myself to meet this mystery man. Do I know him? Oh my gosh, what if he was my childhood principal or something weird?

As I'm preparing myself to meet my mom's side piece, she opens the door and I swear everything in time freezes in place. The dust motes in the air, the leaves on the trees, the bees on the flowers, everything stands still.

It's *him*.

Time thaws.

All the air in my lungs escapes.

My body suddenly weighs less; the slightest breeze could carry me away.

"Hi, Faith," Owen says to my mother. His eyes steal over to me and he clears his throat. "Autumn."

His gaze sharpens as it rakes over my body and I suddenly feel like the universe hates me. My hair is in a messy cascade of curls all the way to my back from my nap and I'm wearing fucking sweatpants. My heart races, my chest heaves, I can't breathe. There is nothing in my stomach, and yet somehow it wants to be sick all over the tile floor.

"Owen." Four letters, and I choke on every one of them.

We stare at each other, and everything flows between us. The love, the pain, the accusations, the years apart, they mix into a concoction of strangling intensity.

I'm not sure how much time passes, because I'm stuck, but my mom's voice breaks through.

"Owen, you changed your mind?"

Um … what? Owen is who my mom normally expects? *Why?* And how often?

He glances at me, then back to her. "Uh, no." He holds up a white paper bag. "I forgot to give you your prescription earlier. I guess I was distracted."

She takes the bag from his outstretched hand. "Oh, thank you. I forgot too."

He stands in the threshold, an awkward silence taking over the three of us.

His dark brown hair is slicked back, freshly show-ered by the looks of him, and he's wearing a nice button-down shirt with dark jeans. Fifteen-year-old Owen was handsome, but twenty-eight-year-old Owen is absolutely yummy. I want to kill him. No one should age that well. How dare he stay so handsome and not gain a hundred pounds and be bald.

Mom reaches for his forearm and pulls him into the house. "You might as well stay and eat," she coos, giving him a smile. "I made one of your favorites."

I nearly choke on my spit. One of your favorites? What the hell has been happening while I've been across the country? Are these two bffs and nobody told me? Do they have matching necklaces? A secret handshake? *This motherfucker stole my mom!*

A surge of irritation flows through me.

I pivot and return to the kitchen. I can't even handle this situation right now; my brain is short circuiting. I don't see this man for ten years and he waltzes into my mom's house like he lives here. And I'm in sweats!

In angry haste, I transfer the caramelized onions to a plate, slice the bell peppers and put them in the pan. Once those are cooking, I chop the chicken like I'm murdering it and season it before adding it to a separate pan. I make sure to slam it good and hard so that the entire house knows I'm pissed. I'm heating tortillas when my mom comes in.

She surveys the scene. "I didn't tell you we were having fajitas."

So, she's totally going to ignore the awkwardness of Owen being here? *Awesome.*

I shrug. "Lucky guess." There is a growl to my tone.

How weird would it be if I went to my room and put on a sexy black dress and full makeup? I want Owen to feel the satisfying pain of knowing he would never have me, but considering I look homeless right now, I'm not much of a catch to lose.

She snorts. "Or you still know Owen's favorite foods."

Dammit, Mom, going in for the kill.

I don't say anything. Instead, I get out the sour cream, the guacamole, the cilantro.

"Honey, I know you don't like to talk about him, so that's why I didn't mention—"

"It's fine," I growl. I'm not mad at her, I'm mad at him and I hope she knows that. I made a rule with my mom a long time ago: no talking about Owen. Now that rule is coming back to bite me in the ass.

Reaching out, she squeezes my shoulders. "You want me to ask him to go?"

Yeah, right, and show how much I care he is here in the first place?

No way.

"I'm totally fine." I tip my chin high and blow a stray hair out of my face.

"Alright, well, I'm going to wash up for dinner," my mom says, leaving the kitchen.

This is fine. I can handle this. Everything is fine. Taking a deep breath, I stare up at the ceiling. I knew I was going to see him. But so soon? I'm not sure I'm ready.

"Autumn?"

His voice reaches out, swirling around me like smoke, curling up my legs, my torso, over my shoulders. For three years, my sun rose and set on the owner of that voice. Slowly, I turn toward him, knowing we have to do this.

Owen stands there, arms crossed. It's a defensive stance, but his expression doesn't match. It's hard to describe his expression, except that it's not angry or hateful like I expected.

That was how he looked the last time I saw him and I expected it to be the same.

But now? I see concern. Apprehension. Nervousness.

Too bad I don't feel the same. Too bad he could drop dead right now and I wouldn't even attempt CPR. Ten years ago, Owen stood in my dorm room in Santa Clara and told me exactly what he thought of me. I'd stayed quiet, absorbing everything he said, believing each ugly word. I thought I deserved it.

The worst part? A part of me still believes what he said. It's funny how a person can know something is ridiculous on the outside, but on the inside anything is possible. Emotions can turn something around and make it believable, acceptable. This is how we believe lies about ourselves, even when we know they are lies.

He takes a step into the room. Two more. I watch him like a lion watches her prey.

He pauses a few feet from me. "I—"

I raise a stiff palm and he stops. I realize in that moment that I'm not ready to do this, I'm not sure my heart can go back in time right now. Not with my mother sick and all of my worry on her.

"I don't know what you're going to say, but I don't want to hear it. I don't even understand why you're here." My insides are shaking. My whole body feels like a snow globe violently shaken by a toddler on a sugar high.

The corner of Owen's mouth quirks up, just like it

always did. I hate that he still does that. I hate that I remember it. "Your mom's prescription," he explains.

I push a hand to my hip, willing the shaking to stop. "Do you hand deliver medicine to all your patients, Owen?"

He squeezes his eyes shut, one hand rubbing the back of his neck. "You aren't going to make this easy, are you?" He reopens his eyes and studies me and I see pain there, just behind the eyes. And just like that I'm taken back to that day ... the day that broke us. The day that stained my soul—the sterile room, the smell of antiseptic, the way we held hands so tightly I thought my fingers would break.

Shaking my head to remove thoughts of the past, I turn back to the food, flipping over the chicken. I'm not sure what there is that I have the power to make easy, and I don't want to ask.

I feel it the second he disappears from the room. I'm reaching for three plates and the intensity evaporates.

Well, *good.*

He can go to the living room and wait for dinner. I don't have anything more to say to him right now. Owen Miller doesn't deserve my grace. I am going to make this as hard on him as possible because he made things hard on me ten years ago and payback is a bitch.

But even as I think it, I feel my resolve softening. What we went through ... it tore us both in two and maybe he deserves a little tiny bit of understanding...

"Where is Owen going?" my mother asks, coming back into the kitchen.

Guilt suddenly gnaws at my gut. "I didn't know he left."

"He just walked out the front door, Autumn." My mother looks at me like I've done something wrong.

"Okay." What does she want me to say? It's not my fault he left, though I do feel bad that any guest would feel unwelcome in my mother's home on my account.

She points to the door. "Go get him please."

"What? No." She had no idea what she was asking me to do.

"This is my house and he is a guest. I don't know what you said to make him leave, but I want him here. So, go get him. Now." Her tone is no-nonsense. She is not to be argued with, not that I want to. I want to make her happy, but if she knew what happened between Owen and I, she wouldn't ask this of me. "Autumn, I raised you better than this."

Dammit, that got me.

I put the plates on the counter and hurry out of the house, making it outside just in time to catch Owen climbing into his car. He sees me and pauses, one leg in and one leg out. He leans one arm on the top of the doorframe, the other on the roof. He doesn't say a word, just looks at me and waits for me to speak. Smart man.

"Where are you going?" The attitude in my tone is heavy. I want to pick up a handful of dirt and throw it in his face, or egg his car, or something immature that I never got to do when I was eighteen.

"It's highly likely my dinner is poisoned. I don't think I should stay."

I have to hold back a chuckle. Owen always had a good sense of humor, but I'm not in the mood. I stare at him for a second, then decide to play nice, for my mother's sake, because she raised a good hostess. I pat my pockets and tell him, "I misplaced my poison. Tonight's dinner is safe."

A smile tugs up one corner of his mouth.

I wish time had been unkind to him, but the opposite is true. He's only grown better looking. His hair is longer than he used to wear it. It has the slightest wave to it. I hate to admit, even to myself, that it's cute. Fuck Owen Miller and his dashing good looks. Meanwhile, homeless Autumn is over here single and pushing thirty.

I tug at my sweatpants and pin him with a glare. "You coming or not?"

He steps away from his car and closes the door. Tucking his hands into his pockets, he walks closer to me, squinting as he approaches, the setting sun in his eyes. "Are you going to stab me with a kitchen knife?"

I didn't even realize I still had the small knife in my hand and now I pretend to consider it. "Probably not. You better be on your best behavior though."

He stops beside me and I hate the zinging sensation in my body. All of me is at attention because he is near.

35

How, after ten years apart, can I remember him so flawlessly? How can he still make my body come alive?

"*Probably* not?" One eyebrow lifts. "You're making one of my favorites, so I'll take those odds." He smiles.

I turn away. There is too much energy between us. I need to cut it off.

"Come on in, before it gets cold."

Owen follows me inside and I wonder what the hell can of worms I've just opened.

Two weeks ago, I was in my apartment in Manhattan. I ate in front of my laptop, working at night after working all day.

Now I was face to face with my past.

Funny how a phone call can change everything.

DINNER WAS … awkward.

I don't think my mom could've tried any harder to make conversation flow. I tried, I really did, but I just couldn't make it happen. A block formed in my brain.

A block made up of memories and pain and judgments. Every time I looked at Owen, every time he opened his mouth, all I could see, feel, and think of was our past. The good and the bad. Everything from the way he kissed, to the way he called me a monster and slammed a door in my face.

I had managed to excuse myself to the bathroom just as we walked in from his car. I ran upstairs to put on skinny jeans, blush and run a brush through my hair.

After we ate, Owen did the dishes. He sent my mom and I to the couch, claiming it was his turn to put in some of the work.

"Dish duty," my mom sang, and they shared a knowing smile.

My chest tightened as I watched the familiarity between them. It made me angry. Owen has been here, spending time with my mom, and I didn't even know it. I was in New York, grinding away, chasing my career dreams. Funny how reality sets in once the shine wears off. I went to New York with my shiny new marketing degree, ready to work at an advertising firm and use my creativity. And I did. It just didn't feel as good as it sounded when I was in college. Not that any of that matters anymore. I'm back in my hometown, ready to take care of my mom and help her win her third battle.

I've been sitting beside her on the couch for the past ten minutes, silent, as some inane show with canned laughter plays loudly on the television.

The irritation at her obvious closeness with Owen beats a rhythm in my chest, until I feel it building up, up, up and it feels impossible to avoid. "How often do you see Owen?" My voice bursts into the silence, and I feel my mom startle against my shoulder.

I scoot back on the couch so I can look at her. She leans forward, grabbing the remote from where it lays on the ottoman, and mutes the TV.

She looks at me, apprehension in her eyes. "Once a week, unless I have an appointment with him, and then it's the appointment plus our Monday night dinner. Unless he's mowing my lawn on Sunday, but that only started last month."

Twice … and, recently, *three* times a week? Holy shit. Anger rolls through me until I steel myself. My mom doesn't know what went down with Owen and me. She had no reason to avoid him.

My lips purse. "Why didn't you tell me?"

She could at least have done that.

"You told me not to talk about him."

I rolled my eyes. "I didn't want you to ask me about him, but I'd like to have known you adopted a new son."

She chuckles, thinking I'm joking.

My mom raises one eyebrow. "Would you have wanted to know?"

"Yes."

She cocks her head to the side and narrows her eyes. She doesn't say anything, and I know she's giving me time to reconsider my response, to respond truthfully.

"Maybe," I spit out begrudgingly.

She nods once, slowly. Still giving me time.

"Okay, fine. No. I hate this." I cross my arms and stare at the TV.

"That's more like it." She pats my knee.

I frown, wishing Owen would just fucking leave. "You still should've told me."

"You were in New York, living your dream. I didn't want to put a damper on it by bringing up something difficult."

"You don't talk to him about me, right?" That was a line I hoped had never been crossed.

My mom raises her hand and tucks the thumb and pinky in. "Girl Scouts honor. Autumn talk is off limits."

Relief floods through me.

"So, you filtered out the truth every time I called you?"

"Lie by omission, I guess."

"Were your scruples always this flexible?"

She barks a laugh. "No. But things change as you age. Facing death challenges perspectives."

With that one sentence, my indignation fizzles out. I am reminded of why I am here—not that I forgot.

Mom looks behind me, placing a smile on her face, and I turn around.

Owen steps into the edge of the living room, looking between us with uncertainty. This has to be weird for him too. He's been coming here once a week for years, and has probably never felt more uncomfortable and unwelcome.

There was a time when he was here constantly. *Mi casa es su casa* was a literal term when we were together.

Without warning, nostalgia sneaks its way into my chest. I don't like how it softens the tension, blunting the edges of the annoyance I feel at Owen's presence in my mother's life.

"Kitchen is clean," Owen announces. He tucks his hands into the pockets of his pants. "Thanks for dinner, Faith. I'll see you on Thursday." He starts for the door.

Something sharp juts into my side.

"Ow," I huff.

"Walk him out," my mom hisses through clenched teeth, her elbow in my ribs. "And *be* nice."

I climb to my feet, shooting a dirty look at the ground instead of at her, and hurry after him for the second time since he showed up unannounced a couple hours ago.

As I arrive at the front door a few feet behind him, he reaches for the handle, letting himself out in the warm summer evening air. Without looking back at me, he says, "I thought I heard your fairy-footed pitter patter."

The inside joke causes a smile to overtake my face.

My damn traitorous face. Fucking nostalgia. It's a powerful bitch.

"My feet are enjoying the break from stomping around in high heels." I'm providing him with an excuse instead of acknowledging the throwback to our past, to the time he told me he liked my light feet, joking how it trained his ears to listen closer for my approach when I was barefoot.

He turns around suddenly and it takes me by surprise. I can't stop my forward momentum in time.

My palms rise to stop the collision, and I wind up with my hands pressed to his rock-hard chest.

He grabs my shoulders, catching me.

My mind screams at me to step back, but my heart wants two more seconds in this space.

"Autumn," Owen says my name softly.

His thick, husky voice snaps me from the moment. I rip myself from his arms. "Don't, Owen. Just don't."

His eyes plead with me. "I have a lot to say, Autumn."

"Don't you think you said enough?"

Guilt rides across his face. *Good*. He should feel bad.

"That's what I want to talk about. I—"

I shake my head and he stops. "I'm here to get my mom through this. I'm here to support her while she fights. I am not here to revisit the past. Don't mistake my presence here as an invitation to take a ride down memory lane."

There. I put my foot down.

A short stream of air bursts from his nose. "You're just as stubborn as you ever were!"

"You call it stubborn. From a different angle, it's strength of conviction." I shrug. "Call it what you want. You drew lines in the sand a long time ago. I'm simply staying on my side."

Anger lights up his face. "You are unbelievable. Fucking unbelievable." Owen sweeps the air around him with one arm. "Welcome back, Autumn. It's about damn time."

He turns to get into his car and I step forward. "What the fuck does that mean?" My words slip through clenched teeth.

Owen spins back around and leans in to me. "It means you should've come years ago."

"Excuse me?" My head reels back. Mr. Fucking Judgy Asshole was at it again. "Don't act like I ignored the situation. I worked harder than any other person in my office just so I could make more money and pay her medical bills. My hard work made it possible for her to pay for *you*, Owen. For the best care, for home nurses, and replacing her income so she didn't have to worry about working while she battled. Don't you act like I stepped back with hands up when she got the bad news."

A little bit of guilt creeps into his face. "Autumn, she needed *you*. Not your money."

Oh, this self-righteous asshole.

"Weekly dinners and now you think you know my mom better than I do?" I step closer to him so that he is well within range if I decide to smack him, "She told me to stay there, Owen. She made it clear where she wanted me to be, and I respected her wishes."

His face carries a mixture of hurt and anger, "Fuck that, Autumn. You didn't want to come back because you didn't want to face me. You let her tell you what you wanted to hear."

There is so much anger inside me that my fingers are vibrating. My lips tremble, but there is nothing left inside me to hurl at Owen. This exchange has depleted me. He has touched on the guilt I feel deep inside my soul.

Tears sting my eyes. Owen sees them, and the angry planes of his face soften.

"Autumn…"

"Don't." I point a stiff finger at his chest. "Don't send any sympathy my way. I want nothing from you."

He sighs and backs up. "For the record," he says, walking backwards and then stopping. "This reunion went just about how I expected it to go."

"Good job accurately predicting the future. Do you know what I'm going to say next?"

Owen stares at me, waiting.

"I'll take it from here. Monday night dinners are my responsibility. We'll see you at her appointments." There is clearly too much history for Owen Miller and I to ever be in the same room with each other again.

His face falls. "I want to check on her after her chemo days."

I cross my arms. "No thanks. I've got that covered too."

Owen's face is a mask of anger as he spins on his heels and walks to his car, pausing when he reaches it. He glances back at me. "Stubborn woman."

"Strength of conviction!" I shout and give him my back.

I don't need to watch him drive away again. This time, he can stare at me as I disappear.

Chapter 4

Owen

FUCK.

That girl drives me crazy. *Woman*, I mentally correct myself. She's a woman now. And what a woman she has grown into. Feisty as hell, stubborn, more than ready to go toe-to-toe with me. She wasn't always that way. She was never a pushover, but she wasn't always so easy to incite. Is it the person she has turned into or is it me? Does seeing me bring this out in her?

Whichever it is, it's maddening. I can't figure out if I want to take cover and hide until she decides to leave again, or press my lips to that pretty mouth of hers and shut her up.

If I did the latter, she'd probably knee me in the balls.

The hate rolled off her in waves just now. I could

feel it, see it, taste it. The worst part is that I don't blame her. I *deserve* it.

I had a chance to patch things up, but when she shut down my conversation, I lashed out and went right for her wounds. I was a grade-A asshole. Autumn brought that out of me.

My grip tightens on the steering wheel as I think of her. Mounds of dark hair curling down to the center of her back. She wore it shorter before, but I like it this way. She wasn't dressed in anything special, just baggy sweatpants before changing into tight jeans, but still as gorgeous as the day I met her. Her arms were slender, but her thighs were muscled, probably from all the walking around in the city. She has hips now too, graceful curves she didn't have before. She looked tired, and not just remnants from her redeye. Probably overworked, like me. Different careers, same pressure.

Funny how we've both let our work do that to us. It makes me wonder what else we have in common. Is she in a relationship? Has she been serious with someone? I'd glanced at her left hand and didn't see a ring. My stomach roils at the idea.

It's not fair. I've dated. Not that I've been serious. The second the girl starts talking about a future, I'm done. It's been hell trying to convince my eighteen-year-old self that Autumn isn't my forever. It's a sad fact that I'm still trying to convince him. Her being back isn't helping the situation either.

I need to blow off some steam, so I reach for my phone and dial Ace.

"What's good, buddy?" he answers.

"You busy?"

"Uh…" He pauses. "Kind of. What's up?"

"Don't worry about it, man." He's probably with a girl. My best friend is always with a girl.

He clears his throat. "Hang on."

The connection falls silent. I'm pretty sure he put me on mute. After a minute, his voice comes through.

"I'm available now."

"Ace…" I know what he did, and I'm sure it didn't go over well.

"You're more important. When was the last time you called me and sounded like a princess in need of rescuing? No way I'm gonna pass that up."

I groan. *Great*. The last thing I need is to be indebted to Ace. He'll call in the favor in the form of making me tell some poor girl that he had to rush into surgery and can't take her out on the date he promised her. No need to mention that Ace isn't a surgical oncologist. It'll just be a part of the story he, and by extension, *me*, will be feeding her.

"Where do you want to meet?" he asks.

"Shoot some hoops?" I suggest.

"For sure, man. Let me stop at home and change. See you in twenty?"

"See you soon." I hang up.

I stop at home too, changing into basketball shorts and shoes, and head back out.

"GIRL TROUBLES?" Ace asks as he approaches.

"You're late," I say, watching him walk up, a plastic bag swinging against his thigh.

He plops down on the bench beside me. "I stopped for some much-needed beverages."

I lean over, peeking into the bag. Two forties of beer knock against one another.

"Forties? What are we, eighteen?" I chuckle, tipping up my head to see my best friend. The sun has finally gone down. Some days I'm grateful for the long summer days, but other days the relentless sun can feel oppressive.

Ace pulls the bottles from the bag. The *crack* of opening the lid fills the air and he hands me one.

"Brother, some days I wish we were eighteen again."

Yeah, because at eighteen he was sleeping with every girl in a five-mile radius of our dorm room. My eighteenth year was the darkest year of my life and you couldn't pay me to relive it.

"Probably shouldn't drink these before we play," I warn, but even I don't listen to the warning. Placing the bottle to my lips, I take a sip. It's cool, crisp, refreshing.

"That's why I got the light beer. More like water than beer."

I nod. "True."

Ace takes a long swig and looks at me. "You gonna tell me why you called sounding like someone ran over your dog?"

I make a face. "That's not how I sounded."

"Sure is."

"Stop enjoying it so much."

Ace chuckles. "Cool and calm Dr. Miller? Sorry, no can do. You're just lucky I wasn't recording you, because if I told anybody how you sounded, they'd never believe me. You don't even believe me." He drinks again, and when he's finished, he says, "So, spill it."

My ankle crosses over my knee and I lean against the back of the bench, clenching the muscles in my shoulders until they coil tightly. "She's back."

Ace sits forward so fast a bit of beer sloshes out of his can and onto his fingers. "She? Like *she*? The one who must not be named?"

Yes, my best friend and I liken Autumn Cummings to Voldemort. It was fitting considering she nearly killed me from heartache.

I run two fingers under my chin and nod. Just saying it out loud makes me want a drink. Lucky for me, Ace thought ahead. I take a long pull and swallow.

"To help with her mom?" he asks.

"Yeah."

"And to see you?"

I snort. "Hardly. She can't stand me. Let's just say we should make sure there aren't any sharp objects nearby when she and I are in the same room together."

My best friend's face turns serious. "So, you've already seen her?"

I nod. "That's where I was coming from when I called you." I sigh. "She hates me."

"No offense, Owen, but she has a pretty good reason." Ace has never been one to mince his words. I like that about him.

I shake my head, rubbing my forehead as shame creeps over me. "I know."

I still grimace when I mentally replay some of the things I said to her that night. Ace was with me that day. He made the long drive out to Santa Clara with me where Autumn was going to college. At the time, we were roommates at University of Arizona. We barely knew each other, but Ace was up for a road trip, and I was too blinded by immature anger to care about who came along to watch me self-destruct and clip the tenuous ties that still held Autumn and I together.

But she hurt me too. After everything we went through, she just fucking ghosted me. Didn't answer my calls, returned all of my letters, deleted my emails. It's like she died and I was left with no closure and an apology that never got to leave my lips.

"I thought I was going to marry her," I say, taking another chug of my beer.

Ace claps me on the back. "There's your problem … you believe in marriage."

That causes a grin to pull at my lips. "You're going to be a sixty-year-old spinster with two girlfriends and half a dozen illegitimate children."

We both chuckle over that, but then Ace's face takes on a serious look.

"Do you want to turn Faith's care over to me?" he asks out of nowhere.

My surprise is evident in my face. "Why would I do that?"

No fucking way. Faith is my patient and I will get her well again. I've done it before, and I won't let personal shit get in the way.

"Gee, I don't know," he says in a tone that tells me I should most definitely already know. "Conflict of interest?"

"It's always been a conflict of interest." This is a smallish town; every patient is a conflict of interest to some degree.

"Right, but now it's a front-line conflict. In a major way. Your patient's closest family wants to grind you into hamburger meat. Do you think that could affect Faith's care? Emotions fuck shit up, man. You know that."

I shake my head. And here I was calling Autumn the stubborn one. I know Ace is right. There *is* a conflict of interest and emotions *do* fuck shit up. But I didn't have any conflicting emotions with Faith. I wouldn't hesitate to make good medical decisions where she was concerned.

Both these things have existed for years; they just haven't been a problem until now. If they even will be at all. I can deal with Autumn, explain to her that she and I need to figure out how to be adults and get along, and as for the emotions part, well, there is no dealing with that. I have to be the one treating Faith, because I need to know I've exhausted every possibility, gone down every path, left no stone unturned. I'll never forgive myself if I don't, and part of that is being the person in charge of her care.

Ace stands, taking the basketball I brought from its spot underneath the bench. "You ready to play?" He tosses his empty beer can back in the bag.

I drain the rest of mine and do the same.

"I'm going to kick your ass," I inform him, just as he throws the ball at my chest. I wasn't expecting the pass and I end up grunting before barely catching it.

He scoffs. "You've never beaten me, asshole."

"Sure," I say, passing the ball back to him. "But there's a first time for everything."

Ace laughs, then proceeds to hand my ass to me. Figures.

I can't catch a fucking break today.

"COMING," I yell at the front door.

I'd just finished dressing when the knock sounded. Early in the morning, I wasn't expecting anybody, which actually told me who it probably was. There's only one person with a habit of showing up unannounced, and now that she's done it so often, it's become her calling card.

"Hey," I answer, opening the door. I was right.

"Hey," Naomi grins, a smile sliding out one side of her mouth. "I just finished my shift and I'm not ready to go to sleep."

She steps inside, not waiting for me to respond. Naomi works nights in the emergency room at the hospital. She's a great doctor and funny as hell. After a couple months as friends, things progressed, and pretty soon we were sleeping together. It's never moved beyond using one another to scratch our itches though.

Normally I'd have no second thought about leading her back to my bedroom. It's a route we've walked dozens of times. But today something is different, and I'm not sure what it is. Or maybe I know exactly what it is, and it drives me insane.

"I'm running late, Naomi. Can we take a raincheck?"

"C'mon, Owen. It doesn't have to take long." She steps into me and I smell her shampoo, her damp hair brushing my cheek. She's ready. She stopped at home and showered, and instead of dropping into bed after a night-long shift, she drove over here. Naomi is good in bed; she knows everything I like and it would be easy to just jump into the bedroom with her real quick.

She pushes her hand against the front of my pants, her fingers curling over me.

It might be nice to fuck Autumn out of my thoughts...

Naomi leans in, brushing her breasts against my chest, a low moan rumbling in her throat.

I swallow hard, fighting biology and my second brain, and step away from her. I'm an emotional wreck after seeing Autumn, and although Naomi and I don't have a serious relationship, I can't bring myself to get involved with her right now.

I offer her a disappointed smile. "I really need to get going."

There is hurt in her eyes. We both know I'm not late for work. She knows what time I'm due at the hospital.

It's the first time I've ever turned her down, and I feel the shift in the air between us.

"Another time, then," she says, plastering a fake, bright smile on her face, and yanks her hand from my pants. She pivots, pulls open the door, and steps back through it. "Have a good shift, Owen."

I'm an idiot. What normal guy turns down casual sex? Ace would have a heart attack if I told him.

I stay in the door and watch her go. Naomi and I were never going to be serious, so why did I just fuck up a good thing? All because a certain brunette blew back into town and reminded me of the mess we made, the mess that's been simmering undisturbed for years, always waiting for the time when we would be forced to give it the attention it's been waiting so patiently for.

Frustrated, I snatch my keys off the kitchen table and shove my wallet in my pocket.

The entire drive to the hospital I try to forget about Autumn and her passionate arguing whenever she's around me… of the sadness in her eyes even when she's angry.

And I fail completely at the pointless endeavor. Mostly I wonder if the underlying sadness in her eyes is there because of me.

Chapter 5

Autumn

"MOM, YOU NEED TO EAT." I make a face, exactly the kind of maternal face she's made at me a hundred times.

How long have I been sitting here watching her push scrambled eggs around on her plate, creating little mounds and then destroying them with her fork? Feels like three hours. In truth, it's only been maybe ten minutes.

She uses that same fork to point at my food. "Take your own advice."

Half of my food is gone. Given the way I feel this morning, it's the most I can possibly eat. Today is her first chemo treatment. First one of this latest diagnosis, anyway.

"More than you," I retort. "I read about all this last

night, Mom. It said you need to eat a light meal before beginning treatment, and—"

I stop when I see the look on her face. "What?"

"This isn't my first rodeo, Autumn."

My stomach drops and the guilt gnaws at me. I should have been here all those other times. Grabbing my glass of water, I bring it to my lips. "No, but it's mine," I mutter into the glass. I was up late reading, reading, reading. Every webpage I could find on how to prepare for chemotherapy. I read until the words bled together.

"After your treatment today, I'm going to run to the grocery store. I made a list last night. We're going to start juicing."

Mom wrinkles her nose. "I don't own a juicer."

"You will by tomorrow. I ordered one last night." Right after I read that dark leafy greens and brightly colored fruits and vegetables are full of antioxidants and cancer-fighting compounds.

Mom eyes me for a moment, then presses flattened palms on the table and pushes up to standing. She places a kiss on the top of my head. "Maybe I should've told you to stay in New York again."

My mouth drops open. "Hey!"

Her lips curl into a smile and she laughs. "I'm kidding, Autumn. Of course I want you here, even if you're going to make me drink spinach juice."

She steps away from the table and starts to leave the room, eggs uneaten.

"Spinach mixed with other stuff," I yell after her.

She waves a hand over her shoulder, like no matter what else is added there is still spinach and that's all that counts. I pull out my phone, open the notes app, and add kale to the list. That way when I tell her there isn't any spinach in the mix, I won't be lying. She won't have to know I substituted.

Daughter of the year.

I clear the table, scraping all the wasted food from our plates into the trash, and mouth the words *I'm sorry* at the small heap. I hate wasting food. It feels like I'm giving Mother Earth and the supply chain that brought the food to me a giant middle finger.

While my mom gets ready, I spend a little time organizing the pantry. She was never a super tidy person, and neither am I, but I need something to do with my hands. I'm antsy about today.

I've come back home to take care of my mom, but doing that means I will need to find a job sooner or later once my savings run out. Even with health insurance, my mom's medications aren't cheap. All of these thoughts zoom around my brain as I put the pasta sauce with the dried pasta and move all of the baking goods to their own shelf.

I've just finished rearranging the canned goods when I see a little piece of paper tucked back between a can of diced tomatoes and the wall.

It's a small white square, maybe six inches by six inches. I turn it over, expecting it to be a recipe, but the handwriting confuses me. The block lettering is definitely not my mom's. My eyes grow bigger as I read.

FAITH,

You're a phenomenal cook. I haven't had a meal like that in a long, long time.

I'm leaving this note here in the pantry in hopes that when you find it,

it will bring an unexpected smile to your face. Those are the best kind.

Tonight was lovely. It may have been the first time, but I hope it wasn't the last.

Love,

Me

WHAT. The. Actual. Fuck?

My mom is seeing someone? Since when? I'd asked her point blank on Monday night when it turned out the person at the door was Owen. Did she answer? I have to think about it, but now that I'm running the scene through my mind, I realize she never responded to my question.

"All set?"

I jump a mile at the sound of her voice and my fingers curl around the note tucked in my hand. Sliding my hand behind me, I act as if I have an itch in the middle of my back.

"Did I scare you?" she asks, laughing at me.

I clear my throat. "Maybe you should wear a bell around your neck."

She moves around the kitchen, and while her back is turned, I look at the note once more. "Mom, are you dating someone?"

She whips around and looks at me, her expression confused. "No. What's that?" Her gaze falls to the folded paper in my hand.

I hold it out. "It's a note … I found this in the pantry."

She takes the note and reads it, a smile gracing her lips. Then she refolds it and tucks it into her back pocket. "This is a few years old. I saw someone briefly, but it wasn't important enough to tell you about."

"Whoa, Mom. You had a lover?" I shake my shoulders and wiggle my eyebrows.

She sends me a stern look. "That's the last we'll talk about *that*."

I laugh at her discomfort. "As you wish. I'm ready if you are," I tell her, stepping out of the pantry and closing the door behind me.

On our way out of the front door, Mom stops at the hall closet and pulls a heavy coat off a wooden hanger. I take it from her, draping it over my forearm. From my reading last night, I know that the cold cap she has chosen to wear in an effort to keep her hair will make her freezing cold during treatment. It strikes me that she has been here before. She is practiced, she has a routine. She has her iPad and a book in a little bag slung over her shoulder.

She is traversing a trail blazed twice already.

My mom is a warrior.

I HAVEN'T DRIVEN to Sedona General in years, yet I still know how to get there. Nestled between large scrubby bushes, the three-story hospital is one of the taller structures in town. This is where I came after a particularly nasty bout of the flu when I was eleven and needed fluids. I remember sitting in the waiting room of the emergency room and looking out the windows, thinking how unfortunate it was that the view from the front of the building was of the boring parking lot instead of the famed red rocks.

"Ready?" I ask, putting the car in park and pausing to look at her across the small space.

"As I'll ever be." Her forced cheerfulness saddens me.

I get out of the car and pop the trunk as my mom bends over, moving to grab the coat and bag. Instead I reach over and get to them first.

"I can hold something, you know," she chastises me.

"You can close the trunk," I tell her cheerily.

"Are you sure? I might break a nail."

"Mom," I start, but I don't know what else to say.

It's weird for me to be protecting her like this. It's always been the other way around.

She sighs, looking up at the sky and closing her eyes. The sun envelops her face and she squints at its harshness. Lowering her head, she looks back down at me. "I might be more nervous than I'm letting on." Her voice is small and it shatters my heart.

The arm I'm not using to carry her things wraps around her shoulders. "You don't have to be strong. I'm here now. Let me carry some of your load, okay?" I glance at the coat wrapped around my forearm and chuckle. "Literally and figuratively."

Mom smiles. "I guess I made the right call asking you to come home."

"Even if I make you drink kale?" I wink.

One side of her nose scrunches. "Kale?"

"Spinach," I hurry to correct.

"Now that I know kale is a possibility, I guess spinach isn't that bad."

I shake my head but I'm smiling. "You ready?"

Mom glances at the building in front of us. "Guess so."

We walk into the front door and my Mom leads the way to the outpatient clinic. She checks in while I take a seat in the waiting room.

The place has had a facelift since I was last inside of it. Larger windows and a fresh coat of paint make it look less like an institution. I imagine this is nice for the people who are coming here for treatments, like my mother. Less like impending doom.

"Nice to see you again, Faith," the receptionist says warmly, then makes a face and tips her head to the side. "Although, I do wish I was just running into you in a coffeeshop instead of seeing your name on today's schedule."

"You and me both," Mom answers.

I have an out-of-body moment then.

My mom is a regular at a chemo treatment center.

That's beyond messed up. Why do bad things happen to good people? Why can't some pedo get cancer and have his dick fall off? Why does my sweet mother have to be in this position? Instead of letting the anger rise up in me, I swallow it down and step away while Mom finishes up with the receptionist.

I glance at the wall between the rest of the hospital and the cancer treatment facility, noticing it's made of glass, allowing for full view of the first floor of the hospital. Which, of course, means everyone out there can also see in here. Just as I'm thinking this, a woman passes by with a little girl, holding tightly to the child's hand. Our gazes meet briefly through the glass. Does she feel pity for me, the person on the other side of the wall? Does she assume it's me who needs treatment? Or does she not give me a second thought, too wrapped up in whatever has brought her to the hospital. It strikes me that unless you're coming to visit someone who has just had a baby, a hospital can be a scary place to be. Depressing, even.

And Owen spends all his time here.

I push the thought away. The tone of that thought was too softhearted, tinged on the outside in a warm, buttery yellow. Feeling sympathy for Owen does not align with my other thoughts about him.

Mom steps up beside me and nods at the front desk. "That's Sandra. She has worked in this clinic for as long as I've been coming here. Her first day was also my first day."

Damn. I don't know why that saddens me so much, but it does. Does Sandra go home and think about my mom and all of the people who don't get well and keep coming back here?

I'm not sure how to respond, so I say, "I don't know if that's cool or really sad."

Mom smiles. "A little of both, I suppose." She points at the wall across from us. "That artwork is new."

I follow her gaze. It reminds me of Picasso, bright and geometric. Does color equal an uplift in spirit? If so, I think that's what the interior decorator who chose the paintings was after.

It annoys me a little. Cancer is the reason everyone is in this room, and that's beyond depressing, and no amount of colorful artwork can cover that up. I know it's better than some drab room, but I'm in a mood to find a problem with everything.

"Faith Cummings," a deep voice calls.

A voice that makes my insides quiver.

I look up to see Owen standing at the door. He's dressed in gray slacks, a white shirt, and a tie. Over all of this, he wears a white lab coat.

A doctor. My freaking ex just had to go and become a doctor. Next, he'd take on a British accent and just top the cake.

My mom and I walk over to him and I can't stop thinking about our little exchange when he came over for dinner. He smiles, but it's directed only at her, which annoys me.

"Since when do doctors do the job of nurses?" Mom asks, her tone a blithe teasing.

Busted. I loved that my mom called Owen on his shit. It was one of her best qualities.

"Melody was on her way to get you but I told her I'd do it." His gaze switches over to me. "Hello, Autumn."

"Hello, Owen." *You handsome asshole.* My response is stiff.

There's a moment of silence where we should probably ask the other how their day has been going or something fake like that, but we don't.

Mom's gaze shifts between us. "You two are beyond words."

We stare each other down for another moment, until Owen clears his throat. "Back this way," he says, pushing the door open with his hand and stepping back slightly, waiting for us to walk through first. As I pass Owen, my wrist hits his and an electric jolt zaps up my arm and down my spine, making my gut clench. Shoving my hand into my pocket, I ignore the way his accidental touch makes me feel.

I follow my Mom into the room and look around, trying not to stare at the recliners set up in rows. More specifically, I try not to stare at the people who are in the recliners.

"Faith!"

We all turn to an arm raised in the air. A woman waves and smiles. She's wearing a cap on her head, and a book lies open on her lap. Her other arm has an IV hanging out of it.

"Linda?" Mom waves.

"How do you know her?" I ask in a low voice.

"I met her the last time I went through this. She was on her first round." Mom frowns. "Looks like she's on her second now."

Fuck. I needed a drink. This was depressing.

"There's a chair open beside her, Faith," Owen says. "Would you like us to set you up there?"

Mom looks at Linda, then points at the open chair next to her. Linda sends a thumbs-up.

Owen gets the attention of a nurse, I'm guessing Melody, the nurse who was supposed to call us back. She's young, probably five years younger than us, with long blond hair and cornflower blue eyes. And those blue eyes are doe-eyed as she listens to Owen. He instructs her on where my mom wants to sit, and what treatment she'll be receiving. The entire time he speaks,

Melody, the Beautiful Young Nurse, fidgets with her necklace, holding on to the gold cross pendant and dragging it along the matching gold chain.

"Got it?" he asks when he's finished.

"Yes, Dr. Miller," Melody, *I want to fuck my boss nurse,* says, her voice breathy.

She'd probably take off her pants and dance in a circle if he told her to right now.

The urge to cross my arms protectively in front of me is strong, but I resist, keeping them casual at my sides. *See, everyone?* I'm feeling *nothing* in response to this girl fawning over my ex. I'm cool. Super cool.

Melody leads us to the recliner beside Linda while my Mom and I follow. When we reach Linda, Mom grabs her free hand and gives it a squeeze. A look passes between the two women, a look of knowing, of disbelief, of *Can you believe we drew the short straw again?*

I suddenly feel like I don't belong here. It's my mom's third time doing this and I'm only just now coming to help. I'm an asshole and I feel like shit for sending money when I should have been there to hold my mom's hand.

Melody gets my mother set up, and the irritation I felt toward her for flirting with Owen ebbs as I watch the kindness with which she treats my mom.

"This is my daughter, Autumn," my mom says, introducing me to Linda. She extends an arm while she speaks, and Melody slips on a blood pressure cuff. "She came here from New York City to be with me."

My chest swells at the hint of pride in her voice. Maybe I could make up for not being there before; my mom certainly doesn't seem to be holding a grudge over it. "Nice to meet you," I say to Linda.

Linda grins. One front tooth is crooked, overlapping the one beside it, and it's endearing. Imperfections are my favorite thing about people. Owen has a scar on his ribcage from hopping over a fence when he was younger; my favorite thing was to trace my fingertips over the rippled, white flesh.

I shake my head as that thought pops into it.

"Nice to meet you too. You have a pretty great mom, you know that? She's a hoot. She made sure I knew what to expect after my first treatment. Thank God for her. I tell you what, I'd have been scared shitless last time had it not been for Faith." She smiles again and takes a big breath.

I like this lady and I really like how much she likes my mom. "I'm glad you had her during a difficult time."

"We had each other," my mom clarifies.

"How's it going over here?" Owen's voice comes from behind me. "Are you getting settled in alright, Faith?"

"Sure am," she responds, tipping her head at Linda and smiling mischievously. "This broad's trying to get me in trouble already."

"Guilty," Linda says, holding up one palm.

Owen laughs, and I feel it, deep down in my core, sliding over my skin. I hate how much I still find his laugh attractive. It's a bit wild and carefree, not the restrained laugh I use with people.

I look over at my mom in hopes of pushing these thoughts from my mind, and I'm just in time to see Melody slip the IV needle into her arm.

Shit. I hate needles. My eyes lose focus, my stomach turns over and all of a sudden, I'm falling.

Strong arms wind around my waist, then I'm pulled into something solid.

"Still afraid of needles, I take it." Owen's murmur vibrates against the side of my head as I realize he's caught me from falling and now I'm flush against his body.

I nod. I can't speak. It might be the needle. Or it might be the fact that I'm being held by the person I've spent years trying to forget. A person who still has this ridiculous, unexplainable ability to make my body react.

It's probably the needle. It'd better fucking be the needle. I spent way too much in therapy for Owen to still make me feel this way.

I take a shaky step away from him. One of his arms is still wound around my waist to steady me. Three curious gazes are on me as well.

Well, two, anyway. My mom knows about my aversion.

"Needles," I say weakly, and my one-word explanation seems to be enough for Linda and Melody.

"Happens all the time." Melody waves a hand around like it was no big deal.

"Autumn, why don't you get out of here for a while?" my mom suggests.

"No. I'm good."

Owen breaks in. "She's right, Autumn. The treatment takes a while. Will you be okay in here for a few hours?"

I glance back at the IV in my mom's arm and another wave of dizziness overtakes me. "Okay, maybe I will step out." I lean down and brush a kiss over my mom's cheek. "Call me when you're done. I'll come right back."

I say goodbye to everyone else and retrace my steps through the room and out into the hall. I'm almost to the door that leads to the waiting room when I hear my name.

"Autumn, wait."

I'm still not used to hearing his voice.

I pause just outside the door and turn around. Owen stops. His eyes are soft with apology. "About the other day ... I'm sorry. I really want this"—he motions between our chests— "to be less contentious. I know we didn't end well, but that was a long time ago. We're adults now. We can do better."

He's right. I hate when he's right. It's been a decade since the dark choice I had to make, since his unforgettable words, and it does no good for me to hold resentment in my heart.

I nod slowly. "So, you want to be ... friends?" Never in a million years would I have thought I'd ever be friends with Owen Miller. Not after what happened between us.

Relief tumbles over his features. "Friends. Friends would be great."

I simply nod and turn back around, opening the door and stepping through. I'm three feet away when I realize I didn't hear the door close behind me.

As I look over my shoulder, I find Owen standing there with his hand propped against the open door.

"What?" I ask, stopping. He has an amused look on his face.

"Are we the kind of friends who get coffee together?" His eyebrows raise hopefully. "I have some things I'd like to say."

Am I ready to go there yet with Owen? Maybe after a stiff drink, but not coffee. Not today.

"Maybe another time." I give him a sheepish smile and he frowns slightly, nodding.

I turn around and keep going until I get to my mom's car. As I slide into the driver's seat and take a deep breath, the tension melts into a puddle at my feet.

He'd watched me until I walked out of the treatment facility and turned the corner. I didn't have to look back at him to know it. I felt his gaze on me, felt the apology I'm certain lives somewhere inside him. Do I have an apology inside of me for him as well? All those times he called after and I never answered. The deleted emails, returned letters. Changing my number, my dorm room and just about anything so that he could never contact me again...

Maybe.

Just maybe I owe him an apology too.

From the look of it, he's been waiting a long time to ask me for coffee and tell me he's sorry about what he said the last time we saw each other.

He can wait a little longer.

Chapter 6

Autumn

I'M glad I let everyone convince me to leave the hospital during the treatment. I needed the sun and fresh air and general lack of needles and blood. Each time I've been around Owen it feels like I'm gasping for oxygen, and that makes me nervous. I was prepared mentally for the anger I felt around him, but not the other stuff...

The car window is rolled down; the air rushing through pushes my hair around my face. I don't have a hair-tie, so I wind it into a loose knot and tuck it into the back of my t-shirt. I'm not sure where I'm going, but I'm heading for Main Street. I make a right turn onto the lengthy thoroughfare and my vision explodes with tourists. They wear hats and visors, loose t-shirts and shorts. Some wear fanny packs. I used to think fanny packs were the epitome of nerdy, but now that I'm older I see the utility in them. Although, I'm not sure if appreciating their function would ever convince me to wear one.

The shops on either side of the street are hard to see because of the sheer volume of people walking around. I pause at a red light, watching pedestrians cross over to the other side of the street. A sullen-looking teenager slouches behind older people I assume are his parents, staring down at the phone he holds inches from his face.

As the light turns green, I ease off the brake.

Where am I going? Where can I go to get my mind off of Owen and my mom? It feels like I'm running from something, an emotion I know too well. Up ahead, I spot the pink Jeep parked on the sidewalk. Seeing it brings a smile to my face. If Sedona is known for its red rocks, then just as iconic are the Pink Jeep Tours.

Trudy's fudge shop sits opposite the pink Jeep, and just seeing it convinces me I need fudge at this moment or I just might die. Running from my ex and right into the arms of chocolate. That should be my life motto.

I put on my blinker and turn, finding a parking spot. The fudge shop also sells ice cream, and the place is packed. I order a pound of cookies and cream fudge, and a half pound of original chocolate. That should last me until dinner.

Stepping outside into the sunshine, I look right and

left. Left will take me further into the crowd so I go right, away from the crowd, and cross the street. There's a shopping center there, one less populated with tourists. It has real stores, the kind of places residents would need. Main Street shops sell Sedona-themed knick-knacks, t-shirts, crystals and geodes. A psychic will reveal your future. All great for tourists, but not so much for the everyday needs of residents.

One of my favorite things about Sedona is that the people who built the place didn't carve up nature to make room for themselves. The hills weren't blasted apart to make everything flat, and so the whole place is full of curves. Winding streets, gently sloping hills. The shops and buildings were built on top of the land, and look as if they were simply set into the existing structure.

What this means for me now is that I have to climb two flights of stairs to access the stores. Not that I mind. My fingers keep dipping into the white paper bag I'm holding. It reminds me of the bags of roasted nuts I'd buy from the street vendor near my apartment in New York City. I'd bundle up and go for a walk in Central Park, one gloveless hand reaching into the bag of sweet mixed nuts. It was one of my favorite things to do in the winter.

And it is *over*. I've leased my apartment and my stuff is sitting in POD storage waiting for me to figure out my next step.

But … maybe I was ready for that part of my life to

be over. I did what my Mom wanted me to do. Got a degree from a good university, moved somewhere and got outside my comfort zone—became a strong, independent woman. It was all her idea, and even though we didn't agree on much, she was so insistent about this one piece of advice that it felt too important not to listen to her. Even as a selfish seventeen-year-old, I felt the gravity of her suggestion. She wanted me to get out and explore, because she never did. And her dream became my dream.

There were far worse things my mom could ask me to do, so I'd applied to Santa Clara University in California. I was in advanced classes at school and my SAT score was high enough that I got in without too much trouble. Financial aid paid for a small amount of my tuition, and I took out loans to pay the remainder. After my first year in the dorm, I moved into an apartment with three other girls. A part-time job in the campus bookstore allowed me to pay my share of the rent without much left over.

New York City was my idea. My mom loved it at first. I think she thought I might just get some work experience and then settle somewhere closer to home like Phoenix or San Diego. It was crazy how fast the years ticked by. I'd only been there a few months when she called and told me about her first cancer diagnosis. The words Chronic Lymphocytic Leukemia sounded foreign and terrifying. I followed my mom's instruction not to look it up on the internet. "Just hear what I'm

telling you. We caught it early and I'm going to be fine."
I was too scared to look it up, too scared of what I
might find. I willingly took her words as gospel. She
told me to stay where I was, that I would help her most
by following my dream. *Our dream*, I thought. I didn't
correct her.

Almost seven years later, she's battling the same
cancer for the third time, and I've finally come home.

I don't know where that leaves me. I only know
where I am right now, climbing steps with sticky sweet
fingertips, the red rock canyon walls at my back.

Just as I reach the main level of shops, my phone
buzzes with a text. Fear spikes through me as I wonder
if it's mom saying something has gone wrong.

When I look down, a frown pulls at my lips when I
see who it's from.

Matt.

New York friend-with-benefits Matt.

Stopping in the opening of a restaurant, I open the
text.

I miss you.

I chuckle. I was pretty sure Matt didn't even know
my last name. He lived in my building in New York
and we met at the gym. We were both dedicated to our
jobs and weren't looking for something serious, so
fuck buddies seemed like a good idea at the time.
Once a week for the past year Matt and I got together
and released our tension. It was nothing more than
that.

You don't miss me, you miss our arrangement, I quickly type back and toss my phone in my bag.

Gym rat Matt misses me. *Hah*, Anna would get a kick out of that. I'd have to call my old roommate later and tell her.

I duck into the restaurant and find the bathroom with the sign on the door that says *For Customers Only*. Once my hands are clean, I buy an iced tea to validate my usage of their soap and water, and keep going down the row of stores. There is an apothecary with hand-made soaps and other items, a coffee bar, a wine shop that specializes in local wine and olive oil.

After buying some peppermint and lavender soap, I duck into the wine shop and buy four bottles of wine. Technically, I only buy three. The fourth is free with my purchase of three. The shop owner, a balding man with a kind smile and a generous middle, also convinces me that I need the garlic infused olive oil that came in yesterday. He tells me it's his biggest seller and the shipment probably won't last the weekend. His appeal to scarcity works on me, mostly because I think garlic olive oil would be amazing with just about every meal I plan to make my mom this week, and last night I read about the potent benefits of garlic.

This shopping therapy is doing wonders for my mood, but I won't be able to spend money with abandon much sooner ... I need to find a job. Sedona isn't exactly the best place for an advertising sales executive and marketing guru.

I walk along, my fudge bag joined by my new purchases, and spot a bookstore.

Oh great. Just take all my money.

A bookstore is the worst place for me to be when I'm engaging in retail therapy.

Funny how that doesn't stop me from walking right in.

The familiar scent is the first thing to greet me. Woody paper and rich ink, musty carpet and stale coffee from a carafe in the corner. There is another scent, one I know cannot be real but still I recognize it: possibility. I smelled it my first night in New York City. I smell it every time I'm in a bookstore. The possibility to learn and grow, all with the opening of a book. Perhaps it's not a quantifiable scent, but for me it is.

"Hello there," a low, throaty voice says. I follow the sound and watch a young woman come from an opening near the back of the store.

I blink, surprised for the shortest second, then gather myself. The gravelly voice had me expecting an older woman, but this woman is probably about my age, maybe thirty but not a day over.

"Hi," I say, smiling at her.

She walks behind a shabby desk that looks like it's used as a register. A can of pens topped with faux flowers sits beside an outdated cash register. She's wearing a cute crop-top and high-waisted jeans, and I wonder if she's from around here. She doesn't have the hippie vibe most others do.

"Welcome to Books 'N' More." She gazes at me expectantly, her voice completely monotone, telling me she most definitely hates her job. "Let me know if you have any questions." Her dark, curly hair just barely touches her shoulders and she wears large gold hoop earrings.

I look around the place, then back at her. "Hey," I greet her. "I do have a question."

She stays quiet but nods her head, giving me permission to ask.

"Why the word *More* in the name of the store? I only see books."

Yes, I'm having that kind of day—desperate to get my mind off of Owen and my mom so I'll chat up some random chick about her store name. The woman grimaces as she steps around to the side of the desk and props a flattened palm on the worn surface. "That would be the work of my crazy grandma. Bless her heart." Her other palm, the one she's not using to balance on the desk, covers her heart. "She owned this place for years. Still does, technically. We didn't realize she was losing it a bit." The woman points to her head and makes a swirl with her fingers.

I wince, in part because I feel bad for the grandma and in part because I'm taken aback by the brutal honesty of this girl.

She notices. "Did I overshare? I'm a say-it-like-it-is person. Blame it on my New York upbringing."

I smile and instantly like her. "No, you didn't overshare. I've spent the last six years living in Manhattan. What part are you from?"

I see amusement trickle into her eyes and her lips curve into a slight smile. "A fellow New Yorker, don't get many of us around here. I grew up in Queens. What's your name?"

"Autumn Cummings."

Not sure I would call myself a "New Yorker," but I'll run with it.

She extends a hand. "Well, Autumn Cummings who lived in Manhattan for the past six years, I'm Olivia Rhodes. But don't call me that, because only my mother does. I go by Livvie."

I like how fast she talks. I like her tough exterior. Taking her hand, I give it a good shake.

"What do you have in those bags?" She peers pointedly at my hands.

"Fudge, soap, wine, and olive oil."

She raises one eyebrow. "You sharing?"

"You want to eat soap and drink olive oil?"

She barks a laugh. "No but I'll take some of that wine."

I look at the front door, certain she's kidding. "Aren't you open for business right now?"

Livvie marches to the door and turns the lock. Then she flips over the *Open* sign and turns back to me. "Not anymore," she announces. "Pop a bottle. I need a drink."

∼

"THAT'S the saddest reason I've ever heard for coming home," Livvie says after I've told her part of my life story and why I'm back in Sedona. She takes a sip of her wine, shaking her head.

We're drinking from paper cups she grabbed from beside the coffee machine.

I take the tiniest sip. I'm supposed to pick up my mom when she's finished. The last thing I need is to tell Owen I can't make it because I've been day drinking.

"And somehow your reason for being here is not just as sad?" A senile grandmother who'd been running her business into the ground unbeknownst to her family makes for a depressing tale too. Livvie jumped in to try and save it, but she's ready to sell it and be done with the whole business if she can't turn it around and make a profit.

Livvie leans back against a row of books. We're sitting on the ground between two bookshelves, hidden away from anybody who might pass by and peer through the store window.

She sighs. "I guess my reason for coming is pretty sad too."

She stretches out her left hand, curling and uncurling her fingers, her eyes focused on the motion.

A huge diamond glints in the dull overhead light. I don't know much about diamonds or weight, but the center stone is the size of a plump blueberry and is surrounded by smaller, yellow diamonds.

"That's quite a ring on your finger," I comment.

Livvie makes a grunting sound in the back of her throat. "If only the man who put it there also cared enough to be around me."

I'm not sure how to respond, but after a beat, I ask, "He didn't come out here with you?"

She shakes her head. "Too busy working."

I hear the heartbreak in the smallness of her voice. Funny how someone can break your heart, even while you're married to them.

"I'm sorry, Livvie."

She looks up at me, pushing back the hair that had fallen into her face. When she does this, two more diamonds peek out from her earlobes.

"Don't be. Sometimes things just go to shit."

I laugh once, an empty, knowing sound.

She eyes me over the brim of her cup. "You know what I'm talking about? Did someone in New York break your heart?"

My head tips up, bumping against the bookshelf behind me. Instead of moving it, I let it rest there. "Someone here," I correct.

Livvie's eyes widen. "Have you seen him since you've been back?"

"He's my mom's oncologist."

"Nooo," she draws out the word in whispered disbelief. "The universe must hate you."

I bust out laughing. Livvie isn't one of those friends who will lie to make me feel better and I like that.

Considering all of my high school friends have either left town or I haven't seen them in a decade, I could use a new one.

"Right?" I ask, joining in her disbelief.

"When did you two end it?"

"A long time ago, so you'd think we'd be over it by now. But it wasn't a clean break … it got ugly."

Livvie clutches her cup tightly. "Go on. I can keep a secret."

Fear and panic rush through me. I don't tell my story about Owen to many people. Any people, actually. It's my deep dark secret that festers inside of me and I don't let it see the light of day. The only people I've told are my college therapist and my old roommate Anna.

Two people. And Owen. And Ace. Four people on Earth know our story. Sometimes keeping it inside of me feels like I'm drowning, like it sits heavy in my throat, begging to be let free, to escape so I can breathe.

I don't know Livvie, so maybe that's why I decide to tell her.

"When I was eighteen … three weeks before I was about to leave for college, I got pregnant." The tightness in my throat eases a bit as Livvie nods in complete understanding. She doesn't say anything, so I go on. "I … chose not to keep it."

The word "abortion" just adds to the shame that I feel, so I try not to use it. Some women don't regret their decision and casually talk about their choice, and I respect that. I envy that.

I'm not that person.

I deeply regret the choice I made, forever altering my path with Owen and destroying our future.

Livvie reaches across and squeezes my hand, her eyes growing misty. Am I going insane? Sharing my story with a complete stranger in a dusty bookshop over wine? Maybe I am. Maybe my mom's return illness and coming home has finally pushed me over the edge.

"After the … choice I made … Owen and I made a pact to return home, here, after college, and get married."

Livvie's eyes are wide and she chugs her wine like it's the only thing that will get her through this story. "What happened?"

So much happened. So much I don't want to relive and won't share. "He got drunk one night and drove up to my college dorm and said things I can never forgive. So, I never came home."

"Ohmygod." Livvie rushes the words together and grabs the bottle of wine, refilling her cup.

I suddenly feel exposed, all the memories flooding into me one by one.

"We were young. So…" I've been telling myself that for years. *We were young.* As if age should provide some kind of salve for the wound.

Livvie nods. "Young love is the worst of them all."

She wrinkles her nose as she reconsiders. "Well, maybe not the worst. But it's wrapped up in a time period when you were extremely selfish and you didn't know any better. And you look back on it with some kind of weird reverence. You love the time when you were allowed to be naive, but you're also annoyed by your naïveté and all the mistakes you made during it."

My lips peel apart in amazement. I've never attempted to define how I feel, but that is exactly it. I've always looked back on me and Owen with fondness, but there's been so much anger attached to the fondness, like a nice memory outlined in angry, violent red. Anger and fondness—I've not been able to tease the two apart.

"How did you just put everything I've been feeling into words I haven't been able to voice?" It's like a weight has been lifted off of me. Telling a complete stranger our story has freed me in some weird way.

"Because I'm married to my high school sweetheart, and our life is nothing like I thought it would be." Livvie tips up her cup and drains what's left again.

Shit, I think I just found my new best friend.

She picks up the bottle that sits between us and refills. When she offers more to me, I shake my head.

I wait for her to say more about her marriage, but she doesn't. And as much as I'd like to stay and keep talking, there's another stop I'd like to make before my mom's treatment is finished.

"I should get going. I need to pick up groceries

before I go get my mom." If I do it now, I won't have to worry about dragging her out with me after picking her up. What if she doesn't feel good or she's too tired? Everything about taking care of my mom during this cancer battle has me on edge.

Livvie stands, grabbing the wine bottle by the neck on her way up, and I stand too. She offers the bottle to me, but I shake my head.

"Keep it," I tell her. "I have three more."

"Wino," she says with a small smile.

"Damn straight," I agree.

"Hah," she barks, smiling so wide I can see almost all of her teeth.

We exchange numbers and a hug, and she walks me to the front of the store before unlocking it. I push it open and give her a long look. I feel like we've shared something special and I only just met this chick.

"Thanks for today." I pause with my palm on the door handle. "I needed to talk to someone who isn't my mom or Owen."

"Owen the oncologist?"

"Owen the oncologist," I confirm with a grin.

"I'm going to use your number," Livvie warns. "But fair warning, I write inappropriate text messages and my meatballs are better than any you had in Manhattan."

"Prove it," I say.

She smiles and I step out the door as it swings shut behind me.

My mood is brighter and I know I didn't have enough wine for it to be that. Livvie was a nice surprise and I hope we can be friends.

My phone rings on the way to the car but it's a number I don't know. The area code is local, so I answer.

"Hello?"

"Autumn, hey." Owen's deep voice trickles through the receiver. "It's Owen."

"I know," I say without thinking.

"You remember my voice?" His tone is light and teasing. And I also hear how pleased it makes him that I haven't forgotten what he sounds like on the phone. For some reason I'm not panicked that he's calling to tell me bad news, but I still want to make sure my mom is okay.

"How's my mom?"

"She's fine. I was calling to tell you my shift will be over about the same time your mom's treatment is finished, so I can bring her home. If you'd like, I mean. I don't want to step on your toes."

My mind flashes back to me telling him I can handle all this, but it would be nice to take my time at the grocery store. And we're supposed to be acting like the adults our age indicates we are, so maybe this is acceptable. Maybe I can let him help.

"Okay," I say, wishing now that I had drank more wine with Livvie.

"Okay, I can drive Faith home?"

I hear the surprise in his question. "Yes," I answer.

"I'll see you after a while, then."

"See you soon," I tell him, and scold myself for the butterflies that take flight in my belly.

I hang up at the same time as I reach the car.

When I get in, I flip down the visor and do a cursory check of my makeup and hair. That's when I see it. The smile I hadn't realized was plastered on my face. I swipe at my mouth as if the grin is a bright lipstick I can wipe off and find myself wondering if it's because of Owen's call or my new friend Livvie.

I have to remind myself that Owen is just a friend, and hardly even that. There is too much pain and history for there to be anything more. And that's the way it is going to stay.

Chapter 7

Owen

My THUMBS BEAT a loud rhythm on the steering wheel of my car as I think of Autumn. The way she narrowed her eyes at me when I'd asked her if we're the kind of friends that get coffee. Then she barked her short answer "another time," before turning on her heel and striding away. The sway of her hips issued a challenge: catch me if you can. She wants to make me pay, and I don't blame her a damn bit. But why do I like pain so much, why do I keep poking the bear? I must have lain awake a thousand nights with Autumn Cummings' name on my lips. I typed that phone number a million times. Kissed those lips hundreds of times. And it all turned to ashes over one night.

"I don't think I've ever seen someone so hyped up."

The muscles in my neck tense at the sound of Faith's voice. I'd been so lost in my thoughts I'd completely spaced that there was another person in my car, enjoying the concert my thumbs were putting on.

I look over at Faith. "What do you mean?"

She shrugs. "You tell me. You're the one who turned your steering wheel into a drum."

My fingers stop, the noise in the car ceasing. "Why are you asking me questions? I should be the one asking you questions. How do you feel?"

Faith has a keen sense of how a person is feeling inside. She missed her calling as a shrink.

She frowns. "Fine. Now, let's talk about why you're so nervous. And don't tell me you're not, because I've known you for a long time, and I like to think I know a lot about you by now."

"You do," I confirm, but a twinge of guilt scrapes at me. She doesn't know what really went down between Autumn and me. She is, however, the only person besides Ace who knows about what I'm going through with my dad.

"I think my daughter has something to do with your nerves. Or maybe she has everything to do with it." Faith raises an eyebrow and I chuckle. If that woman had it her way, Autumn and I would be married with two-point-five kids and living next door. That was the plan ... always the plan.

"Seeing her again isn't easy," I admit. I still

remember taking pictures the night of senior prom. Faith looked so proud to see Autumn and I make it through high school together.

Faith makes a sarcastic noise in her throat. "No kidding?"

I wonder what Autumn has told her and it reminds me of all those times I called Faith's house freshman year of college begging her to get Autumn to return my calls.

"She told me if I speak your name again, she'll disown me. What did you do, Owen?" Faith had growled. Having a woman I considered to be a second mother ask me what I did wrong really fucked with my eighteen-year-old head. That's when the guilt and shame turned to anger. Anger at Autumn for not giving me a chance to right my wrongs, for leaving me to deal with the choice we made and no one to talk to about it.

"We talked today. We're going to do better. Be adult about it all," I said proudly.

I'd chased after Autumn in the hospital earlier as Faith, Melody, and Linda had looked on. It wasn't my finest, most professional moment. I did my best to appear in control as I strode through the treatment room, but I don't know if my air of collectedness fooled anybody but me. "Collected" is the last thing I am when I'm around Autumn. In her presence, my blood boils, my stomach churns with guilt, my heart turns over in my chest. That woman drives me mad and it doesn't help that she's gotten even more beautiful with age.

"Maybe what you two really need is an honest conversation about how you ended," Faith says matter-of-factly. "Air your grievances and get the ugliness out in the open where it can be dealt with. How can you move past it when you're both still stuck inside it?"

A lump forms in my throat at the thought of having Autumn alone, sitting across from her, finally apologizing for everything I said … it would feel so good. But it would also bring up what happened and I'm not sure either one of us ever wants to revisit that again.

Unless she wants to, unless it would help both of us heal…

Maybe. Clearly time hasn't erased her memory. She seems to have a razor-sharp grasp on the last time we saw each other, which makes me so ashamed.

My hand captures my lower lip and I squeeze it so it bunches together in the middle. I'm considering Faith's suggestion.

The hard part will be getting Autumn to hear me out. How am I going to make that happen when she so clearly doesn't want to hear what I have to say? And once I start talking, she's bound to interrupt me in anger and the whole thing will become a big shitshow.

At the next light, I make an unplanned right turn, causing Faith to send a questioning glance my way.

"Ice cream," I explain. "To celebrate you beating this again."

A grin tugs at her mouth. "Isn't it a little premature?"

"Nah. We're putting it out into the universe that you're going to make this cancer your bitch."

Faith bursts into laughter and tosses her arms in the air. "Salted caramel for me!"

I love this woman, and Ace's comment about me being too close to properly manage her care gnaws at my gut.

"THANKS FOR CARRYING THAT IN, OWEN." Faith holds the front door open for me and I step through, three grocery bags in one hand. I head for the kitchen and set them on the counter.

"No problem," I tell Faith as she begins pulling items from the bag. We stopped at the store for ice cream but ended up with a few more things Faith needed. Typical. When does anyone ever actually leave the grocery store with the one thing they ran in to get?

"Do you mind if I use your bathroom?" I ask, thumbing over my shoulder and down the hall.

"Of course not," Faith says as she bends to place something in the fridge.

I leave Faith in the kitchen, and just as I reach for the bathroom doorknob, it turns and the door flies open.

"Fuck," Autumn says, shocked, her fingers curling

over the fold at the top of the towel wrapped around her.

"Shit … sorry." I step aside to let her pass. My eyes find the floor so she doesn't think I'm a creep enjoying an eyeful. She takes a moment to gather her bearings, then steps around me. The smell of cucumber and vanilla hits me hard as she passes and it's like I've been punched in the gut.

She still uses the same shampoo, which takes me back to prom night and the shower we took together after…

I hurry into the bathroom, but before I close the door, I look at her. I can't help it.

She's standing at the entrance to her bedroom, watching me. Her long brown hair lies damp on her back, her shoulders bare. Her makeup-free face is more beautiful than I remember and I can't help but eye her lips.

Her eyebrows raise as I take her in. "How's the view?" she asks sarcastically.

My neck heats up. "You'd look too if I came out wearing only a towel," I say, trying for confidence and good-natured humor and hoping she doesn't take it wrong.

She smirks. "Maybe ten years ago, but I don't know what's under there anymore." She points to my stomach. "Could be a beer belly." Then she steps into her room and closes the door.

Hah! Is that a challenge? Because I'll rip my shirt off right now and show her the six pack Ace helped me get in the gym. God, I fucking love her little sassy attitude. It's a problem.

Stepping into the bathroom, I shut the door and I'm left with her scent. It's … well, mouth-watering. A little too delicious for my own wellbeing.

After finishing up in the bathroom, I get back out to the kitchen. Nobody is around, but from the kitchen window I catch sight of Faith in her small vegetable garden. Day one of chemo, most patients would be napping, but not Faith. She's a warrior.

From a cabinet I pull out three small mismatched bowls. Just as I'm dropping the first scoop of ice cream into a bowl, Autumn walks in.

Her hair is still damp, the moisture causing it to appear even darker than its normal chocolate shade. Her face is slightly pink, probably from the hot shower she took. Certainly not because she's flushed thinking about my supposed beer belly. It's painfully clear the effect I used to have on her has disappeared.

I, on the other hand, can't stop thinking about what is under that towel.

She ignores me and walks to the door that leads outside, staring out at her mother. My ice cream scoop stops midway between the bowl and the carton. The afternoon sun shines off Autumn's profile, illuminating her face and my heart twists as I take her in. She is so familiar that my fingertips remember what it felt like to run them up her arms, over her shoulders, down the valley created by her breasts. But there are parts of her I don't know, a newness that intrigues me. Where she used to be narrow, her hips have taken shape more like the bottom half of an hourglass. Her cheekbones are more defined. On her face I see her strength, the determined set of her eyebrows, but fragility lives there too. What happened in New York that made her fragile? Or is it being back here that has done it?

Her eyes are trained on her mom. Her thick lashes blink once, twice, then she opens her mouth: "How was today?" she asks, not looking at me. Her voice breaks the spell and I glance down at my hand suspended mid-air. Small drops of melted ice cream dot the counter.

I clear my throat, more from discomfort than actually needing to clear my throat. "Good. Your mom is a warrior, you know that?"

I keep spooning ice cream and glance up when she hasn't yet answered. Her arms are crossed and she's watching me. I get the feeling I've done something wrong. In her book, anyway.

"What?" I ask.

"I went to the store today and bought a fridge full of healthy food."

"Oh… okay." I guess ice cream was a bad idea.

"People with cancer need a diet rich in cruciferous vegetables. They need dark leafy greens and bright colors for antioxidants. No sugar." She points to the ice cream I wield like it's a weapon.

I hear conviction in her voice, but there's a vein of desperation running through it.

I swallow my sigh and dip my head down so my eyes are on the counter. How can I tell her that I don't disagree with her, but at this point there isn't much a diet like she's describing is going to do for Faith.

Been there, done that—didn't work. Faith's cancer coming back a third time means it's aggressive, and although I'm hopeful I can get her into remission again, it could all go south in an hour and we would have to change our plan.

After Faith's first diagnosis, I got on a first name basis with a farmer and his wife at the local farmer's market. Every Sunday, Faith and I went and bought them out of vegetables and summer fruit. Faith hated juicing, but she pinched her nose and drank. I learned that adding lemon made it all more palatable.

Months later, she was declared cancer-free and we celebrated with ice cream.

And then it came back. *Twice.*

Autumn is seeing this all for the first time. She's coming here with guns blazing, ready to jump into action with acai berries and God knows what else. Faith and I are beaten down and scarred from previous battles, but Autumn doesn't know that, and I don't think Faith has told her daughter how much I helped around the house in the past.

I balance two bowls in one hand and one in the other, walking slowly to Autumn and handing her a bowl.

"I agree with you. And after this bowl of ice cream, you can start her on the diet you're talking about. Wherever you learned it, you're not wrong. But keeping her spirits up is just as important as anything else, so can you please let her enjoy this before you start giving her liquid spinach for dinner?"

Autumn takes the bowl, her eyes squinting at me in suspicion. "You know she hates spinach?"

I feel like there are other questions lying beyond that one. What she's really asking is, *Do you know she hates spinach because you tried this with her already?*

I feel it only fair to let her know just how close her mother and I are.

"I've been eating dinner with her for a long time, Autumn. It only took one time of me making sun-dried tomato and spinach-stuffed chicken to learn about her aversion." It's not a lie, that really happened. Still, I feel bad, because it's not the full truth. But it's what she wants to hear. I don't want Autumn to know the juicing and healthy diet failed. Hope is important in cancer recovery, even if it's the family member who carries the hope.

Relief trickles into Autumn's expression, and I feel a tiny bit better about my omission.

She steps aside and motions out the door. "I'll let you do the honors," she says.

I'm surprised she hasn't kicked me out yet. It's a big step in our new "friendship."

I nod and smile, stepping through the back door and out into the yard. Faith looks over and eyes the bowls I'm holding, then her gaze moves over to watch Autumn step out and come to a stop beside me.

"A little treat to start this all off," I yell to her. "And then it's greens tomorrow. Doctor's orders."

Faith comes over, a smear of dirt across the front of her shirt. She takes the bowl I have held out to her and pulls out the spoon. Then she dips her spoon into Autumn's bowl first, and then mine, taking ice cream from each of us.

She grins. "If I'm going to look like the Hulk from eating all those leafy greens, I might as well go out with a bang."

"COME ON, Autumn, you know you have some good stories." Faith pushes her empty dinner plate out of her way and leans her forearm on the table. "Spill."

Autumn pushes a lone piece of zucchini around her plate. She made roasted vegetable enchiladas that were a thousand times more delicious than anything I made for Faith in all the time we've eaten together. I'm not sure what has shocked me more since I brought Faith home from chemo: Autumn's cooking ability—which she claims is just following a recipe, not real talent—or her inviting me to stay for dinner.

Autumn twists her lips and tips her head, looking at the wall behind me as she thinks. Her eyes light up, and she looks back down to me, then to her mother, her lips curling into a fond smile.

"There was a homeless man who hung out by a fountain near my apartment. Sometimes, if I was stopping to grab something to eat on my way home, I'd grab food for him too. Usually just the same thing I was getting. But this one Saturday morning I was on my way out to run an errand, and I asked him if there was anything specific he would like me to get for him, and..." She pauses, looking at us intriguingly. "Do you want to guess what he asked for?"

I look across the table at Faith, seated beside Autumn. She grins and says, "Condoms."

Autumn's eyes widen and I laugh. "Mom, for real?"

Faith shrugs. "Is it so farfetched?"

Autumn thinks about it. "I guess not. But ... well, no. That's not what he asked for."

"My turn," I declare, making a show of rolling my shoulders and clapping twice, like I'm ready to go. "I think he asked you for a dozen eggs."

"Hah!" Autumn belts out. "No, but you're in the ballpark. He asked me for organic soy milk."

My mouth drops open. I was kidding about the eggs.

"Organic scmorganic, what's the obsession with this

organic stuff?" Faith bellows, and I grin. "If you tell me to go gluten free, you're fired."

Autumn's brows knit together. "We may have to consider gluten free, Mom."

I can see that the comment triggers Faith and I don't want them to argue. I want Autumn to stay happy and carefree, so I quickly get back on topic.

"How did he keep it cold? The homeless guy?"

"No idea. But I did as he asked. And it made him happy."

Faith smiles and sits back, thawed since the gluten free threat. "That was nice. Better than the story you told me about that time the guy on the street in New York shoved a CD into your hand as you passed him and then Matt—"

"Oh, right, that was crazy," Autumn breaks in. She gives Faith a warning look. It's subtle, but I didn't miss it. There was a story there that she didn't want me to know.

All I can think is: *Who the fuck is Matt?*

I stand, taking my plate with me as I go. When I make a grab for Autumn's plate, she reels her hand back too quick, pulling it from my reach without a word of explanation. Then she takes Faith's plate too but doesn't make a move for mine.

Okay...

I turn around and head for the kitchen and feel Autumn right behind me.

She pulls up next to me at the sink and places her small stack of bowls beside my single one.

"I'll do the dishes." My voice is gruff. I can't help it. The second the dude Matt's name left Faith's lips, it turned me inside-out with jealousy. I'm not an idiot; I don't expect Autumn turned into a virginal princess when she and I broke up. Until now I've tried to never, ever consider her with anybody else. Given what it's doing to me right now, that was a good call on my part. But now I'm wondering if she has a boyfriend back in New York.

Faith and I came to an agreement years ago: we don't talk about Autumn. Now I'm wondering if that was wise.

Autumn frowns at me. "Are you okay? You seem … off."

I don't want to admit what's going on, so instead I reach around her for the scrub brush and snatch up the soap. Who the hell is Matt? An ex? A current? A friend? Matt had better be short for Matilda because this was seriously stressing me out. Honestly, I was shocked she wasn't wearing an engagement ring. Twenty-eight and still single? She was going to get snatched up quick.

"I'm fine. Just tired," I growl.

"I'll do the dishes," Autumn mutters, jaw muscles flexing as they tighten.

"No, I'll do the dishes," I argue back, squirting soap onto the brush. Too much comes out. Blame it on the anger I feel bubbling just below the surface. Anger I don't even have a right to feel because Autumn hasn't been mine in a very long time. Maybe I should have slept with Naomi this morning. Why didn't I?

Autumn crosses her arms, standing so that she faces me. "I'm sure you have other things to do, Owen. Thanks for driving my mom home." Her tone is pointed, insinuating, and her anger is back. God, she's so fucking angry at me all the time. It's a wonder she can hold it together for five minutes and be cordial. I know she wants to ream me over what happened between us. She's like a volcano, constantly simmering yet somehow not yet exploding. One day she will and I just hope we survive the aftermath.

She looks down at her bare feet and I do too. Her toenails are painted a bright orange-red, and even her feet are fucking cute.

A long stream of air comes from my nose. I'm trying to calm the chaos inside me. Autumn's head lifts and our gazes lock. She stares up at me; I stare down at her. I think of the Autumn from before, the girl who softened before an argument could become a fight. We never fought; we disagreed but it never became disrespectful or escalated. Not until the very end, until I messed everything up. She left for Santa Clara, and we weren't sure where we stood anymore. For that matter, even when I showed up at her dorm, she didn't fight me, didn't offer a single word in her defense. She just stood there and took my verbal onslaught, the memory of which has my throat tightening with emotion and my head hanging in shame.

Right now, her hardened gaze shows no sign of softening.

My jaw twitches, and I think it's me who's softening, melting like a damn stick of butter left in the hot sun.

I wrench my gaze away before she can spot the weakness. At the same time, a ringing fills the air. Stepping away from the sink, I pull my phone from my pocket.

The name flashing there fills me with dread. I don't want to answer this in front of her, but I have to.

"Hello?"

"Hey, buddy."

His voice is jovial. A good sign. He hasn't crossed over into aggression. *Yet.*

"What's going on?" I ask. Normally, I would say, *What's going on, Dad?* But Autumn really liked my father, and I don't want her to know what he has turned into.

"Just headed out to Mickey's. Thought I'd see if you wanted to join us for a beer."

Mickey is my dad's best friend. He lives two streets over and has turned his garage into a bar. It's a BYOB system, but Mickey has the place stocked with essentials so you can pretty much drink what you desire when you're there and stumble home. As long as what you desire is a basic liquor and one mixer. None of the twenty-two-dollar martinis Autumn was probably drinking in Manhattan all these years.

I look at Autumn. She's attacking a pan with the scrubber, her arm muscles flexing. Her whole body is rigid. It's probably best if I leave, like she suggested. This thing we're trying to call friendship is already stretched taut. No need to see how much weight it can support.

"I'm on my way," I say into the phone.

"What?" My dad says, shocked. "Oh, great."

His surprise at my agreement is understandable. I used to go with him to Mickey's when I thought it was just a father and son spending some time together. I quit accepting his invitation once I realized he had a problem. Mickey's was an alcoholic's Disneyland and I didn't want to enable him, but tonight I could use a drink.

My hands tuck into my pockets of my work slacks and I roll back on my heels. Autumn's back hasn't lost even a fraction of its rigidity. "I'm going to take off," I tell her, hoping maybe she'll try to ask me to stay for a drink or at least go out on the porch and talk.

I have so much to say to her...

She doesn't move. "Thanks for driving my mom home. And for earlier." She glances at me for the shortest second, then her gaze dances away. "With the, uh, needle."

I don't say anything, but I have the strongest urge to reach out, to hold her the way I did at the hospital this morning. It couldn't have been more than five seconds she was in my arms, needing me, but each second stretched out into a minute. I went straight back to being seventeen, to the time before everything between us went to shit.

"No problem," I grunt.

Autumn stays in the kitchen while I say goodbye to Faith.

Then I go to find my drunk father and settle in for a night of babysitting him.

Chapter 8

Autumn

"SINCE WHEN DO you go to church?" I give my mom a skeptical look.

"Since I started going," my mom shoots back.

I'd been lying on the hammock in my mom's small back yard with one of her romance paperbacks when she walked outside and told me to go get changed.

"And I have to go with you?" I ask from my prone position, hoping she'll let me off the hook. My entire life we attended church services twice a year: Easter and Christmas.

"It would be nice if you'd go." I can tell she's trying not to put too much pressure on me, but she can't keep the hopeful look off her face.

She's wearing a flowy gauze skirt and top. She's

blow-dried her hair using a round brush and it looks full and beautiful. I'd heard the hair dryer blasting on my way out of the house a half hour ago when I'd walked out back with the book tucked under my arm, but I didn't think much of it. I don't know her routine yet; maybe she always gives herself a blow-out on Sundays.

Turns out, her routine includes something else I never saw coming.

God.

The old man upstairs and I are on weird terms right now, and I'm not keen on stepping into a church anytime soon, but I'm not going to deny my mother anything while she's going through her chemo treatments.

"I'll go with you," I relent, trying to cover my reluctance. I scoot over and swing my legs off the side, swaying a little as I stand.

"You can't wear that to church," she tells me, her eyes running down my bare legs.

"Shoot," I say, snapping my fingers. "It's either this or that lingerie I sleep in."

"Very funny," she responds, jostling me with her pointy elbow.

We go in the house, and I do as I've been asked and manage to make it happen in the twenty minutes I've been told I have to do it in.

"Will this do?" I ask, walking into the living room,

where my mom is seated on the couch. My hands are held out to my sides, palms up. I'm wearing the black slacks that were a staple of my work wardrobe and a royal blue blouse.

Mom stands. "You're perfect. Let's go."

She's quiet on the way there. Well, technically, that's not true. She doesn't speak, but she's not quiet. She taps a finger on the center console and plays piano on her knees. Even her pursed lips make sounds when she finally has to take a breath. Is she nervous or in pain or something? Maybe side effects of the chemo?

"All good?" I ask her when we park.

She nods. Clears her throat. Adjusts the sleeve of her top. "All good."

"Okay..." I draw out the word, trying to understand why she's acting so strange.

Heat rises from the hot asphalt parking lot, and I swear I feel it seeping into my heels. The temperature isn't too bad yet, but the asphalt retains the heat, baking us all from the bottom up.

As we walk, people wave to my mom. They say hello and call her by name.

What the hell?

Oops. Good thing that was in my head.

"People know you, Mom," I murmur, nodding at someone who looks at me with curiosity.

"Mmm hmm."

I wait for more, but nothing comes. My mom is a

full-blown churchgoer! This thought fascinates me. We enter the large front doors and my mom parades me around, introducing me to person after person. They all know me. Or … they know *of* me. I'm asked over and over what it was like to live in New York City, and if I'm glad to be back home.

It was a great experience, and yes, I'm thrilled to be back with my mom.

I say it over and over. I say it until I realize it's not just lip service. It's true.

Despite being forced to face Owen again, and the reason I've moved back, it is good to be home, to step away from the hustle and bustle and breathe again.

My mom leads us from the foyer into the sanctuary, where everything is polished oak. The pews are covered in a soft-looking, deep red fabric. It reminds me of Christmas—because, ya know, that used to be when we went to church. When we sit down, I run my finger along the seat cushion. Velvet.

Around us I hear hushed conversations, until all at once the hushed sounds disappear. As I look forward, I watch the man who stands at the center of the stage, the one responsible for quieting the masses. He's wearing a dark gray suit and navy-blue tie and he greets the room with a booming voice. I look at my mom to find that she has a serene look on her face. Maybe that's how I look when I'm practicing yoga. I hope so. If this gives my mother something she needs, then I'm all for it.

For the next hour, I do as I'm supposed to.

I stand when I'm supposed to. I bow my head as I'm instructed. And I pray. It's been so long since I prayed that I don't know if I'm doing it right, but the pastor says there is no wrong way, and I hope he's correct.

When he's done talking, the choir comes back out and we sing one more time. The pastor closes the service with a final prayer, and then dismisses the congregation.

Whew, I didn't burn up. Maybe this God thing isn't so bad after all. My mom stands, but she's a little slow to get to her feet.

"Are you okay?" I ask, reaching for her.

"I'm fine," she answers, gently pushing away the hand I've offered her. "You try sitting in one position for an hour when you're my age and tell me if your bones don't protest a bit."

She's only fifty-five. If it weren't for the cancer, I'd tell her she's too young to be making statements like that. Maybe that's what it is, and she just doesn't want to say it.

We walk from the sanctuary and melt back into the crowd once more. There is more chatting. More people to meet. And then I'm introduced to the man whose voice I just listened to for an hour.

"Pastor Greg, this is my daughter, Autumn." Mom rests her palm on my upper arm and smiles warmly at me.

"Well, Autumn, it's sure nice to meet you. I've heard

a lot about you." He extends a hand, grinning in this earnest way that makes me like him automatically. He's probably about my mom's age. His blond hair is thinning on top, and he reminds me of a cuddly teddy bear. He's not overweight, but he looks soft.

"It's nice to meet you too, Pastor Greg." I'd tell him I've heard about him too, but, well, I haven't. And I can't lie while standing in church, directly in front of the pastor. God might smite me.

Pastor Greg turns his attention to my mom. "How'd you like the service, Faith?"

One side of Mom's lips turn up into a rueful smile. Pastor Greg shakes his head and clucks his tongue. Clearly I'm missing something, but I just watch their interaction instead of asking.

"Would you tell a chef if you didn't like his food?" the pastor asks.

"Probably not," Mom answers, still grinning.

Pastor Greg chuckles. "So I can't count on you for an honest answer about my sermons?"

"Probably not," she repeats.

Pastor Greg laughs again, but I'd call it a chortle. Loud enough to make some people standing nearby look over with interest.

Was my mom flirting with the pastor?

Go Mom.

Before I can think any more about it, he looks my way and tips his head. "It was nice to meet you. If you'll excuse me, there are some other folks I need to talk with."

He shuffles away, and I watch him go.

"He wasn't wearing a wedding ring," I say off-handedly, thinking about how much I was expecting him to.

"What?" My mom seems surprised by my comment. "Oh, he's been divorced a while back. That was before I joined the church."

I open my mouth to respond but someone else fills the empty place the pastor left behind. She's an elderly woman named Margaret, and once she learns where I've just moved from, she talks at length about the time she spent living there and working on Broadway. Of everyone I've met today, she's my favorite.

Mom taps my shoulder, signaling she's ready to go, and I'm relieved. There is only so much churching I'm capable of and two hours is my limit. I extract myself from the conversation as politely as possible.

"Will you be here next week?" Margaret asks hopefully. I look at my mom and she looks hopeful too.

"Sure," I tell her.

Oops. I may have just lied.

We finally make it out to our car after more goodbyes.

"You're the belle of the ball," I comment, backing out of our parking space.

"They know I'm sick," she answers, waving me off.

"So if you weren't sick, they wouldn't talk to you?"

Mom flicks my thigh with the side of her hand. "You know what I mean."

"Yeah, I do. Are you hungry?"

"Starving."

I smile. "Creamed spinach it is."

"Autumn Marie…"

"I'm kidding, Mom." I can't help the chuckle that escapes me.

We settle on pizza and salad. Unfortunately, she doesn't eat much. I see her pop an anti-nausea lozenge into her mouth after two bites … the chemo effects I'd read about must be finally bothering her. I want to ask about it, but she doesn't say anything and I wonder if she just wants a normal Sunday lunch with her daughter, so I don't mention it.

When we're eating, Mom tells me there's no way the pizza in New York City could be any better than it is at this place. I tell her she's right, it's better here because when I ate it in NYC I didn't have her sitting across from me. She tears up, which makes me tear up, and she tells me to quit saying sweet things.

It's something she would have said to me years ago, but aside from the words themselves, everything about her delivery is all wrong. The tone, the tears, the expression on her face.

This time, I don't believe her.

LATER THAT NIGHT, my phone buzzes with a text and I inwardly groan. If it's Matt again I'll vomit. He tried to send more *I miss you* texts, but I've just ignored them. His most recent text said, *I'm starting to get the hint*. Hopefully by now the hint has been fully received. I blow out a relieved breath when I look down and see it's from Livvie.

Livvie: I don't know about you, but I could use a drink.

Me: Perfect timing. My mom just went to bed.

Livvie: Orange Peel Brewing Company? I don't want fancy wine. I'm in a cold beer mood.

Me: I can be there in twenty.

Livvie: See you soon, baboon.

Me: Is that one of the inappropriate texts you warned me about?

Livvie: No. I'm just feeling you out to decide how receptive you are to jokes in general. Starting slow, you know? Like, just the tip.

The water I'm drinking catches in my throat and I cough while I'm laughing. It burns.

Me: Ahhh there it is.

Livvie: That's what she said. See you soon!

I PULL on comfortable jeans and my Converse shoes. No spiked heels for this meetup. Livvie is my keep-it-real girlfriend, one who I can be myself around. Maybe

I'll wear heels again, but right now it's difficult to imagine a scenario in which I'll need them.

I get to the brewing company first and grab a booth. Livvie walks in a few minutes later. She's dressed like me.

"Tell me the truth," she says, sliding in across from me. "You thought about skinny jeans and heels too, didn't you?"

"Of course," I nod. "But Chucks arc one thousand times more comfortable. What were we doing going out in heels?"

"Rookie mistake. Blame it on youth." She eyes me. "How old are you? I know you're younger than me." She points at her eyes. "You don't have fine lines yet."

"Oh stop. I'm twenty-eight but lately I feel forty-five."

She makes a disgusted sound in the back of her throat. "Neophyte."

"You don't want fancy wine but you use a fancy word?"

She shrugs. "I learned it today at the bookstore. It was empty because, shocker, it's ugly as sin in that place with fuck-all to do in the way of fun. Anyway, I was reading a book and that word was in it. I had to look it up, and now my vocabulary has grown by one word."

I high-five her, grinning. "How old are you?"

She narrows her gaze. "It's impolite to ask that question of your elders."

I give her a pointed look and she says, "Thirty-five."

I gasp and pretend to be horrified. She looks around for something to throw at me, but there isn't anything on the table except our forearms. Seriously, she looks amazing for her age. I thought she was only a year older than me.

She sticks her tongue out at me, then looks around for a server. When she spots one, she signals them over.

"I'll have the amber ale in the coldest glass you have," she tells the young guy in the black polo. "And a food menu."

He looks at me, gaze expectant.

"Two, please."

When he leaves, Livvie starts speaking: "I need to talk, but I can't until I've had a sip of beer."

I nod, considering her words. "Then I'll talk while we wait. I went to church with my mom today. Apparently she goes every week, and she has been doing so for some time. I had no idea."

"Is it a big deal that she's going to church?"

"No. It's just that I didn't know, and things like this keep happening. It's not like I moved away and didn't speak to her. We spoke often. I even came back here to visit. They weren't long trips, but it's not as if I left and never came back."

"You're hurt she didn't share more about her life?"

I shake my head. "No."

Maybe.

"You sound like your feelings are hurt."

I chuckle. "Maybe a little."

The server walks up with our drinks. He tosses down two cardboard coasters, then sets down the beers, followed by two menus. "I'll be back for your order."

Livvie's arm shoots out, stopping him. "Wait a sec," she says, quickly scanning the menu. "I'll have a basket of green chili fries."

He nods and looks at me.

I shake my head. "Nothing for me, thanks."

"Do not tell me you're on a diet," Livvie says as he gathers the menus and leaves. She says the word *diet* as if it's responsible for a heinous crime.

"I already ate," I explain. "It's nine and I'll get heartburn if I eat a basket of chili fries right now and go to bed."

"What does that have to do with anything? Fries are fries." She lifts her beer and knocks it gently against mine. "To neophytes and their elders."

I grin and sip my drink. It's crisp and cold. "So?" I urge Livvie. "Talk."

"My husband is an asshole." She takes a long drink. "A giant asshole."

"What happened?" I ask.

Livvie drains half of her beer. "Jeff, my husband, wants kids."

"And that's bad because…?"

"A long time ago, we agreed not to have kids. We

wanted big careers, the kind of careers that make it hard to have a family. We both work on Wall Street," she explains. "I didn't want to give up my career for a family, and he didn't either."

Sounds familiar. I definitely fall into the workaholic type of personality. Well, I did when I actually had a job.

"You could get a nanny." As soon as I say it, I feel stupid. Livvie and Jeff have probably thought of everything. She doesn't need me to point things out needlessly. "Sorry, I'll shut up and listen."

Livvie laughs and drinks her beer. "Neither of us want to have kids and watch another person parent them. And that is what we would be doing. Now, out of the blue, Jeff wants kids, but when I asked him if he planned on being a stay-at-home dad, he laughed. He said he thought maybe I'd grown tired of my career and I was ready for a new scene. He asked why I didn't want to look like the other moms pushing expensive strollers around the park. As if I have some sort of defect for not wanting that."

"I'm so sorry," I tell her, pushing my hand across the table. She knows what I'm doing, so she meets me halfway and accepts my squeeze. What an ass that he expects her to drop her career and take care of a new baby.

"I came out here to help save my grandma's business, but I discovered how much I like Arizona, and I don't want to go back now. Earlier today, I asked him to come out here. To give it all up. We could get jobs here, or even in Phoenix. There's so much we could both do there. We could work normal hours. I'd be open to getting a nanny because we wouldn't need her 24/7. I'd be open to kids..."

"What did he say?" I lean forward.

"He said no. He's not willing to give up his job. He has worked too long and too hard to quit now."

Asshole.

I lean in closer. "What are you going to do?"

She sighs. "I don't know. I hung up on him."

I wish there was more I could say or do to make her feel better.

"Now he got all up in my head, and every time I pass a baby something kicks my ovaries until I stare at the baby with heart emoji eyes," she says, and I grin.

This conversation is hitting a little too close to home, so I squirm in my seat and give a nervous laugh.

Someone drops off the fries and we both murmur a thank you without looking up. Livvie takes a few, shoving them into her mouth. After a few moments of companionable silence, our server comes over and she orders another beer. I try like hell to stop eyeing those fries. After a few minutes of them sitting between us, I can't take it anymore.

"Fries are fries," I say, grabbing a few. Livvie laughs.

Fuck heartburn. It's worth it.

"Please tell me about your problems. I can't stand

mine anymore." She eats another fry. "What's the deal with Owen the oncologist?"

"I'm not sure. I saw him a few days ago. He drove my mom home that day after she had chemo. The day I met you. And he stayed for dinner that night. I thought we were doing okay, being civil and all that. But then things got weird when we were cleaning up the kitchen, and he got a call and left abruptly."

To be fair, I all but pushed him out. He was acting cagey and weird. I sensed he wanted to get into our past and I wasn't feeling it.

"Some broad?"

I shrug. "Maybe. If it was, it didn't sound like a new relationship. His tone wasn't sweet enough for that."

Did Owen have a girlfriend? I had no idea.

"You think it was an old relationship? Like one he's been in for a while?"

The thought makes me sick and I don't know why.

"Wouldn't my mom have said something though?" Probably not, since we had a no-talking-about-Owen rule for ten years now.

"The same mom who didn't tell you she was going to church?"

I nod. She didn't tell me she'd been having dinner with Owen weekly either. It makes sense she'd keep something like Owen having a girlfriend from me. "I see your point."

"So, what if it was a woman on the other end of that

phone call?" Livvie's eyes bore into mine and I suddenly regret sharing.

If Owen had a girlfriend, would I really care? I mean, sure, he was a good-looking doctor who I had history with, but who cares? We both moved on. *Right?*

"I don't know."

"You don't know? Or you're not being honest with yourself?"

A shadow passes over my soul as my mind goes right back to what Owen and I truly share: three good years together that exploded like a supernova in one day. The memory of the foul things he said to me that day in my dorm floods my mind. How Ace stood by and watched in horror as Owen spewed verbal diarrhea all over me in an effort to mask his own pain.

I grab two more fries, using my fork to scoop up green chili. "He hurt me, Livvie. Badly."

"How badly?" she asks cautiously, clearly noticing the change in my mood.

"Not physically," I assure her. "No, nothing like that. It's just..." My palms come to meet in front of me. "When things went south, it got ugly. He said things, and they left a mark."

I finish my beer and take one more fry.

Livvie must sense I'm done talking, because she doesn't say more. Her second beer arrives and we move on to less emotional topics. We're knee-deep in a discussion about the best cannoli on the Upper East

Side when a commotion at the bar stops us mid-sentence.

"You need a new set of eyeballs, friend! I'm just fine!" a man hollers with slurred speech. I look up and see a clearly drunk man with his back to me, swaying on his feet. Another man, bald and wearing a collared shirt, hovers near the drunk. Baldy turns slightly, and I make out the emblem of the restaurant embroidered on his shirt, so he must work here. As he reaches for the drunk man, the old guy shoves him off.

His voice … it's raised the hairs on my arms.

Where do I know that voice?

That's when the drunk turns and I get a clear picture of his face. He's older, his hair salt and pepper, but I recognize him immediately.

I bolt up from the booth, heart hammering in my chest, and Livvie follows.

"What are you doing," she asks, right on my heels.

"I know him," I tell her, and walk right up to the two men. The guy with the collared shirt, who is clearly a manager or something, is trying to explain something.

"Sir, we can't serve you any more tonight. Now, if you'll just tell me your name and address, I'll be happy to call a car to drive you home."

"This is ridiculous. I came here to spend my hard-earned money and you're turning me away?"

"Hey there," I say, stepping up to the two men.

The manager puts a hand on my forearm. "Ma'am, I don't think it's a good idea to get in the middle of this."

I ignore him and focus my attention on Owen's dad. "Mr. Miller?"

He blinks two heavy-lidded eyes at me. "Autumn … is that you?" His face brightens a little and I'm relieved he remembers me in his inebriated state. But now that I'm close, I see how the years have aged him: thick red skin, wrinkles—time hasn't been good to Mr. Miller, and I don't think this is his first time getting kicked out of a bar.

I offer a small smile to the manager. "I've got this, sir."

He looks uncertain. "Are you sure?"

"Yes. I'll take him home. I know him."

He nods once, then steps away. Given how quickly he walks away, I'd guess he's grateful he doesn't have to deal with this situation any longer.

"Can we go somewhere and talk, Mr. Miller? I haven't seen you in a long time and I'd love to catch up."

He glances back to the bartender, who's shaking a cocktail in a metal shaker but is still keeping an eye on Owen's dad.

"I guess so," he says gruffly. "Not much point in staying here."

I look to where Livvie stands a few feet from us. "Go ahead," she says quietly. "I'll get the bill. You buy next time," she says when she sees me begin to protest.

"Thank you," I mouth. I wind my arm through Mr. Miller's and hope he doesn't realize I'm providing him with support in case he can't walk. To cover up what I'm doing, I look up at him and ask if he still has that old collection of baseball cards.

"Sure do," he says. "Wouldn't sell those things for the world."

I ask him which one is his favorite. He talks about the card, how he got it, and what he paid for it. This conversation gets us all the way out of the place and into my mom's car.

"Does Owen know you're back?" he asks as I start the engine.

"Yes, Mr. Miller. He's my mom's doctor."

They must not talk much, and that hurts my heart. I had no idea. Mr. Miller was always an unemotional man, but he and Owen had a decent relationship.

"Call me Mike, Autumn. Feels weird to be called Mr. Miller." He coughs and adjusts his seat. "I'm sorry to hear your mom is sick."

"Yeah, me too. Thanks."

Mike reaches around behind himself, struggling, then his arm reappears with a silver flask. He unscrews the top and tips it to his lips, then offers it to me.

"No thank you," I tell him, trying to keep the surprise from my voice. I can't remember ever seeing him have more than a couple beers the entire time I was dating Owen. What happened?

"Do you still live on Liberation Lane?" I ask.

"Yep. I guess not much has changed since you left," he laughs as he says it.

I smile, aware of how wrong he is. "Guess not," I say.

By the time I turn onto his street, he is slumped against the passenger door, passed out. His head is tipped back, soft snores falling from his open mouth.

Well, *shit*…

How am I supposed to carry an unconscious grown man inside?

Chapter 9

Owen

MY FINGERS CURL around the cold beer bottle. For hours I've been looking forward to opening my new science fiction book, sitting back in my favorite chair, and drinking a cold beer. It's my preferred way to unwind from a long day at the hospital when I find it difficult to settle down my brain. Going into a fantasy world is my favorite form of escapism.

I sink into the chair and put my feet up on the matching ottoman. I paid an obscene amount of money for this chair, but it's already paid for itself in the amount of relaxation it brings me.

I'm one paragraph into my book and two sips into my beer when my phone rings. My gaze flicks across the room and I stare at the device on the coffee table.

I'd love to ignore it, but I can't. It could be the hospital. Or my dad. In either scenario, my help may be needed.

With a deep, irritated sigh, I close my book and set it on the small table beside my chair. My beer comes with me and I can feel the frown on my face.

I have a sixth sense for bad news. Comes with being a cancer doctor. And this call feels like bad news.

Grabbing my phone, I see the name flashing across the front, and my frown deepens.

"Autumn?"

"Hey," she responds. Her voice is uncertain.

"Is everything okay?" Something must be wrong. She wouldn't call me for any other reason. The last time I saw her she stood at Faith's kitchen sink, her anger apparent.

"Um, no. Not really … I need your help." She sounds reluctant, but presses forward anyway. "Your dad is passed out in my car and I can't wake him up. And I certainly can't carry him into his house alone."

What. The. Fuck?

My eyes close slowly, my chin tipping up to the ceiling. My grip on the beer bottle tightens, the muscles in my fingers straining as embarrassment washes over me.

Dammit. What the hell did he do now? How did Autumn get roped into it?

"I'll be right there." I hang up without waiting for Autumn to answer.

My old man has a problem, and I've known for a while. But how do you help someone who doesn't want help? He's sixty, retired, and not keen on taking advice from his young son.

I go to the kitchen, empty the rest of my beer into the sink, then toss the bottle into the recycling bin, staring at it for a full second and wondering if I could ever be like my dad and have a drinking problem.

Running into my bedroom, I change quickly from my ratty basketball shorts into jeans and a long-sleeved shirt, then grab my keys and phone and head out.

I had no intention of telling Autumn about my dad. Guess that desire is out the window. I wonder what she thinks…

AS I PULL into the driveway beside Faith's car, I kill my lights. From what I can tell in the dark, there is only one person in her car, and my guess is that it's not Autumn. Something moves in the shadows on the side of the house and I recognize her petite frame.

Climbing from my car, I close the door, heading around the corner.

"Hey," she says softly as I come near. She's leaning against the house, blocked from the view of the street, hands tucked in the front pockets of her jeans. A swath of moonlight cuts across her face and I try not to think about how beautiful she is.

"Hi." I come to a stop a few feet away. "Sorry about my dad."

She waves me off. "It's no biggie."

It is a biggie to me. A huge fuckin' biggie. Local doctor's dad becomes the town drunk. It's embarrassing.

We're both silent for a full minute and I'm trying to figure out how to get him into the house without her helping when she speaks.

"How long has he had a problem?"

Her question rankles me. I feel defensive, even though I know he needs help. I hate what he's turned into, and of all people to see it, it's Autumn...

"You can leave now," I say, looking out into the distance and avoiding her question. I know she doesn't want to be here. "I can handle it from here."

"I can't leave, Owen. He's in my car."

Right.

"And I wouldn't leave you with this alone. Why do you seem mad at me?" A guarded edge has crept into her voice and I hate that she looks hurt on my account. I've hurt her enough for ten lifetimes. I don't intend to do any more of that.

I press the spot at the bridge of my nose and avoid her gaze. "I'm not mad at you. I'm mad at him. Where did you find him?"

"I met a friend at Orange Peel Brewing Company. Your dad was there ... creating a scene. I stepped in because the manager was two seconds away from calling the police."

"What friend?" Of everything she just said, it's the

entirely wrong place to focus. I can't help it though. "Have you met someone here already?" I'm completely shocked by the jealously lacing through my voice.

She balks. "What does it matter to you if I have?"

"It doesn't." The lie burns my teeth as I tell it.

"I didn't think so." She crosses her arms and steps closer to me, bringing the heat of her body with her. "Besides, you're the one who went running the other night when your phone rang. Someone has *you* on a short leash."

I'll be dammed. Autumn Cummings is jealous. This one shred of information does crazy things to my stomach. Could we pick up where we left off? Would it be that simple? No, but it was proof that everything wasn't dead between us.

"What does it matter to you?" A sly grin pulls at my lips and her gaze sharpens like an eagle ready to hunt.

"It doesn't," she says, just a little too harshly. A little too intense. The hallmark of a lie. I would know, seeing as how I just did the same.

I take a step forward, grazing my body against her, my gaze on her face, watching her reaction. Her expression is steady, and if it weren't for the slight widening of her eyes, I'd think my proximity had no effect on her.

One more step puts me fully flush against her, and I'm delighted when her breath hitches as she presses herself closer to me. Her chest rises and falls with a single, deep breath. The scent of her skin wafts over me, covering me like a blanket, bringing memories to the surface like sunken ships pulled from the depths by a hurricane. I cannot deny how much my body wants her. How much I want to make her moan the way I used to. I want to rediscover her.

Cautiously, I reach out to touch her and she watches my hand but doesn't back away. With one fingertip I trace the edge of her tank-top strap. Her eyes go half lidded and my finger trails across her collarbone and then up her neck to trace her jawline.

Was that a small moan? I can barely fucking contain myself; I want to explore every inch of her, but I stop as her sharp exhale fills the already thick air between us.

"It doesn't matter to you that I left your house after a phone call?" I want to test her, to see if she still cares for me.

She levels her heated gaze on me. "It doesn't matter to you that I met someone tonight?"

Fuck. It's a stalemate. We both know each other's hand but neither will admit it.

My fingers travel up her neck, feather over her jaw, disappear into her hair. She swallows hard as I lean closer, ducking my head and placing my lips on her neck. I don't kiss her, but I hold my lips there, taking in the familiar scent of her skin.

I'm completely floored that she hasn't racked me in the nuts by now. She wants this … like I want this … and that thought brings everything good about our love back to me. The way we used to be, like two magnets that could never part.

I drag the tip of my nose up her neck, near her ear, across her cheek. Her heart hammers against my chest. We're nose to nose, forehead to forehead, my lips hovering over hers.

"I missed everything about you," I whisper.

"I missed nothing about you," she shoots back with a halfcocked grin.

Lies. All lies. And we both know it.

In that moment my lips crash down on hers, I can't take it anymore. I can't take her refusal to admit we still have something. I want to kiss it out of her, remind her what we had before we hurt each other.

So I do. I cradle the back of her head with my palm and I kiss her the way I've been dreaming of since the day I walked away from her. She moans, threading her fingers into my hair as she opens her lips to deepen the kiss. We're tender at first, careful with one another. The gentle meshing feels like an overdue apology.

But then it changes. The apology gives way to anger. Resentment. Pain. Years of all this, pent up. Autumn kisses me hard, pressing her lips deeply into me as I match her. I feel her lips trembling, her hips ramming into mine. It's one of those aggressive movie kisses that you never think are real, but this is the realest fucking kiss I've ever had. She reaches under my shirt, her warm hands skimming my torso. Then I feel her nails dragging over the skin of my back and I contemplate leaving my father to sleep off the night in the car while I take Autumn into the house.

This kiss is more than a kiss, it's our goodbye, our hello, our everything. It's ten years of not speaking after we shared one of the deepest and darkest moments a relationship can ever have. I need Autumn like I need air, and her signals are all green light.

Keeping my lips on hers, my hands travel down, finding the top of her jeans. I unbutton them and push a hand inside, sliding down over the soft cotton of her underwear. Waiting a moment to see if she rejects me, I'm pleased when she tilts her hips harder into my hands. I push aside the fabric and find her center.

Fuck me, I can barely keep the groan off my lips as my finger dips inside and she covers me in heat and moisture. It's further proof that she wants this, likes this.

A mangled cry comes from deep within her throat, and I swallow it. Of all the times I've done this with Autumn, I've never been anything but gentle. Except for now. There's a roughness to this, a primal instinct in the way I pleasure her. Her fingernails dig into my back as I use my hand against her, rotating in small circles.

She lifts her face to mine, and when she kisses me the fight is gone from her. It's gone from me too. A breeze picks up, pushing her long hair off her shoulder, and I kiss her skin where her tank-top has left her bare. The roughness of my touch has disappeared. Muscle memory has kicked in and I move expertly, remembering what she liked all those years ago, hoping it's what she still prefers.

It is.

Under my hand, her body comes to life. Her breathing picks up in pace, until I feel her breasts push against my chest and her back arches. My mouth comes down onto hers and I devour her sounds. Her breath is heavy as she jumps up and straddles my waist. I catch her ass with one hand and hold her against me as we kiss, my other hand moving faster inside of her. I don't know what's come over me, but I'm suddenly determined to give Autumn an orgasm. To prove that I can still pleasure her? To bring her some amount of bliss after years of pain? Whatever my motive, I move my fingers harder and then brush my thumb in circles over her most sensitive spot.

"Owen." She clenches against me and starts to shake. "Holy fuck." She screams as I back up and slam her against the wall of my dad's house. Autumn rocks against my hand, tightening over my fingers as her orgasm pulses in my hand.

I'm so turned on I can't even think straight. She finally collapses against my neck and huffs a huge contented sigh along my earlobe. Slipping my hand out of her pants, I lower her to the ground and adjust my hard-on as she buttons her jeans, face flushed red.

I wipe my hand on the inside of my shirt and she smirks.

"That used to embarrass you," I say, reaching up and

tucking away a piece of hair that has blown into her face.

"I've grown up a little since then."

I cup my palm around her cheek. "I can see that."

Suddenly, looking at my neighbor's house, she seems to realize where we are.

"Did you just finger me in your dad's driveway?" She grins, looking young and carefree, like the old Autumn.

I'm still breathing heavily, wondering what it would be like to make love to her. I'm no longer mad that my dad's a drunk, because it made this happen.

She looks up at me. "The person I met tonight was a girl. I made a friend."

I laugh once, a relieved sound. "The person who called was my dad. He wanted a drinking buddy..."

One side of her mouth curls into a small smile and I know this is the perfect moment for our talk.

"Autumn, I'm so sorry for what—"

Her face falls and it stops me short. "Owen, don't."

My brows furrow. "Don't what? I've been waiting ten years to apologize to you and you're not going to let me? Why?"

She chews her lip. "Because I'm afraid it won't do anything."

Shit. Afraid it won't fix anything, she means. Afraid that even the most heartfelt apology can't make her love me again. If that's not the most depressing thing I've ever heard, I don't know what is.

She looks into my eyes and I can see the questions floating around in there. They mirror my own.

"Autumn—" I try again.

A garbled yell comes from the front of the house. "Owen?"

Panic takes the place of questions as I remember my father. I step away from Autumn, reaching down to adjust the front of my pants a final time as Autumn runs a hand across her shirt, smoothing out wrinkles that aren't there.

"Coming, Dad," I yell back, grabbing Autumn's hand and pulling her along behind me.

I round the corner and find my dad standing in the space between Faith's car and my own, eyebrows drawn together in confusion.

"Owen, did you know Autumn is in town?" He looks at Faith's car, a thick slur to his voice. "This is her car. Where is she?"

Autumn steps around me. "Right here." She waves slowly, cheeks bright red.

Dad sways in the moonlight and I realize he's drunker than usual tonight. "For a second there I thought I dreamed it." He shakes his head and starts to stumble forward. Autumn and I rush forward, but I get to him first.

He crashes into me as I wrap an arm around his shoulder. Embarrassment flushes through me. "I'm going to take him inside. I'll be right back."

This is my moment with Autumn and my dad is ruining it.

Autumn nods.

I get my dad to the front door, use my key to unlock it, and walk him to his bedroom. He insists he can dress himself, so I wait outside his bedroom door for him to do so. After a few minutes, he pulls open the door. He's wearing a checkered button-up shirt and plaid shorts. He looks like a drunken golfer and my depression deepens.

"Don't let me keep you, Owen. Go out there to the girl you've never been able to get over."

He closes the door and I listen. Imagine, my dad giving me good advice for a change.

Excitement thrums through me as I walk back outside, thinking of what happened on the side of the house with Autumn. We have a lot to talk about, but we've taken a step forward. It's everything I've been waiting on for years. It's proof that what we had can never really die, no matter how scarred our past.

I walk out to the driveway, a smile the size of Texas on my face.

But my smile is washed away like a wave at the sea.

Autumn is gone.

Chapter 10

Owen

ACE COMES UP BEHIND ME, clamping a hand on my shoulder. "You ready for this, buddy?"

"You bet," I mumble grumpily. That shit with Autumn last night was a mindfuck. We finally come back together only for her to pull a typical Autumn and run away without a word.

Ace settles in beside me at the silver metal basin and pumps soap into his hands. We scrub and scrub, then we scrub a little more, under our fingernails and up to our elbows. I'm so mad at Autumn that I scrub my fingernails harder than usual, but I need to rein in my emotions because today is a big surgery.

When we're finished, an operating room nurse slides on our gloves. They are tight, almost suffocating, but after a minute I forget they are there.

Ace and I are sitting in on a surgery today. It's a tough case. A tumor wrapped tightly around a liver. The patient is a ten-year-old girl…

Ten years old. It always messes with me to see kids that are the same age as the child Autumn and I decided not to have. It's my biggest regret in life and the darkest weight I carry on my soul. Truthfully, I wanted the baby, but Autumn made her choice and I wanted to be supportive, so I swallowed my opinion and held her hand through it all. That swallowed opinion has eaten me up inside for a decade.

"Doctors…" a different nurse nods in greeting, and gets the door for us as we step into the OR. I blink twice at the bright lights, eyes slowly adjusting. The patient is already there, lying on a gurney in the center of the room. She is tiny compared to other patients I've seen in this same room.

My heart lurches and my step falters. Ace gives me a quick elbow to the side.

"You going to be okay?"

He knows the weight I carry, what Autumn and I went through.

I nod, swallowing my emotions and propelling myself forward. Dr. Maple stares us down from her place beside the patient. I can't see much of her besides her eyes, but those are steely and narrowed, watching me. Dr Maple is a hardass. She's been a surgeon for thirty years; her knowledge is extensive. Being a surgeon in a smaller town means learning to perform an array of surgeries. I'm lucky to study under her, even if she is mostly unpleasant to be around.

"Are you ready, Dr. Miller?" Her tone is laced with impatience.

"Yes, Dr. Maple," I say with confidence I don't feel. From the corner of my eye, Ace dips his chin just slightly. I hear what he isn't saying.

You got this.

And I do. I manage to pull myself together. The air in the room becomes heavy, thick with our fierce desire for the best possible outcome. We all know the stakes. If we aren't successful, the little girl will be air-vac'ed to Phoenix Children's Hospital. Right here, right now, we have the best possible chance of saving her liver; otherwise she goes on a transplant list.

I love watching Dr. Maple work. She is precise, calm, and if she has nerves, she doesn't show them. Not even a twitch of her hand.

We reach the end of the surgery and Dr. Maple looks up at me. "Close her up," she instructs. I freeze for the shortest second, then move into action. I know what to do, so I push any emotions I have for my patient to the back of my mind and rely on my training. An OR nurse hands me a threaded needle as Ace looks on. I'm aware of the eyes on me, on the needle I'm holding.

I take a deep breath, but I do it slowly, trying not to let anybody see the telltale rise and fall of my chest. Just as I've been trained to, I slip the needle into the skin, telling myself it is *the* skin and not *her* skin. She is a patient. Amorphous. Not a little girl. I push away the details of who is lying here and focus solely on what I'm doing. When I finish, I tie off the sutures and step back.

"Perfect sutures," the anesthesiologist says from her place near the little girl's head.

"Thank you," I nod at her. She's been around the hospital for fifteen years longer than me. Her compliment means something.

The nurses take over, and Ace and I leave the OR. We strip down and discard our gloves, washing our hands again.

"You did great, man. Really." Ace pats my shoulder as we walk away from the sink. "I know kids are tough for you."

I nod. "Yeah."

"Is it harder than usual because Autumn's back?"

Last night floods my mind. I can't get a handle on what happened on the side of my dad's house. So many emotions swayed between us, each one fleeting. Desperation, attraction, anger, none of them getting the air time they need.

Bottom line: Autumn and I need to have an honest conversation. And soon.

"Maybe. But it's hard every time it's a kid."

"Especially one that age," Ace points out, forcing me to face that fact.

"Right," I agree. "I'll type up the report, okay?" I veer off without waiting for him to respond.

In my office, I spend a few minutes with my head in my hands, going over everything from the surgery. Reliving it helps me with the details so that I can write an accurate report. Even if it hurts to remember her smallness, I have to do my job.

After I finish typing my report, at nearly the same time my stomach grumbles. Unfortunately, I don't have time to eat. I have three more patients to see this afternoon. So, I pull open the top drawer of my desk, push aside some papers, and find the protein bar I threw in here last week. It's the best I can do for the next few hours.

I'm on my way out of my office when my phone buzzes. I'm in a rush but I stop short when I see it's a text from Autumn.

My mom would like to know if you're coming over for dinner tonight? It's a Monday, so...?

I sigh. Is it only Faith who wants to know? Or Autumn too? Is there any reason for me to hope? Or is it the most dangerous thing I could do?

I want to type her back: *What the fuck happened last night?* but I don't. I know she's struggling inside and I don't want to push her. I got a glimpse of what we could be like again last night and I don't want to fuck it up.

I type out my response. **Tell your mom I wouldn't miss it for the world.**

It's true. Autumn or no Autumn, Faith is important to me.

"YOU'RE LATE."

Autumn leans against the doorframe, arms crossed like a guard denying me entry. All I can think about is my fingers inside of her as we were pressed against my dad's house in the dark of night ... the way she moaned in my ear and tilted into my hand, begging for more.

I clear my throat. "My last patient needed some extra time." I rub my temple with two fingers. I should ask her where the hell she went last night after she disappeared on me, but I don't have it in me to start that discussion right now. I'm exhausted, and I'm starving.

Autumn must sense that I'm not a worthy opponent right now. She steps aside and I walk in. If I were more awake, more spry, I'd brush against her as I walk past, but I'm not, and I don't so much as graze an inch of her.

"Hey, I was fucking with you. You okay?"

I flinch, I don't know why, but I do, and she retracts her arm.

"I had a rough day with a pediatric patient." I flick my gaze up to hers and her face falls.

"Oh." I can see the shadows cross over face, haunting her, and I regret telling her about my patient.

I'm so pissed she hasn't said anything about

running off last night that I just keep walking until I reach the kitchen.

Faith is in there preparing a salad. I peer over her shoulder to see what we are eating. Kale, with sliced apples, almonds, and grapefruit.

"Very healthy," I comment.

Faith startles. "Geez, I didn't know you were there, Owen. I'm sorry. I was daydreaming."

I settle back against the edge of the counter. "I hope it was a good dream."

She smiles. "Pretty good."

Also known as, *I'm not telling you about it.*

"How are you feeling after chemo?" I ask.

She nods. "About as good as can be expected."

That meant some nausea and fatigue no doubt.

Autumn walks in, glancing at me hesitantly before going to the fridge and opening it. She's wearing black leggings, a loose top, and her hair is wound into a messy bun on the top of her head. She's stunning and she's not even trying. Typical Autumn.

"The grill should be ready by now," Autumn says, pulling away from the fridge with a tray. On top are three large salmon filets. She doesn't ask me to come outside with her, but the meaningful look she gives me conveys her message.

From the window above the kitchen sink, I watch her walk to the grill, and after what I think is probably enough time, I follow.

"Do you need help with the fish?" I ask, coming up

to stand beside her at the grill. She has set the tray on the small attached workspace and is folding the foil around the salmon so it creates something like a pillow. My guess is that she brought me out here to talk about what happened last night, but I'm not sure how to start the conversation.

"I'm sorry," she says, not looking at me. She sets the foil packet on the heated grill. "I freaked out and took off last night."

Wow. An apology from Autumn Cummings. Never thought those words were capable of leaving her lips. She picks up a pair of tongs and uses them to push the foil to the center of the grill before stepping back. I reach around her and push the lid down over the grill to be helpful.

"I understand," is all I say as I watch her toss the tongs on the now-empty tray. "But I was disappointed." I'd wanted to hold her, touch her, kiss her, make her listen to what I have to say. I've waited a fucking decade to speak and she still hasn't let me.

"I didn't know what to say or do after ... you know." Pink blooms on her cheeks. "It was just so unexpected. I still can't believe I let it happen like that."

I still can't believe I let it happen like that. My stomach drops in my gut. That sounds like regret. Or embarrassment that we let our passions get the better of us?

I study her profile as she stares out into the yard. Clearly there is still attraction between us, as strong as it ever was, maybe even stronger now. "Don't be embarrassed, Autumn. I ... liked it." What a lame way to finish a sentence. I want to tell her that I didn't just *like* it. I *loved* making her come apart at the seams, knowing it was me who was taking her on that ride.

She eyes me. "It's backwards..." she says and I get her meaning. "I don't know what to say or do now either."

"Neither do I." I rub my eyes, the exhaustion of the day creeping in.

"Did you have a bad day?"

My hands run through my hair. "No. Not really a bad day. Just a hard one."

"Why was it hard? Because ... it was a kid?"

"Because the patient was a ten-year-old girl."

"Oh." Not just any kid, a kid the exact age ours would be.

Her lower lip trembles. A few seconds later, tears well up in her eyes. "Is it always like that for you? When it's a child" she asks. She is trying so hard to be brave, to stumble through the anguish that still plagues us both.

"Yes. You?"

"I don't have much interaction with children. But yes, sometimes it happens."

We look into each other's eyes, and the stare is full of everything we've been holding back. We've held it in for years, knowing it lies dormant, resurrected only by one another.

"I'm so sorry," Autumn says, a guttural sob escaping her. Her shoulders slump and her head dips.

I rush in, wrap my arms around her. "I'm sorry too, Autumn. So sorry. I was just a kid. What I said—"

She shakes her head against my chest. "Please don't go there right now, Owen. I can't take it." She sniffles and wipes her eyes, taking a step back. "Maybe we can talk on your next day off? I'm sure we have an audience right now."

I look over and Faith darts away from the window.

I frown. "You're right, we do."

She smiles ruefully. "My mom is dying to know what happened between us."

"Do you think you'll ever tell her?"

Autumn sighs. "Maybe one day."

"She might take it better than you think."

"You think you know my mom pretty well, don't you?" A defensive tone creeps into her voice. It's the same tone she uses every time she thinks I'm insinuating I know her mom better than she does.

"I know her well enough to know she has lightened up a lot over the years," I tell her.

Autumn frowns. The conversation is moving away from where I want it to go, and I have to get it back.

"I have the day off tomorrow. Can we get that coffee?"

Autumn nods and reaches for the handle to lift the grill, but I get to it first.

"Let me."

She steps back and I take care of the fish. Out of the corner of my eye, I see her run her fingers under her eyes one more time, wiping away any evidence of upset.

"You ready?" I ask, pausing with the tray in my hand.

She nods and follows me back across the yard and into the house. Halfway through dinner, Faith sets her fork down and says she doesn't feel well.

"What's wrong?" I ask her, leaning forward. The doctor in me is examining her appearance; the human in me feels the cold whisper of my own fear.

"Just some nausea, that's all."

She does look a little pale. "Can I get you anything?" I ask.

Chemo is a necessary beast. It borders on killing everything good inside of the patient while killing everything bad.

She pushes away from the table. "I think I'll just go lie down."

"Faith, hang on." I stand up, coming around the table to stand in front of her. I lift my hand, hovering it in the air in front of her forehead. "May I?"

She nods, and I place the back side of my hand against her forehead. She's warm, but not hot. Not a real fever, at least not one that's concerning. Chemo-therapy side effects are to be expected. Even though my rational doctor brain knows all this, I still feel a trickle of concern.

"All good," I tell her. It's not a lie. I'm managing her stress level, and I don't have a thermometer. What I know is that she's not burning up.

She steps around me, but stops when she gets a few feet away. As she turns back around, she looks at Autumn. "Thank you for dinner, hon. I never thought I'd actually like kale."

Autumn musters a smile, but I can see the worry in her creased forehead. Faith leaves the room and I begin gathering dishes from the table.

"Why don't you go hang out for a bit and I'll take care of the dishes." Autumn takes them from me.

I start to protest, but she stops me with a swift shake of her head. "You're clearly exhausted, Owen. And I know you're worried about my mom." She glances in the direction of Faith's bedroom. "I am, too. I'd feel better if you stayed for a while. Just to make sure she doesn't suddenly get a high fever or something."

Tension I didn't know I'd been holding melts away. I like the idea of staying here for a bit and monitoring Faith.

"Okay," I agree, leaving the kitchen and going to the living room. I find a baseball game on the TV and sit back in Faith's recliner. I'll give it an hour and then I'll check on her.

Chapter 11

Autumn

AFTER WHAT HAPPENED last night with Owen, and then what happened in the back yard with him earlier, I need a little space. That's why, when I finish cleaning up the kitchen from dinner, I don't immediately go to find him in the living room. He's watching baseball. I can hear the booming voices of the announcers.

I pour myself a glass of white wine from the bottles I bought last week and take it outside. My mom has set up a covered sitting area near the back of the yard. It's not big, just large enough for a love seat and little round coffee table. Potted geraniums flank the love seat, giving it a nice spring feel. Instead of a wall, the backside is a trellis. A vining flower, I'm not sure what kind, grows unrestrained, winding its way through the diamond-shaped holes. The flowers are a brilliant royal purple and they lighten my mood the tiniest bit.

Glass in hand, I settle into the center of the love seat, tucking my legs underneath me and laying one arm across the back. My mom's house sits at the top of the gently sloping street, and from this spot I can see past her wood fence and out into acres of pinyon pines and juniper trees. Other homes are tucked in among the trees, but from here it looks like nothing but green. The sky is a dark orange and soon the stars will decorate the sky. If I turn off all the lights inside the house, the sky will twinkle spectacularly. Sedona is a certified dark sky community. Light pollution is taken very seriously here, and it shows. It's part of what makes Sedona so special.

My heart twists as I realize how much I've missed this place.

When I left here at eighteen, I didn't walk. I ran. I'd had a problem, something bigger than me. A problem I created.

But I guess it wasn't just me who created the problem. Owen had a hand in it. A pretty big one.

When I left Sedona, I wasn't sure where we stood. He showed up in Santa Clara. After my first day of classes, I dragged myself back to my dorm room to find Owen sitting outside my door. Beside him was a guy with dark hair that flopped over his forehead. This person was a stranger to me, and then Owen stood up and turned into a stranger before my eyes.

I blow out a breath and take a drink.

I can't even begin to make sense of what happened to us back then. Or what happened last night. What was I thinking? Did the dark shadows that hid us from detection dim my brain also?

Or was it Owen who took away my common sense?

Whatever it was, what happened was probably a bad idea. A bad idea that felt so, so good. Not just how Owen made me feel, bringing me a release I'd desperately needed, but having him at all. Being touched by him. Being back in the arms of the man who was my everything. First kiss, first love, first heartbreak, he was all of it.

I sit quietly, finishing my wine and looking out at the darkened sky. The baseball game must be good. Owen hasn't come to find me, something I hate to admit I was hoping for when I came out here. An uncomfortable feeling unfurls inside me. I don't like that I wanted him to notice my absence, to search for me.

Getting up from the love seat, I walk inside, depositing my wine glass on the counter beside the sink and stepping into the living room. Owen, sitting back in my mom's chair, is fast asleep. The TV casts a whitish-yellow glow on his face as I walk closer. His lower lip has pulled away from his upper lip, and a heavy, rhythmic breath slips in and out. A wavy lock of his hair tumbles down over his forehead and I'm entranced by how handsome he is.

Should I let him sleep? I'd hate to wake him. He was exhausted when he arrived and he looks adorable. His broad shoulders take up so much of the chair. He has it reclined; his feet hang off the end. Looking at him now, it's nearly impossible to remember the way his face twisted in an angry mask that day in front of my dorm room.

"I'm sorry," I whisper, so quietly it's almost soundless.

Will he ever know how sorry I am? How deeply I grieved my choice? How much I still do?

I grab a blanket and cover him before clicking off the TV and walking to my room, tears running down my cheeks, my arms wrapped around a womb that once held our baby.

HE'S GONE when I wake up.

The blanket I laid over him last night is folded, hanging neatly over the arm of the recliner. A note lies on top of the gray knitted wool.

A,

Thank you for letting me sleep. I needed it.

Coffee at ten.

O

"I see you got your note," my mom says, coming up behind me.

I turn to look at her. She's wearing pajamas, the ones I sent her for Mother's Day two years ago. Pale pink, trimmed in ivory lace. They swim on her.

She brings a cup of coffee to her lips and blows across the top, eyebrows lifted, waiting for me to respond.

"Yeah," I say, tucking the note into my palm. "How do you feel?"

"Fine." She inclines her head at my curled palm. "Did he sleep here?"

I knew there was no way she was going to let it go.

I nod. "He fell asleep watching TV and I didn't have the heart to wake him. He was exhausted, and he looked so peaceful."

Mom turns, walking back to the kitchen, and I do too.

She pours coffee into a mug for me and hands it over. "Thanks." I take it, adding a little oat milk from the fridge.

"You know," she says as soon as I lift the cup to my mouth, "last week you wouldn't have let Owen stay and watch TV, let alone allow him to sleep here."

I nod slowly. "Probably not."

But then he fingered me on the side of his dad's house and suddenly I'm feeling forgiving I guess.

I'm not ready to talk to my mom about Owen yet. I'm still trying to figure it out for myself.

She sets down her coffee and pushes it across the counter until it's out of her way, then reaches into the cupboard and pulls out the bowl she uses to mix pancakes. It's the same bowl she's been using since I can remember. It's olive green, with a flower decoration. It's hideous, but right now the sight of it is filling me with warmth.

"Is coffee with him today a date?"

"No." I shake my head and go to the pantry to retrieve the pancake mix. She looks me in the eye when I hand the box to her, but I look away so I don't have to see the hope nestled there.

"I know you don't want to tell me what happened between you two, and Lord knows I've hinted enough to both of you that I wouldn't mind having some idea what went on. But even your silence says something, and it's telling me you two hurt each other pretty badly. Am I right?"

This time, there is no avoiding her gaze without being rude. I sigh. "Yes, Mom. You're right."

"Has either of you apologized?"

"I think that's what coffee today is about. Finally saying the things we've been holding in for years." I want to throw up just thinking about it.

"Hmmm." Mom dumps in the mix without measuring. She adds an egg and milk without measuring the milk. I guess after years of making pancakes, eyeballing becomes its own precise measurement.

"What?" I ask her, because I know I'm supposed to after she makes a sound like that.

She removes a whisk and pushes it into the mixture in the bowl. A little puff of white flies into the air. "Maybe that's not all your coffee date is about."

"Not a date," I remind her.

"Oh, please." She pauses her whisking to look at me. "I see the way you two look at each other. He caught you before you hit the deck when you saw that needle last week and it took the breath away from both of you when you touched each other. Not to mention how he chased after you."

I frown and shake my head as I bend down to pull the griddle from the back of a cabinet. "It didn't mean anything," I tell her. If only she knew what happened two nights ago while his dad was just fifteen feet away, passed out in the front seat of her car. We were like two horny teenagers again. *Embarrassing*. I lay the griddle across two burners on the stove and turn them on.

Stepping back, I ask, "Mom, do you know if Owen's dad is okay?" I lean one arm on the counter and watch her pour pancake batter onto the griddle. A soft sizzling fills the air, along with the smell of batter.

She glances at me as she pours, distracted by my question.

"Mom..." I nod at the griddle. The pancake she has just made is twice the size of the others.

"Oops," she mouths. She tips the bowls over again,

giving the oversized pancake two ears. "Minnie Mouse pancake, like I used to make for you."

"Thank you," I tell her, smiling. As sweet as her gesture is, it hasn't escaped my attention that she is avoiding my question.

"Owen's dad?" I press.

She reaches for a spatula and holds it poised in midair over the pancakes. "I think that's a story for Owen to tell you."

Shit. My stomach sinks and now I'm wondering if that wasn't just one night of bad drinking … if it's every night.

"Is it bad?"

She shrugs. "Depends on your definition of *bad*, I suppose."

"Well, in your definition of the word, is it bad?"

She purses her lips and looks at me. "Yes."

My teeth capture the inside of my cheek. I was afraid of that answer. Owen didn't seem shocked to find his dad passed out.

"That's sad," I murmur, taking a drink from my coffee because I don't know what else to do or say. My heart hurts for Owen. The only parent Owen has ever known is hurting himself, and in turn, hurting Owen. And Owen takes care of him, because that's what Owen does. He's a caretaker, right down to his core. But who takes care of Owen?

I blink hard, twice. That is a dangerous thought, one I have no business entertaining.

I watch her flip pancakes, then get out plates and forks, butter and maple syrup.

We eat, and talk about the garden she wants to plant. No mention of Owen or his dad, her cancer or my lack of a job. There is no shortage of depressing topics of conversation, but we manage to avoid them all.

When we're finished, I clean up from breakfast, then go get myself ready for coffee with Owen.

The not-a-date coffee. The maybe-an-apology coffee. The coffee I thought would never come.

Here it is.

If only I felt ready for it.

Chapter 12

Owen

My slick palms slide down the front of my shorts, my eyes trained on the front door of the coffee shop. It's opened three times in the past four minutes. Each time my breath has caught in my throat, and for nothing.

Autumn's almost ten minutes late. I'm not worried that she won't show. Autumn has plenty to say to me, tucked back behind her cool exterior. This is her time to let it all out.

Five minutes later, the breath catches in my throat once more, and this time Autumn steps in, eyes sweeping the place. Her gaze lands on me, and I see her throat move as she swallows.

Seeing her nerves relax my own, but only just slightly.

I leave my table and go to her. When I reach her, I lean down, and although I mean to give her a hug, something in me takes over and I end up with my lips pressed to her temple.

Her shoulders stiffen and I pull away. An apology is on my tongue until I see the look in her eyes. Longing and sadness swim in the blue-green color.

I don't know how to act around her, so I clear my throat and take a step away. "Would you like something to drink?" I motion to the blackboard listing their house specialties.

She shuffles from foot to foot, gathering herself. "Sure," she murmurs, leading the way to the register. She orders first, something that sounds complicated, but the guy behind the counter doesn't bat an eye. I order my plain black coffee and remove my wallet to pay.

"I can get it," Autumn says, her hand disappearing into her purse.

"No, I've got it."

"This isn't a date," she says, her voice sharp around the edges.

Great, she's more keyed up than I thought she would be. I'm mentally preparing myself for the verbal ass kicking she's going to give me.

"I'm aware," I tell her, my own voice taking on a razor quality. I hand cash over to the barista and we move on to the pick-up counter.

While we wait, Autumn spins the delicate gold

bracelet she wears on her wrist. "I'm sorry," she says softly, not looking at me. "For the whole 'not a date' thing back there. My mom said something before I left, and I guess it put me a little on edge."

Wow, that's the second time Autumn has apologized to me. She's grown from the headstrong teenager I once loved. It also shows me how much she cares.

I nod, hands tucked in my pockets, watching the barista make Autumn's drink. "What did she say to you?"

Autumn's gaze finds me. "That she thinks today is about more than just us meeting to talk things out."

She says the words so matter-of-factly, I can't get a read on what her mother's opinion means to her. "Did you tell her she's wrong?" The barista appears in my peripheral vision, sliding Autumn's drink across the smooth stone countertop, mine comes right after it. I pick up hers and hand it to her, before taking mine, then lead her back to the table I sat at to wait for her.

"Yes. She's stubborn though." The corner of her mouth turns up as she talks about her mom.

"She certainly is," I agree, taking a sip of my coffee and trying not to wince at the heat.

"You've grown a lot closer to her since I left," she says, attempting a relaxed tone. She's not fooling me. I know she doesn't like how close I am with her mom.

"I saw her on and off before I became her doctor—when I came home from U of A to visit my dad, and during summer break."

Autumn nods. "I guess I'm glad she had you all this time."

"You don't sound like you mean that."

Autumn laughs. "I do … sort of." She stirs the little wooden stick around her drink. "I'm just jealous. You know that, right?"

"I do." I push up the sleeves of my shirt until they're bunched near my elbow. Autumn's gaze falls to my forearms. Her eyes widen as she looks over my tattoos.

"Those are new," she comments, nodding her head at the ink.

"New to you. Not to me." I can't believe this is the first time in these past few weeks she's seen my tattoos.

She nods. "Right." But her eyes don't leave my arms. "When did you get all that?"

"Over the years. It started with you though." I rotate my arm to show her the bare tree, the red and orange leaves floating down to join the pile at the base. I still remember the day I got it—six months after our dorm room blowout, when I realized she was never going to talk to me again, when I knew we were over in her mind. I needed closure, I needed to know what we had was real.

Her fingers lift, covering her lips, and a low, mangled sound comes from deep in her throat. "I had no idea you did that."

"I wasn't in the best place. It was a couple months after the last time I saw you." I raise my eyes to find hers, forcing her to look at me directly. "Look, Autumn … I'm sorry. For everything I said to you. I didn't know it at the time, but I was grieving. It just came out as anger instead of sadness."

She pushes her hair back from her face, then props her chin on her hand. "I understand."

She's letting me off the hook too easily and I don't deserve it. This is her chance to hold me accountable, to remind me of what I said to her. *You killed me too.* It was a cruel thing to say. I was hurting, and I wanted her to hurt alongside me. I wanted to blame her for everything even though it was *our* choice. I never spoke up and said what I felt, so it was my choice too. Silence is a choice.

Even though she's not asking for it, I keep explaining. "You left for college right after the abortion, and you just seemed so … composed. I felt like I was the only one who'd had their heart broken. I lashed out."

Autumn flinches at the "A word" and her shoulders shake, just these tiny micro movements. "Maybe on the outside I didn't look like the picture of grief you expected me to be. I was in shock, I think. But on the inside, I was a mess. I took everything I was feeling and tucked it away. I promise you, everything you felt existed inside me too. It still does. Every day I live with the guilt of my choice, whether it was the right one to make or not."

"*We* made that choice, Autumn. Not just you. We

decided together that an abortion was the right choice for us."

She shakes her head again. "That's where you're wrong. *We* might have made the choice, but *I* went through with it."

"I was with you in that room when it happened. I was as involved as I could possibly be."

She lifts one shoulder, dropping it back down, and when she looks up at me, I see so much malice in her gaze. This is her moment, the one she's been waiting for, and I steel myself.

"Until you screamed stop," she seethes.

Fuck. I'd forgotten that. I'd blocked out most of the procedure and focused more on the aftermath of what we did.

"You started crying and..." I grab for words, fumbling as the memory of Autumn weeping during the procedure resurfaces.

"You can't change your mind in the middle of a fucking procedure, Owen! Do you have any idea what that did to me?" Spittle flies from her mouth as her fist slams down on the table and I flinch. "It's been ten years and I can still hear you screaming 'Stop!' in my head. It *broke* me."

My face must completely be drained of color, because I feel lightheaded and I can't keep my hands from shaking. "Fuck ... Autumn. I'm so sorry. I was just a kid."

Tears line the edges of her eyes and she sets her coffee on the table.

"So was I, and I needed you to be strong. I'm sorry, I can't do this." She stands and the chair goes screeching backward, causing every gaze in the place to land on us.

The guilt I feel right now is like a cavern opening in my chest. This whole time I'd been focused on how what I said in her dorm room at Santa Clara might have affected her, but I hadn't given any thought to the procedure.

Autumn bursts out through the door to the coffee shop and I tear after her, heart pounding in my chest.

I rush outside only to be pelted with rain and my gaze scans the parking lot for her mom's car. "Autumn!" I shout when I spot her jogging to the small sedan.

I run as fast as I can towards her and jump in front of her car door before she can drive away for another ten years. Everything is crystal clear now and I know exactly what I need to say, what she needs to hear to heal the wounds inside of her.

"I only said stop that day because you were crying and I didn't want them to hurt you. I fully supported your choice though."

There. I said it. I took the weight off of her feeling like she was the only one who made that choice. It's a complete lie and I don't care. I'll do anything to see her never cry again. What's done is done, there's no going back, but I can try to heal whatever is broken inside of her.

Rain falls onto her face, rolling down her cheeks so I can't tell if she's crying or not.

She shakes her head in disbelief. "You can't fully understand, because it wasn't your body. If a man wants a woman to have an abortion, he's just a selfish asshole. If a woman wants an abortion, she's a killer. *That* is what I live with every day."

You killed me too. That day in her dorm room, I made her out to be a murderer. What did that do to a person? How could I ever fix that?

"Autumn..." Her name rides on a pained whisper. I reach for her and my fingers grip the sides of her waist. "What I said was inexcusable. There was no reason for it. And I'm sorry. I'm so fucking sorry." My nose burns and my vision swims as rain pelts around us.

Autumn's lower lip quakes but she pulls it in, pressing it tightly to her upper lip to keep from crying. "I have one question for you."

I nod. "Anything."

Her face searches mine. "Do you regret our choice as much as I do?"

My heart stops for a few beats and I wonder if a healthy twenty-eight-year-old is capable of a heart attack. She's spoken aloud the one thing I've never said, and it feels so good to know I'm not alone. I knew she didn't enjoy the choice she made, but I never knew if she regretted it, if she wished there was a ten-year-old little boy or girl standing beside us now calling us Mom or Dad.

"Only every day," I admit.

My throat catches. I'd thought Autumn hadn't struggled, hadn't cared very much. She so easily cast me aside and I thought she moved on. I was wrong. So, *so* wrong. Of all people, I should've figured it out by now. Between watching patients lose the battle against cancer and telling new patients they have it, I see grief every day. It doesn't look the same for everybody. I know this as surely as I know there isn't a pot of gold at the end of a rainbow. So how is it that I never applied this knowledge to Autumn? Never stopped to consider it was her grief that kept her stoic when I was falling apart?

Autumn stares down into her coffee. "Despite knowing how impractical it would've been to start a family, I still envision what it would've been like. I picture crayon drawings held up by magnets on a fridge. Sticky fingerprints everywhere. Toys in cute, labeled containers."

A sad smile tugs up one corner of my mouth. "Do you think we could've been a family?"

That was our plan. Go off to college, come back and get married while Autumn followed me off to med school. Then fate took a different course, and right before we left for college everything blew up into a thousand unbearable pieces.

She shrugs despondently. "Maybe. But we were so

young, Owen. We were terrified when that stick showed a plus sign. I know my mom has chilled out a lot now, but do you remember how strict she was? How desperately she wanted me to get out of Sedona? If we'd kept the baby, would you have made it down to Tucson for college? And through medical school? Through residency?" Her head shakes. "No way. I wouldn't have made it to Santa Clara, or anywhere else for that matter." She takes a deep breath. "And even with all that practicality, guilt still hangs over me like a little black cloud following me wherever I go. I know I made the right choice for me at the time, but the weight of the choice is sewn into me. It's stitched onto my DNA." She palms her chest. "And that's what I mean when I say the choice was mine."

I want to tell her that I think we could've done it, that even if our life looked completely different, it would've been the life we created. I don't say any of that though, because tears are escaping through her dark lashes and rolling down her face, mixing with rain. I pull her into me, tucking her into my chest.

"Despite all that, a part of me hates myself for going through with it. Do you hate me too?" Her voice is tiny, fearful.

My first instinct is to deny, to shield her from any more pain. But then I remember that last summer, when I didn't say how I felt, when I told her I supported what she thought was best. On the inside I begged and pleaded for her to say she wanted the baby we made; on the outside I stepped into the role of supportive boyfriend. I helped her make a choice, and then I resented her for it.

"I don't hate you anymore," I say into her hair. She slumps against me and my hand rubs across her back.

In fact, I'm pretty certain I still love you.

Chapter 13

Autumn

"I DIDN'T TAKE you for a hippie." My mom grins, laughing at her own joke. She's carrying a walking stick and wearing a necklace with a large purple crystal pendant.

"I didn't know you were into energy work," I shoot back, bending over and lacing up my tennis shoes. I'm still sitting in the car. Mom's standing beside it, impatiently waiting. To be fair, she did tell me to put on my shoes before we got to the trail. I didn't listen.

"I'll take all the help I can get," Mom says, scuffing her toe in the dirt. A little puff of reddish-brown wafts through the air.

"All set." I stand up and reach back into the car for my water bottle and hat. Pushing the hat down over my head, I start for the trailhead, my mom in step beside me.

We make it roughly five minutes before she asks about Owen: "Are you going to keep telling me coffee yesterday was *fine*?"

I sneak a glance at her. She looks okay enough for this hike. It's not strenuous and I'm actually surprised at how well she's doing with the chemo. We're here for the vortex. Supposedly it has healing powers, or some New Age mumbo jumbo like that. I grew up here and never felt the subtle energy people come here to find. I've heard people talk about feeling a tingling in their hands, a rush of energy, or a buzzing throughout the body. Personally, I think it's all in the mind. If a person wants to feel something, they will.

But when my mom asked me to accompany her on an energy vortex hike, there was no way I was saying no. I'd just hoped Owen wouldn't be a topic of conversation.

"Coffee really was fine, Mom."

It was both heartbreaking and a giant relief to finally say those things to Owen. He held me in the rain and then we both had to go. And now I don't know where we stand. It was painfully awkward considering our little driveway finger-banging session a few nights ago. This whole thing with him is ass backwards and I don't know what to do about it.

"Mmm hmm. And what was it besides *fine*?" This time she accompanies the word with air quotes and an eye roll. For a second I'm stunned, but I recover quickly. I'm still getting used to this relaxed, sarcastic version of my mother. This is not the person I grew up with. She used to tell me sarcasm was a poor man's wit.

"He apologized, for one."

"What did he have to apologize for?"

I shoot her a look. I know she's curious, but damn I'm not sure I'm ready to tell her.

"Fine," she says, drawing out the word and giving me a look that shows how pleased she is to be turning the table and using that word on me.

"He has tattoos," I tell her, hoping this tidbit will be enough to quench her thirst for answers.

"I've seen them," she answers.

"Did you know one of them is for me?"

"The tree?"

I nod.

"I noticed it, but I never asked. I figured it was for you, with the fall colors and the leaves falling off the branches. If his ink was a poem, it would be titled *Autumn Left* or something dramatic like that." She barely manages to conceal a smile. "Or maybe it would be called *Autumn Right.*"

"You're full of jokes, huh?" This new Faith Cummings is weird to me, but I like it.

She shrugs. "I'm always good for a dad joke."

She had to be my mom and dad, so that makes sense.

We get a little further on the trail and Mom stops to take a drink. "Did he touch you?" she asks, her water bottle poised at her mouth.

My eyes bulge. *Did he touch you?* isn't exactly something you want to hear come out of your mother's mouth.

"Yesterday?" I ask, trying to calm my racing thoughts.

She scrunches her eyes as she drinks. "When else?" she asks after she swallows.

Oh, gee, I don't know, maybe when we hid in the shadows beside his dad's house and he put his hands in my pants like we were teenagers again...

My cheeks get hot, and it has nothing to do with the sun beating down on us.

"He hugged me yesterday. I was upset. From talking about it all, you know?"

"No," she snaps. "I do not know. Because you have yet to trust me enough to tell me."

Whoa.

My heart falls at her bold share session. My mom and I don't usually go this deep. It's work and bills and her health, but she doesn't really dig into me like this.

I stop and sigh, and my Mom stops too. She's about a foot away from me, and even though she's wearing a hat, she lifts her hand to the brim, giving herself just a few more inches of shade. "Honey, I'm your mother. You can tell me anything."

I suddenly feel like I'm carrying a thousand-pound

weight and it's crushing me. Honestly, I'm sick of keeping the secret. Sick of being the only person who knows, of clinging to my choice and letting it define how I see myself. I've toiled over it for so long it feels like a part of me, but I feel better after talking to Owen and Livvie. Maybe I'll feel better if I tell my mom what really broke me and Owen. Maybe, if I start chipping away at the pieces of my secret, it won't be so heavy inside me anymore.

"Would you really like to know what happened between me and Owen, Mom? Even if it makes you look at me differently?"

She frowns. "Did you cheat on him?"

"No." I swallow hard, preparing myself to tell my mother my darkest secret.

"Did you fall in love with someone else while you were with him?"

"Isn't that cheating?"

"You can fall in love with someone and never touch them."

I frown. "My answer is still no."

"Did you learn his biggest secret and then blab it to the world?" It's like she's on *Jeopardy* trying to figure out an answer with rapid-fire speed.

"No, Mom. Why are you trying to guess?"

"So you don't have to say the words, because they obviously hurt." Sweat beads her brow and I wonder if I should ask her to sit on a rock or something before I drop the A-bomb.

"That's sweet." I reach for her hand, pulling her to the side of the trail. "Normally I'd tell you to sit down, but there isn't anywhere to sit. Are you ready?"

She nods but I can see the fear in her eyes.

"The summer before we left for college, Owen and I got pregnant."

My mom blinks rapidly, her mouth dropping open just enough to reveal the top of her bottom teeth.

"We decided to get an abortion. Even though it was a choice we made together, we were both devastated, and the weight of it tore us apart."

Did we decide together, or did I say I wanted one and Owen went along with it to be supportive? I always wondered that but I'm too scared to ever ask him.

I study her face. She is being careful, I think, not to react too strongly. But I wonder if inside she is experiencing what I always feared she would feel: horror, disgust, soul-crushing disappointment. This is all compounded by the fact that she's been going to church weekly now. I wonder if she's already condemned me to hell.

I steel myself, ready for it all, but it doesn't come. She takes me by surprise when she grabs my shoulders and pulls me in, hugging me into her thin body. "I'm sorry you went through that without me. I would've liked to have been there for you. I made mistakes, and I know why you didn't come to me … why you felt you couldn't."

"Thank you," I whisper. My worst fear has evaporated. Just like that. And now I feel stupid for holding it in for so long.

Mom keeps hugging me, and two sets of hikers pass us. She releases me, but not before she leans in and places a swift kiss on my forehead.

"Are you ready to step into the vortex?" she asks, winking.

"I think I already feel it," I answer.

"I know you're kidding, but it is possible to feel it already. It's said energy vortexes can be felt as far as a quarter-mile away." She starts walking, and I follow.

I wasn't kidding about the vortex. There is something different inside me right now. Maybe it's the spiritual energy source, infiltrating me and filling me with the buzzing feeling. Or maybe it's the fact that I no longer have to hide from my mom. When you keep a secret so big, it's like covering yourself in a sheer veil. Sure, she could see me, but there was something between us. Between me and the world. Not that I'm planning to staple a note with my confession to my forehead; the relief I feel from telling my mom might be all I need.

We reach the creek and walk along, where my mom says the vortex is supposed to be felt the strongest. She pauses, placing one palm over her heart, and then a second palm over the first. She motions her head for me to do the same, and, unlike putting on my shoes before we arrived, this time I listen.

We fall quiet, listening only to the soft sounds of gently flowing water and the occasional call of a bird.

"Do you feel it, Autumn?" my mom asks. Her eyes are closed.

My eyes are supposed to be closed too, but they're not. I'm watching her, taking in her peaceful expression, absorbing her stillness.

All of a sudden, I'm hit with a weird feeling. A sense of impending doom. If cancer takes my beautiful mother from me, I'm not sure I will survive it. I only just got fully back into her life. I want thirty more years with her at least.

"I love you, Mom," I tell her, swallowing the softball-sized lump in my throat.

She turns her chin to me, her eyes fluttering open. "I love you too, baby girl."

"I'm sorry I didn't come back until now." My voice cracks. "I was fleeing Owen. Not you."

She removes one hand from where it lies on her heart and uses it to palm my cheek. "I know that, baby. Besides, I told you to stay there. And I meant it."

"I didn't have to listen."

"No, you didn't. But I'm glad you did. You had what I never did: a bigger life, a dream that was just for you." Her eyes grow wide as she speaks.

"Mom, what is it?"

"The abortion ... you had it because I was pushing you so hard to leave Sedona. You didn't want to disappoint me." She says this as if she's had a sudden real-ization.

My head is shaking even before her sentence is finished. "No, Mom. *No*. Owen and I made that choice on our own, without anybody else, okay? Don't blame yourself. You weren't the reason I decided not to have a baby."

She drops her hand from my cheek, appeased, but her eyes hold a flicker of doubt.

"Well, we should probably—" Her words are cut off by a retching noise as she tears her hand out of mine and falls forward.

"Mom!" I shout.

My mother falls on her knees, panting on all fours as the contents of her lunch come up onto the hiking trail.

She waves me off, wiping her mouth. "I'm okay. Chemo," she whispers, as if this would pacify me.

It doesn't.

"Should I call 911?" Why the fuck did I agree to this hike? My mom has an aggressive form of cancer and is undergoing chemo and we are acting like we're training for the Ironman.

My mom laughs, rocking back on her heels, and looks up at me. "No, baby, just give me some water and haul me up."

God help me. This is her life now, falling over and vomiting in vortexes. It isn't fair.

I pass her the water bottle and she takes a swig, swishing it in her mouth before spitting on the ground.

Next, I hook her under the armpits and haul her up.

Did my telling her about the abortion overwhelm her emotionally? Is that why she vomited?

Her gaze flicks to mine. "Autumn, stop it. I see you overanalyzing." She points to my wrinkled forehead. "I'm fine. This is chemo. I'll have a nap and be okay."

I wind my fingers through hers and give her a nod. "Okay, Mom."

"That was some powerful vortex energy," she jokes, trying to force a smile out of me.

I don't know about vortex energy, but I definitely got more than I bargained for when I agreed to this hike.

WE GET BACK to my mom's car and I find a missed call from Owen. There's also a text from him, so I open it up and read as my mom straps into the passenger seat.

I have an idea, and it might be my worst idea yet, but here goes... Do you want to have dinner with me tonight? Just as friends, obviously. Quit trying to lure me into dark shadows.

I smile at my phone. He's just as playful as he ever was. That was what got my attention in the first place when we were fifteen. I mean, yeah, his broad shoulders and messy hair drew me in, but when I saw how much of his personality was light and fun, like a curious puppy who could suddenly morph into a strong male, that's when I knew I was a goner.

My fingers fly over the keyboard, texting out my response. **A girl does need to eat. And as I remember it, you're the one who kissed me first. I was merely in the wrong place at the wrong time.**

Three dots pop up automatically, then his message comes through. **I'm sure you meant to say right place, right time.**

The muscles in my upper thighs clench. My legs cross at the ankles and I pull them in as far as the confines of the sedan will allow, trying to get control of myself. Could Owen and I ever have another loving and trusting relationship? I have no idea. But could we have some amazing sex? Yes, yes, we could.

A quick glance at my mom tells me she hasn't noticed my sudden change—thankfully. I start the car and pull out onto the road that leads back to our house.

I have to change the tone of the conversation before I spontaneously combust. **Pick me up at six?** I shoot the text back, before dropping my phone in my lap.

Owen must pick up on my change, because he responds in the same vein. **See you then.**

"Is that Owen?" Mom asks, and I can tell from her voice that she's sleepy.

I balance my phone facedown on my thigh and nod. "He asked me to get dinner tonight. Will you be okay on your own?"

I don't want to leave her, especially after she threw up on the hike.

She gives me a withering look. "Autumn, I'm a grown adult. Of course, I'll be okay having dinner on my own."

"I just wanted to make sure. Because I can cancel. It's just a dinner between friends. No big deal." My hands lift in the air as if I'm pleading my case.

"Go to dinner. Have fun. Forget about your problems."

My problems. *Damn*. Why did she have to remind me? Jobless, hanging with my ex and watching my mom get sicker by the day.

"If that's what you want…" I tell her.

She laughs. "It's an order."

When we get home, she goes to her room to lie down. I go into the bathroom, turning on the shower and waiting for the water to warm. As I wait, I lean against the bathroom counter and think about what I should do about tonight.

I can't figure out if it's a good idea to let this happen. A friendship with Owen feels inevitable, but is it a *good idea*? Maybe not. Will it stop me from going? *Nope*.

I climb under the hot spray of water, but I don't have all the time in the world to let the water wash away my nerves. A drink wherever we're going should do the trick.

After stepping out of the shower, I towel off, then

start on my hair. It takes forever to dry because it's too long, and I make a mental note to get a trim. Moving on to curling it, I blend it into loose waves. I move on to my room, where my makeup bag lies on the dresser. Some women love makeup. I am not one of them; however, I do see the merit in a good pressed powder and swipe of mascara. Since I'm going to dinner, I add a dab of cream blush to my cheeks and a little eyeshadow and eyeliner.

Tonight is about two people who are hungry deciding to break bread together. Nothing more. But, just to be safe, I select a romper from the closet and pull it on, hoping it will function as a modern-day chastity belt. I'm not sure one can ever really prepare for something as unexpected as what happened the other night at Owen's dad's house, but at least this way I feel I've taken some measure of precaution in case things get out of hand again.

Or, in hand, I suppose.

My little joke makes me chuckle. Standing in front of the dresser mirror, dabbing some Chapstick over my lips, I slide a couple gold bracelets onto my wrist.

"Autumn," my mom calls from somewhere beyond my door.

I grab my purse from my bed and thread my arm through it, then leave the room.

Owen stands in the foyer, making small talk with my mom, and nerves claw at my gut. He looks up when I walk in and I watch him take me in, his Adam's apple bobbing when he clears his throat. I take him in too. He's wearing dark-wash jeans and a tight powder-blue polo that shows off his tattoos. He looks absolutely yummy. *For a friend...*

"All set?" he asks, eyebrows raised.

I point down at my bare feet. "Just need shoes."

I walk to the sandals I dropped by the front door when we came in from our hike. But to get there, I have to walk by Owen. He smells like manly body wash, virility, and desire.

Pushing the scent out of my nostrils with a quiet huff, I slip my feet into my sandals. "Ready," I sing, turning around and holding my hands out to the side.

Mom smiles. "Have fun, you two."

I lean in, brushing a kiss on my mom's cheek. "What are you having for dinner?" I feel bad making her eat alone. I'm here now. She shouldn't have to eat by herself.

"Spray cheese and ultra-processed crackers."

Owen explodes with laughter, shaking his head as he tries to catch his breath, and I scowl at the both of them.

"If that's true, you'd better eat it all in one sitting, because when I get home I'm going to search high and low for that contraband."

Mom laughs, placing her hand on my shoulder and gently shoving me to the door. "Seriously, go. I'm fine."

I open the door and step through, pausing on the other side to wait for Owen. He offers my mom a high-five, probably congratulating her for ribbing me, and walks out.

"Feeling better from before?"

She nods. "Yep."

"What happened before?" Owen asks, his body tensing.

"She threw up," I tell him.

Owen's face relaxes. "Ahh, chemo."

"She wanted to call 911," my mom tells him, and he bursts out laughing again, before seeing my glare and turning it into a cough.

"Chemo is harsh stuff."

"Alright, you two. Have fun and don't worry about me." My mom shoos us away and closes the door.

"You encourage her by laughing, you know that?" I tell Owen as we walk down the driveway to his car.

Owen shrugs. "She's funny. I laugh."

"I'm still getting used to her sense of humor." We reach his car and he follows me around to my side, opening the door for me.

"Thank you," I tell him, sliding in. He's done that since high school and it still makes my belly warm.

On the drive, Owen peppers me with questions about my job. Old job? Former career? I don't know what to call it.

"It was fun, I guess. Kind of like a puzzle. Figuring out the target demographic for a given product. Working with different clients." I think back to my building, the high-rise I walked to every morning and walked away from every night. It wasn't especially beautiful, not like other buildings Manhattan is known for, but it was a part of the skyline, and it made me feel special.

Owen makes a right, taking us off the black tar road and through a curved entry, his tires now bumping over cobblestones. Giant sycamore trees tower over us. Two-story buildings all around, ivy vines that curl and stretch, covering the thick stucco walls.

"Owen," I breathe, unable to take my eyes off my favorite place.

Tlaquepaque.

Tucked away behind a low stucco wall, it's not so much a hidden gem but one that requires a longer gaze to be discovered. It's not just a place, but a Spanish Colonial village. Tlaquepaque sits high above the bank of Oak Creek.

I know what I will find once we leave Owen's car: columns and arches, intricate ironwork and patterned tiles artfully decorating little spaces here and there. And everything, absolutely everything, built around the sycamores that stretch high throughout the village.

Owen has brought me to my favorite place, the very place we had our first date, back when neither of us could drive and my mom dropped us off here. In the courtyard, under the glow of white lights that wrapped around trees and the balconies of second story shops, Owen pressed his lips to mine for the first time.

I get out of the car, leaning back slightly and gently

resting against the frame. If there is any place that could make me feel the word *home*, this is it.

Owen reaches for me, but only for a moment, the pad of his thumb brushing the inside of my wrist. "I was hoping you hadn't come back here yet."

My head turns and I look at him: at his strong chin, his angular nose, the freckle on his earlobe.

"I didn't bring you here to walk you down memory lane." The words trip from his mouth, his eyes bright with the hurry he feels to justify why we are here. "I just know how much you love the Mexican restaurant."

I'm stunned, trying to catch up to the feeling slipping through me, but Owen takes my silence for something else.

"We don't have to go there," he reassures me. "Other restaurants have opened since you've been here."

"El Rincon," I assert, my eyes still trained on his. It is our place. "I want our table, if possible."

AT THE WORDS, *our table*, Owen's lip peel into a sly grin and he nods swiftly. Gathering one of my hands in his, he leads me away from the car, across the cobbled street, and through an arched hallway. We spill out into the main courtyard. In the center, a stone fountain gurgles. People mill about, stepping over the places where Sycamore roots have pushed against the pavers laid atop them. I look around, drinking in the architectural ingenuity, the sheer beauty of a place capable of transportation. In here, the desert we live in is but a distant memory.

"Walk first?" Owen asks me, pulling my attention from a second-story shop. "Or eat first?"

"Eat," I respond without hesitation. The hike with my mom wasn't strenuous, but the sun still has a way of sneaking in and stealing energy; it made me hungry.

The front door of the restaurant is visible from where we stand. We walk there together, and though he doesn't need to, Owen keeps a firm grasp on my hand.

And I let him.

I'm holding hands with Owen Miller. What kind of alternate universe is this?

We request a table on the patio in the corner, under an orange umbrella. Our table. When we sit, I adjust the wicker chair, dragging it closer to the table.

"It hasn't changed a bit," I remark, one finger bumping over the terra cotta tiled tabletop. Even the plants in the planter boxes along the gated patio look the same, deep green and waxy.

"No," Owen agrees. "But we have." His gaze, which is on the menu he holds in his hands, lifts to meet mine.

I don't know what to say to that, and so I choose to say nothing at all.

It's true.

Our server comes, and we place an order for two prickly pear margaritas.

I smile at Owen when the waiter walks away, feeling a bit like I've done something naughty. "That's the first time I've ever ordered a real margarita here."

He grins. "Not for lack of trying," he reminds me.

"Oh gosh," I laugh, my eyes half-rolling. "That was embarrassing."

"It was funny," Owen corrects.

"Maybe for you," I say, picking up my menu but still peering at him above it. "I hope that server didn't get into too much trouble for serving me alcohol. I felt terrible."

It was silly, just a bet between Owen and me. He didn't think I had the guts to order a margarita and not say the word non-alcoholic while doing so. I showed him just how wrong he was. The flaw in the plan was that I didn't account for a gullible server. I assumed the server would take one look at my seventeen-year-old face and call bullshit. But no. So I decided to roll with it. The manager, however, was not as gullible as the server, and he came over before I could take a drink, apologizing profusely for their error in serving a minor who most certainly had not intended to order a real margarita. By his third *I'm so sorry*, which was accompanied by his over-the-top acceptance that the mistake was their fault, I realized his tone was more sarcastic than apologetic. And that he knew exactly what the seventeen-year-old girl in his restaurant had been trying to pull.

Despite the embarrassment of the night, we

returned over and over. Can't keep a couple teenagers from their beloved chimichangas. We never saw that manager again.

Our drinks are dropped off. They are hot pink and sugar-rimmed. Owen lifts his, waiting for me to do the same. As I reach for mine, I get a swipe of sugar on my finger in the process.

"To old times and favorite tables."

I echo him and carefully clink my glass against his, then bring it to my mouth. It's cold and sweet. Refreshing. "This," I say, keeping the drink in the air so he knows what I'm talking about, "was worth waiting for."

"Yes," he responds, his tone gruff. "It was."

Something tells me he is not referring to the margarita.

Instantly, the empty third seat at our table is filled. Not by an uninvited person, but by a ghost. The shadow of our failed relationship sinks down into the wicker, uninvited but nonetheless expected. Did I really think we could get through a night at our old spot without it?

Chapter 14

Autumn

FOR MOST OF DINNER, we've managed to ignore the phantom at our table. Our conversation leans toward the basic, giving any possibly touchy subject a wide berth.

But our time is running out. I can feel it. And by the shift of his torso in his seat and the changing of positions of his legs, Owen can too.

"Thank you." I smile graciously at our server as she drops off my wine. A Spanish red. Owen has opted for a second margarita. Classic this time, not pre-made prickly pear. He said he was only allowed one hot pink cocktail a week, and had therefore reached his limit.

Our plates are cleared and we've declined dessert. There is nothing left but us, our drinks, and a conversation that, for all its meandering, has been headed in the one direction since I climbed into his car.

Owen picks up the straw from his drink, pinching it between his thumb and pointer finger before suddenly dropping it back into the glass. He looks at me, intensity burning in his gaze. "Why did we break up, Autumn?"

And here we are. The rest of the shit we haven't hashed out has arrived.

I squirm. "You know why. We discussed it at coffee." I know it's not possible to move on without talking about this, but a girl can dream.

Owen shakes his head like a child refusing a parent's request to clean up toys. "I mean *why*. Not what happened that caused us problems. I want to know why we couldn't handle what happened."

Why couldn't two eighteen-year olds handle an abortion? Gee, let me think…

"I … don't know." As insufficient of a response as it may be, it's the truth. I honestly don't know what went wrong after that day, only that I could no longer look at him the same. Could no longer see us together.

His dark lashes fall and I see the hurt my lack of an answer causes, so I try to explain. "I used to think about it a lot. But I could never really pinpoint exactly what it was that ended us. There was no great big swipe of a blade … it was just everything."

"Death by a thousand cuts," Owen says, the admittance both nostalgic and forlorn. It makes me sad for our younger selves, the teenagers who bit off more than they could chew, who tried to be adults and instead of cautiously stepping into the water, jumped in headfirst and drowned.

"I suppose so." I look at my wine. It's half empty but I don't remember drinking it.

"You ghosted me." His voice is small. "We promised to go to college and meet back here. I ... waited for you."

My heart breaks in that moment and I reach across the table to squeeze his hand.

"I'm sorry." I meet his gaze. "Every day after the abortion, we chose not to acknowledge it. We buried it alongside our grief and pretended we weren't heartbroken. We lied to each other, and the whole time we were slipping further and further from one another. Then, when you came to see me at Santa Clara, you exploded."

His head hangs in shame. "I know. I'm sorry."

I shrug, pulling my hand back. "It's okay, but it's the reason I ghosted you."

There, I said it. I admitted he was to blame for some of this whole thing and it felt good.

He nods. "The entire time, the only thing I wanted was to take you into my arms and hold you." Owen struggles to get control of his voice.

I push away the burning in my throat. "And I thought you were disgusted by me. By my body and my choice."

"Never." Owen's denial is delivered on a fervent whisper. "I felt so far removed from you. I didn't know how to help you, when I couldn't even help myself. And to make it all that much more fucked up, I couldn't even identify why I felt the way I did. We only had each other to turn to, and instead we turned away."

"I couldn't look at you," I choke out, my eyes watering. "I couldn't even stand looking at myself."

Our server approaches, ill-timed, to drop off the check. I use the break in intense conversation to look off to the side, surreptitiously wiping my eyes and checking the moisture on my fingers for runaway mascara.

Owen pays the bill, and this time I don't argue.

On the way out the door, I thank him.

"Would you like to walk around?" he asks. Behind him, the courtyard has come alive with strings of white lights, and somewhere nearby I hear the strains of live music. He offers me a hand, waiting for my answer. I'm not ready for the night to end.

I nod, slipping my warm palm into his. We walk along, admiring the many artist galleries, the boutiques, the store that sells only gemstones and minerals.

As we walk on through the village, the pedestrian traffic is moderate. Tlaquepaque is so beautiful it draws locals and tourists alike. One visit provides a taste of what it has to offer, but I could never tire of its unique beauty.

"Are you ready for dessert?" Owen asks, pointing to an ice cream shop.

"Most definitely," I say with more exuberance than intended, making Owen laugh at me. On the way in, I notice the storefront beside the ice cream shop is dark, and for a quick second I wonder what used to be there. The thought is quickly replaced by the smell of sugar.

Owen scoffs when I order. "I can't believe you still order peanut butter chocolate."

I frown as they hand him his cone over the case. "Says the guy who ordered vanilla."

"It's classic," he argues, head bent to lick the side.

"It's boring."

I'm handed my cone, and this time I pay.

Finally, I win the argument.

We take our treats outside, seeking out a bench near yet another water fountain.

"I love that sound," I say, tipping my head back and closing my eyes, a bite of ice cream melting on my tongue. When I open my eyes, I find Owen's gaze piercing into me, leaving no room for me to wonder what he's thinking.

"I wish you'd gotten ugly," he whispers.

"What? Why?" I ask, my tongue coming out to lick at the corners of my lips. There isn't any ice cream there; it's anticipation I feel.

"Because now I have to do this." He tosses his half-eaten cone into a nearby trash can and gently cups my cheeks with his palms.

His lips are soft, searching, and I yield to him auto-matically, offering myself without reservation. As our tongues sweep against each other, heat pools between my legs. Our kiss is cold, and tastes like sugar and absolution.

When Owen pulls away, he drags his lips across my skin. "Do you want to come home with me?" His invita-tion, his smell, his tone of voice, they are enough for me to get drunk on.

"Yes," I murmur into the summer air.

Hopefully, this chastity jumper is about to get torn off me.

Owen kisses me again, stealing all my breath, until my hand turns into a sticky mess from melting ice cream.

"I FEEL like you're a real adult," I muse, looking out the car window at Owen's house.

We've just pulled into the half-circle driveway and he's cut the car's engine. He owns his own house, a nice house in the good part of town, and it's weird to think of Owen with a mortgage.

Owen throws a smile at me. "And you're not? You moved to Manhattan. You *stayed* in Manhattan. Until now."

I guess that does seem pretty adult-ish of me. I certainly felt like an adult striding around the office, working late hours, climbing the ladder. But then I come back to Sedona, jobless, and back to square one. Owen has a career and a house. What's next? A family? Judging by the size of this place, that's the next step in a natural direction.

"True," I agree, peering out the windshield at Owen's house. It's a beautiful home in uptown, close enough to the shops and Main Street, but not too close. Like Goldilocks, it's just right.

"Do you want to come inside? I have wine. Or not. Whatever you want." Owen's hands splay the air between us. "Shit, I'm nervous," he mutters, rubbing the back of his neck.

"Hey." My fingers find his thigh, pushing down until he looks over at me. "I want a glass of wine. Inside. Preferably with a view of the stars, if you have it."

Preferably with you naked and doing that yummy finger stuff from before.

His face softens, his frustration melting away. "I can do all that."

He climbs from his car, and as he's rounding the back, I flip open the visor mirror and do a quick check. My door opens and Owen's palm hangs in the open space, offering to help me out. Grabbing my purse, I take his offered hand.

He pulls me from the open door and closes it behind me, spinning me around once, slowly.

"Were you always such a gentleman?" I tease.

He was. Always. But I'd forgotten.

I let go of his hand, only to loop my arm through his, and we walk up the steps to his front door.

"I don't think so," he replies, pulling his keys from his pocket. "I was a horny teenager who only wanted one thing."

My shoulders shake with quiet laughter. "How is that different from right now?"

The lock slides out of its spot, and the sound is thunderous. Or is it my heart that I hear, beating away furiously in my chest?

Owen's eyes find mine, and they are so full. Of longing, concern, and a primal hunger. We are stuck here on the threshold, balancing on a precipice, dangerously close to falling over.

I don't know what tomorrow will bring. I don't have next steps. I've left behind my job and my life in NYC to come home and care for my mother, and instead I've found my old life waiting right where I left it.

But I do know what I want tonight.

Owen.

So I'm the one who turns the doorknob and the first to step into the dark house. And Owen follows behind me.

He understands what I've done, the statement I've made, and takes over. He steps around me in the entryway, flipping a switch. Light floods the living room. This place may have been built thirty-plus years ago, but the inside is recently remodeled. The floor is a ruddy reddish color, the tiles enormous. The walls are light, the furniture contemporary. The cathedral ceiling with exposed beams is the perfect complement to the style of the home.

"It's gorgeous," I tell him, impressed.

"Thanks. I can't take the credit though. Not really. I had help."

My stomach seizes. I nod, but don't ask. I don't want to know who has been beside him during the years I've been gone.

Owen leads me deeper into the house, and I follow. He steps into another room and turns on another light. The kitchen.

There is a large, butcher-block island, and the cabinets are navy blue with copper-colored handles. I hate how much I like what *she* picked out, whoever *she* was.

"Red or white?" Owen asks from where he stands beside the stainless-steel fridge.

"White," I answer. I'm feeling warm. I need something cool.

He opens the fridge, and I watch him reach in, all the way to the back. His shirt pulls up, revealing just a peek of skin, only a few inches, but what I see is tan and toned. My tongue sweeps through my mouth, moistening the sudden dryness.

He pulls away from the fridge, bottle in hand, and walks to a cabinet. After opening it, he selects two stemless white wine glasses and pours us each a drink.

Walking over to me slowly, he hands it to me. "I believe the stars were your next request?"

I swallow the lump in my throat and nod. I was the brave one, taking the first step, the biggest step, over the threshold and into his house. Now he's the one taking over. And I like it. I need it.

Nerves are creeping in, poking at me like little cactus needles. It's been a long time since we were together. What if it's a letdown? What if our memories have built up something that's impossible to reach?

"Come," Owen says, walking from the kitchen and motioning for me to follow. We walk through another room, but Owen doesn't turn on the light. In the soft glow cast by the kitchen I make out the shape of a pool table and I smile. *Bachelor move.*

Owen slides open a door and we step outside.

"Oh," I say without thinking, my voice a low, surprised moan. The sky is inky black, shot through with twinkling stars. Of course I knew it would be, but still, it's breathtaking.

"I know," Owen says, not needing an explanation. He settles into a seat on the outdoor couch, placing his drink on the table in front of him. I sit down beside him, close enough that we're separated by only a few inches, but I can feel the heat from his body. I lean back, and Owen tucks an arm over my shoulders.

I can't believe I'm at Owen's house, snuggling on his couch and watching the stars with a glass of wine. What that actual fuck is happening? I like it. I like grown-up Owen and I like grown-up us. His fingers graze my arm, leaving goosebumps in their wake.

His hand falls from my shoulder and touches my lower back, slowly stroking my skin through my clothes. The sensation of his fingers, even through the fabric, sends tremors down my spine. I snuggle deeper into him and his eyes darken, and when he speaks, his voice is deeper, huskier, causing my toes to curl.

"That's Venus," he points to a star in the sky, "the goddess of love, beauty ... and sex."

My heart hammers in my chest, an unsteady and irregular beat.

I place my glass on the table beside Owen's, and when I look back at him, what I see in his eyes steals my breath.

Unconcealed lust, curling through his brown eyes, darkening them to nearly black.

"Owen..." I murmur his name, one word meant to convey so many. *I've missed you. I'm sorry we messed up.*

With the hand he still has on my back, he urges me forward. I comply; he grips my hip with his other hand, guiding me onto his lap so that I can straddle him.

I sink down onto him, feeling his bulk even through his jeans, a low, distorted moan slipping between my teeth.

"Autumn," he growls, cupping my neck and trailing his hand over my collarbone, down across my chest and into the chasm between my breasts. "So fucking beautiful."

My back arches and I push down harder onto him. His hand drops lower, winding its way around my back and stomach, his fingers searching for an opening in my romper.

"Can't get in," he grits, and it makes me smile.

"I wore it to prevent this from happening," I admit, biting the side of my lip and raising my eyebrows. I don't stop pushing down on his length, grinding against him as if we're fifteen again.

He crooks a grin. "How do I get you out of it?"

"Top down," I breathe.

His hands are at my shoulders, wasting no time. His fingers slip beneath the fabric and I gasp. His touch is searing, and I know, somehow I know, that this is dangerous.

To my heart.

To my head.

The threat is not enough to stop me. I want Owen. I want this night. I want to make up for all our long-ago wrongs.

The thousand cuts that took us down.

Chapter 15

Owen

SHE'S STUNNING, sitting on top of me like this.

Her mouth opens and she sucks in a breath as my fingers dip under the fabric at her shoulders, tugging it down. For an article of clothing worn specifically to keep her bottom half out of reach, it gives surprisingly easy access to her top half.

The cloth slips over soft skin.

Down.

Down.

Down, until it rests in the crook of her bent elbows. Her bra is white lace, see-through. Her hardened nipples strain against the material. She doesn't lean forward to kiss me, just continues to sit where she is, pushing against the strain in my jeans. She is not shy like she once was, back when we were fumbling hands trying to work out where to put what.

Autumn pulls her arms through the romper and it falls to her waist, exposing her taut, lean stomach. She reaches behind herself, unclasping her bra and pulling it away from her body, dropping it on the couch beside us.

I'm confronted with more beauty than I remember. Her dark hair spills over shoulders, cascading in soft waves down to her breasts. Pert, pink nipples become even stiffer in the open air. My eyes travel lower, down to her bellybutton. There is a small, round scar in the place where a piercing used to be.

Autumn arches her back again, grinding against me, offering her chest. "Touch me, Owen."

I don't need the direction. I'd only been admiring her alarming beauty and my luck at having her here again, but it's good to know how much she wants this. Wants me.

I reach up, cupping my hands around her full breasts, brushing my thumbs across her nipples.

A whimper slides from her. "More," she gasps.

My hand runs the length of her back, and in the same way I urged her closer to me when she was seated beside me, I urge her body into the space between us. At the same time, I lean forward, gripping tightly to her waist, softly sucking the bud of her breast into my mouth. First one, then the other, and Autumn's hands are in my hair, fingernails dragging.

We are in the cover of darkness out here, nobody to see us except the stars overhead, but I want to take her inside to my bed. As difficult as it is, I wrest my mouth from her skin and wrap my arms beneath her ass, hoisting her into the air as I stand.

"Oh," she says, surprised, her legs tightening around me.

"Bed," I grunt.

"Yes," she whispers, pressing her mouth to my neck as I walk to the back door and into the house. I use my foot to close the door behind me, capturing her mouth with mine at the same time. Our wet tongues clash with urgency as I walk, and more than once we bump into the wall. Each time makes us laugh, but not for long. This hunger, this thirst, is too needy.

Finally, we make it my bedroom. I set Autumn on the edge of my bed and take a step back. She watches, halfway undressed, as I reach behind me and pull my shirt over my head. Her eyes travel over my skin and she reaches out, beckoning me closer. As I step into her reach, she grasps my jeans, unbuttoning, then unzipping, sliding them down my body.

She sticks out a bent leg, using her foot to push my jeans all the way to the ground. Reaching down, I remove my underwear, and here I am, standing in front of her fully in the knowledge that, just like me, she's seeing the person I've become since we've been apart. I'm not just bigger, stronger, tattooed. I've had experiences, grown, learned lessons. Just as she has.

Leaning over, I push gently against Autumn's shoulders until she is lying down in the center of the bed. My hand glides up the inside of her leg, and when I get to the apex, still sheathed in clothing, her muscles tighten. I cross over, dragging my hand down the inseam of her other thigh.

Autumn's hands fist my sheets. "I can't take it," she says, her tone pleading.

A sly grin crosses my face as I bend, placing my lips at the inside crease of her knee, feathering kisses up her thigh. Heat radiates from her center, and when my lips reach that part of her, I breathe deeply, adding my own hot breath. Her hips lift, the fabric of what's left of her outfit pressing against my mouth.

I grasp the bottom half of her outfit in two hands and swiftly pull it down over her hips, taking her matching white thong along with it.

After discarding them, I stare down at her. She is naked, gloriously naked, and in my bed. How many times have I envisioned this, only to be overtaken by reality, a reminder that my chance at my greatest love had passed me by?

Reaching out, she grabs my hardness and starts to softly stroke it up and down, making me lose all train of thought. Autumn's tongue darts out to wet her lips, and she bites the bottom one gently. As new as this grown-up version of Autumn is to me, I know what this means. She is done talking.

Well, *good*. So am I.

I lean forward, one knee coming to rest on the edge of the bed. Both hands scrape across Autumn's smooth skin, riding up her thighs, gliding over her hips and into the middle of her body. My eyes on hers so I can watch her, my fingers drift down lower, dragging through her wet heat. Her legs splay open wider, her gaze urging me on. Soft mewls drip from her mouth, and when I can't take it anymore, can't go another moment without feeling her, I sit back, reaching into my nightstand and grabbing a condom.

Autumn lifts her head, watching me roll it on. A memory creeps in, reminding me of before, of how she always looked away at this part.

The memory disappears as swiftly as it appeared.

I hover over Autumn, hands on either side of her head, pressing into the mattress. We are nose to nose, pounding heart to pounding heart.

Autumn's fingernails dig into my shoulders.

"Are you ready?" I ask, lightly nudging her nose with the tip of my own.

"Yes," she says, the word fractured by her heavy breath.

With one thrust, I fill her, and I'm transported to a time when life was easy, when loving Autumn and going to class was all I had to worry about. She moans with pleasure, her nails raking down my back.

Her body feels just as I remember.

I seize her lips with my own, kissing her deeply, my tongue searching.

Her mouth tastes just as I remember.

We part for a breath and I inhale deeply, my nose pressed to her hairline.

She smells just as I remember.

"Owen," Autumn moans, her hands gliding over my back, down over my ass, gripping me. "You feel so good. Better than I remember."

"For me too, love," I murmur, a small part of me realizing I've just called her the name I used to use before. If she notices, she doesn't say anything.

I'm not fast. I'm not slow. This isn't fucking, or making love. It's two battered hearts meeting in the middle, finally finding solace from pain caused long ago.

I reach between us and swipe my thumb over her most sensitive spot, rubbing small circles there. Dipping my head between us, I lap my tongue over her nipple and she moans, deep and guttural.

Autumn's legs press into my thighs and her muscles begin to quake as I continue my rocking motion. Her breath comes in waves, one on top of the other, her chest rising and falling in faster tempo. I increase my pace, setting a fierce rhythm, and Autumn explodes beneath me. I hold her, kiss her mouth, swallow her sounds, making certain I've drained her of every last drop of her orgasm.

She kisses me with ferocity, winding weak legs around my lower back. I try to hold off, working to bring her to another high, but I've just held my love in my arms while she went to pieces beneath me, and I can't stop it from happening.

Forehead pressed to hers, I fill her completely one last time, my heartbeat erratic. My muscles stiffen and jerk, and this time Autumn kisses me, drinking in my pleasure.

Sticky, sweaty, sated, I collapse on top of her with my heart beating wildly in my chest. Autumn keeps her legs wrapped around me, running her calf up and down over my backside.

We're quiet as we lay there, our thudding hearts slowing. I press a kiss to her temple and roll off her, walking to the attached bathroom and stepping inside. I discard the condom and wash my hands, then walk back out.

Autumn has climbed under the covers, sheet pulled up to her chin, but when she sees me, she pulls it away and climbs off the bed. She passes me, beautiful body and a smile on her face, and goes into the bathroom.

I'm not sure what to do now, but that smile on her face was encouraging. In an effort not to appear overeager for round two, I pull on some shorts and lay on the bed, on top of the covers.

Autumn comes out of the bathroom as naked as she walked in.

She hops on the bed and climbs under the covers. "I sleep naked," she tells me. "When I'm not living with my mom, anyway."

"Thank God," I say to the ceiling, shucking my shorts and joining her.

I pull her into me, her ass pressed to my length. It stirs, and though it seems too soon, it's somehow ready to go.

Autumn shimmies against me, laughing.

"You better be careful," I growl lightly in her ear, taking a nibble of her earlobe. "Spooning leads to forking."

She bucks again, pressing into me. "Care to make that statement a reality?"

Challenge accepted.

I roll her over so quickly she blinks in surprise. It's a look that's quickly replaced by lust.

As fast as I can, I pull on a condom and sink into her. She hoists one leg over my shoulder.

Okay, this time we're fucking.

I DID IT.

I was the creeper who watched Autumn sleep. I couldn't help it. Those full, pretty lips, parted in slumber. Steady, rhythmic breaths, lifting her breasts up and down. The sheet was bunched at her waist, and as much as I thought maybe I should pull it up for her, I didn't. She looked like a painting.

I left her sleeping and went to make coffee. I'm not sure what she'll eat for breakfast, but given the groceries she has been buying for her mom, I'm thinking a veggie scramble on whole grain toast. Hold the cinnamon rolls.

I'm buttering the toast when Autumn comes into the kitchen wearing last night's clothes. Disappointment trickles through me. I'd hoped she'd pull on one of my shirts, and then maybe I'd take it off her after breakfast. That romper thing she's wearing is more difficult to navigate—although I did discover the quick access to her breasts.

Maybe the romper isn't so terrible.

"Good morning," I say, cautious, afraid that the sun has shone light on more than just the morning. *Please don't let her tell me last night was a bad idea.*

"Coffee," she mumbles, looking around, bleary-eyed. Once she spots the carafe, she grins in relief and says, "Good morning."

I grab a cup and pour, handing it to her. "When did you start drinking coffee?"

"College," she answers, lifting the cup to her lips, inhaling quickly before taking a drink. "You?"

"Same."

She peers around me to the stove. "What're you making?"

"Veggie scramble. I thought given the kale situation at your place you'd want something healthy."

She chuckles softly. "Kale situation ... getting her to eat it hasn't been so bad." Autumn pulls a chair from the island and sits down. "It's funny how we've changed roles, in a way. Me cooking for her, trying to guide her diet. Her being problematic. When I hand her a juice, she turns into a petulant teenager."

I load the plates with our food and slide it across the island, one to Autumn and one to the spot beside her. "I think she's actually enjoying the attention."

"Yeah." Autumn's voice grows small as she scoops a bite onto her fork.

I know why, and it reminds me of what I said her first night back in Sedona, how I told her it was about time she came home. Even ten years later I'm still putting my foot in my mouth when I'm upset. Maybe I should work on that.

"I shouldn't have listened to her when she told me not to come before," Autumn says between bites. "Why did I listen to her?"

I sense the question is rhetorical, so I keep my mouth shut. I don't have an answer to give anyhow.

We keep eating, until Autumn scrapes the tines of her fork across her plate and looks at me. "Last night…" A blaze of pink blooms on her cheeks.

My muscles clench, readying myself for the words *was a mistake* to come from those delicious lips.

"…was amazing," she finishes.

My entire body melts like a snowman in a hot yoga class into the chair. "Yeah?"

"Oh yeah."

I fist pump close to my chest in celebration. An

incredibly dorky thing to do, yes, but I'm too relieved to care. Autumn smiles.

"Are you almost done with breakfast?" Her eyes dart back to my bedroom.

I stand quickly, the legs of my chair making protesting noises against the floor. Grabbing the arm of her chair, I yank it, causing it to rotate toward me. She laughs as I lean in, lifting her from the seat and over my shoulder in a fireman's carry.

I'm just about to take her to the bedroom but the doorbell ringing stops me. My stomach sinks.

There's no one else who drops by this early without calling…

Naomi.

"Expecting anyone?" Autumn slides down my chest, plants her feet on the floor, and looks up at me.

Fuck. Fuck. Fuck.

I'm so fucked. I can't breathe. I don't know what to say. The doorbell rings again and I'm standing there frozen like an idiot.

"Owen?" Naomi's voice comes through the door and Autumn's eyes go from sexy sultry to axe murderer in two seconds flat.

I gulp. "So … I had a casual thing with this doctor friend, but I haven't touched her since you got home," I ramble, trying to explain the situation.

Autumn looks so angry, I swear she's going to turn into the Hulk. "Okay … should I go?"

My head reels back in shock. "No! Are you crazy? No. I'll tell her what's up."

I hurry to the door, praying my hard-on goes away in the next eight seconds before I open the door and tell Naomi I've moved on.

I feel like such an asshole right now. Yanking the door wide, I see Naomi in her doctor scrubs, looking tired but smiling wide now that I've answered.

"Hey, I have an hour to burn if you're up for it." Her voice drops three octaves and her fingers reach out to stroke my chest.

Autumn clears her throat behind me and Naomi stills.

Oh shit.

Can I just die of a heart attack and not have to deal with this? As a physician, you would think I could deal with conflict and stress well, but apparently it doesn't extend past hospital walls. I hate this stuff.

"Naomi … can we talk?" I step outside and she backs up, her face falling when she sees Autumn behind me.

I leave the door open a few inches as Naomi steps out onto the front porch. She hugs her chest and tries to look cool, but I can see the hurt all over her face.

"I should have called first."

I run my hands through my hair and try to think of what will hurt the least. Maybe just the truth.

"That woman in there … is my high school sweetheart. She came back home and ... I didn't expect it to happen."

Her body relaxes a little when she hears that I haven't just hooked up with some random chick. "So ... is she moving back to town?"

I realize she's asking me if she and I can continue our hook-up once Autumn leaves.

"Yeah..." I hedge. "She lives here for now and I'd like to see if she and I can work things out."

Her unemotional doctor's mask slips down over her face. The hurt leaves her eyes and is replaced with a cold, stern glare. "Okay, well, this was ... fun. I'll see you around, Owen." Spinning on her heel, she walks to her car and I cringe at the thought of seeing her at work now.

"I'm sorry!" I yell after her, unsure if I hurt her or not.

She just waves, jumps in her car and peels out, the tires sending a screech through the entire neighborhood.

Yep. I hurt her.

When I spin back around, I catch a glimpse of Autumn's brown hair dashing away from the door.

She heard everything.

I step inside and prepare for a fight. Fifteen-year-old Autumn was incredibly jealous, and I expect nothing less now. I just hope I haven't ruined things.

The second I step inside, she's standing there in my entryway awkwardly.

"Shit, Autumn, I'm so sorry that just happened. I … well, she and I aren't serious. We had … an arrangement, if you know what I mean. But I just ended it and—"

She steps forward and cuts my words off with a kiss. "It's cool. I heard everything," she says as she pulls away.

I'm shocked. Legit floored that she didn't just smack me and walk out. "Really?"

She nods calmly. "I had a little friend-with-benefits in New York as well. No worries."

Just like that, jealously flushes through my veins. "I'll kill him," I say loudly, and only kind of joking. A peal of laughter leaves her beautiful mouth.

"I believe we were busy before we got interrupted?" Her gaze is hooded, and just like that her fuck buddy and mine are gone from my mind. Reaching out, I lift her into my arms and she straddles my waist.

I'm just glad Autumn didn't marry anyone. I walk only a few feet, just around the side of the kitchen island, and I set her down on top of it. "The second I saw this island, I thought about having sex on it."

Autumn throws her head back, laughing, her long hair brushing the cool granite. "Don't let me stand in the way of making your dreams a reality." She pulls down the straps of that complicated piece of clothing she wears, shifting her hips and removing it completely. She leans back on her forearms, her legs splaying open. She is so familiar, her dips and her curves, her center, but she is also new to me, this person she has become while we were apart.

I want to discover every inch of her.

And, with the sunshine streaming in, illuminating us both in ways that make it impossible to hide, I do.

Chapter 16

Autumn

"THANK you for driving me home. I know you're late for work," I tell Owen as he pulls his car into my driveway.

Owen waves away my words with his hand. "I called and told a nurse I'm running behind, and she told me my nine o'clock already called and said the same." He grins impishly. "She said there must be traffic in town, and I let her think that."

I rest an elbow on the console and prop my chin on my hand.

Owen brushes his fingers across the back of my palm and thoughts of last night flood my mind. *And this morning*. We'd always been compatible in the physical department, but this was on a whole new level. Everything was better, heightened by being unafraid, certain of what we were doing and how to do it. And even though it was beyond enjoyable, I appreciate what it was when we were teenagers. So sweet, so innocent. Kids stepping into adulthood.

Aside from his friend-with-benefits dropping by this morning, it was an incredible night with Owen. I was mad about her at first, but then I realized with what I had with Matt, I didn't really have room to talk. After hearing him completely cut things off with her in order to see where he and I could go, I was totally on board.

Last night was purely adult. And this morning was ... just wow. Owen had dipped his head between my legs, staying there until my back arched off the cool granite beneath me and my vision blurred.

That was new. Something we hadn't done before...

"What are you thinking about?" Owen asks, and when he sees the flame that sweeps across my face, he smiles proudly. He leans in, his breath tickling my ear. "You better believe I will be thinking about that today," he says in a low voice.

I turn my head, my lips dusting over his. "Do you want to come over for dinner tonight?"

He nods, his lips rubbing up and down mine. "And I'll see you at the hospital in a few hours."

What?

Oh. Chemo day. I hadn't forgotten. It had just been misplaced in my brain.

"Right." I sit back. Owen kisses the knuckle on my

middle finger, then releases me. I grab my purse and the door handle at the same time. "I'll see you soon."

As I open the door and put one foot out, Owen says, "Last night meant something to me. Is that okay?"

I freeze, turning back and looking into his eyes. Apprehension pools there, but it's not alone. I see hope in there, too. "It meant something to me too, Owen."

It's scary and exciting, but true. This man is capable of bringing me untold joy and also dropping a bomb on my heart and obliterating it.

We smile at each other across the confine of the car, then I climb out and shut the door, waving at him as I walk to my front door.

The key turns the lock and I open the door quietly. My mom probably isn't still sleeping, but if I'm lucky I can sneak to my room undetected and change, then come out as if I came home late last night and am just now getting up.

As I tiptoe down the hallway, I'm quiet as a church mouse. Just before I reach my bedroom, I smell something out of place in the house. Men's cologne, maybe? Or aftershave? Something manly. I tuck my chin, smelling the fabric at my shoulder. It definitely smells like Owen, which makes me smile. I reach my bedroom door and hurry in, taking great pains to let it softly fall into the doorframe. Moving quickly, I change my clothes, then duck across the hall into the bathroom to wash my face. When I emerge, I look like everyday Autumn, not Autumn who had mind-blowing, reality-altering sex three times in the past twelve hours—with her high school sweetheart—who she is supposed to hate … but no longer does…

Is it time to call my therapist? Or maybe just Livvie? I need a reality check to make sure I'm not going insane.

I find my mom out back, sitting in a chair with a book open on her lap. Birds chirp, hopping from branch to branch of the nearby tree.

"Hey, Mom." I walk toward her. She looks up at me, shielding her eyes from the sun.

"Good morning, hon. You must've come in late."

I sink down into the chair next to hers. "Yep."

So late. Like, five minutes ago.

She closes the book and sets it on the table bedside her. "Don't keep me in suspense. How was your date?"

I think back to Tlaquepaque … El Rincon … walking around, eating ice cream. "It was pretty great. Incredible, actually."

A pleased, knowing smile pulls up the corners of my mom's mouth.

"He has never stopped loving you, Autumn."

I fidget with the frayed hem of the jean shorts I changed into. "I hurt him, Mom."

"You were hurting too, remember?"

"Yeah." It doesn't feel the same though. Pain you cause yourself cuts differently than pain you experience at the hands of someone else.

"I think you're being given a second chance. You can

do what you never did before: let one another heal the wound." She folds her hands in her lap.

"When did you get so wise?"

She winks. "You've already asked me that question."

"I know." I shrug. "I guess I'll just wait for the day when I'm wise like you."

"You're wiser than you think. And braver too." Mom reaches out and tucks a piece of hair behind my ear. "And I love you."

A little piece inside me cracks at her words. "I love you too, Mom."

She nudges a dry leaf under the table with her foot. "Can you make me breakfast? You slept in and I don't know how to use the juicer."

I stare at her. "For real? You're asking for juice?"

"Don't make a thing of it," she tells me, squinting at me.

I stand. "Yes, I will make you juice. And then we'll get ready for chemo, okay?"

Mom sits back in her chair, closing her eyes and letting the sun drench her face in light. "Mmm hmm," she agrees.

I go inside and whip up a lean, mean, and green juice for the both of us. Just before I step outside with a drink in each hand, I notice a man's two-tone gold watch peeking from behind a basket on the counter.

I walk outside, hand her the drink, and ask about the watch.

"No clue," she answers, taking the drink I'm holding out to her. "It must be Owen's."

I stare at her for a beat, searching her face for any indication this watch and the note in the pantry are related, but she just tips her juice back and chugs. Only the slightest bit of panic crossed her face when I first showed her the watch, but it was also when I'd handed her the green drink, so it might just be that. The watch being Owen's makes sense. He's a man who's been coming here weekly for years. I decide to let it go

"Cheers," I tell Mom, holding up my glass.

We finish our juice in the sunshine, then go inside and get ready to face the day.

LINDA, my mom's friend at chemo, smiles at me. "It's nice to see you again, Autumn." Her cold cap is already on her head. My mom sits beside her, hair not yet tucked into the cap, and I wonder if we'll have to shave her head. She lost her hair both times before with the chemo, so I'm trying to mentally prepare myself.

The beautiful nurse from before situates my mom, making sure she has what she needs.

"Do you want me to stay, Mom? I can." I pat the purse resting on my hip. "I brought a book."

"No, no." Mom gestures with her hand. "You go. Call that new friend you've made and ask her to lunch."

My lips pinch as I consider her suggestion. I haven't

seen Livvie since the night Owen's dad needed help, and I wonder how she's doing. I also don't love the idea of seeing my mom poked with needles.

"That's a good idea," I agree, shifting to my other foot. "Text me when you're ready, okay? Or if you need anything?"

Mom sends me the thumbs-up sign as she leans over to Linda to see what magazine she's paging through. I head out of the room, surreptitiously looking around for Owen. I'd been hoping he'd make an appearance at my mom's appointment, but so far, he hasn't been around.

On my way out of the hospital I pull out my phone and text Livvie, asking if she can meet for lunch.

She writes back immediately: **Do WASP's play croquet?**

I bark a laugh. If I never lived in the Northeast, I don't know if I'd have understood her joke. Either way, Livvie is hilarious and I'm glad she's in town for the time being.

We agree to meet at the cafe near her bookstore. It doesn't escape my attention that it's the middle of the day and as far as I know she is the sole employee of her business. Which means she's turning over the "open" sign in the window to meet me for lunch.

Bad business management or living life to the fullest? I'm not one to judge, seeing as I'm currently jobless.

When I arrive at the restaurant, Livvie is already

there. She wears a black maxi dress, and several gold bangles on her right arm.

"You look beautiful," I tell her when I get to the table. She stands up to greet me, pulling me in for a quick hug and kiss on the cheek.

"Do you think it will be enough to make my husband come to his senses?"

I stop with my napkin in mid-air and stare. "Is he here?"

She picks up the phone lying facedown on the table and glances at it, then replaces it. "His flight arrives in a few hours. I'll drive down to the valley and pick him up after we eat."

I adjust my seat and take a sip of water. "Are you excited?"

She captures her lips with two fingers and twists. After a moment, she lets go and says, "Yes. But I'm nervous too. What if this is it? What if he comes out here and decides he hates it? He might, you know." She picks up the small menu. "This feels like a turning point for us. I still can't believe I convinced him to leave work for a few days and come out here."

"What are you hoping for?" I ask her.

She stills, thinking about it. "That he'll want to move to Arizona, work only eight hours a day, and we can have kids and settle down." Her voice is small when she says it, like it's the first time she's spoken her hopes out loud.

Reaching across the table, I squeeze her hand. "Then that's what you ask him for. Don't settle."

She grins, looking confident, and gives me a nod. I move the conversation along and ask her how it came to be that he decided to come out here, and what she will do with him while he is here. She says they're staying at a resort in Phoenix, and she's going to show him that Arizona isn't full of tumbleweeds like he thinks. We order lunch, and continue small talk.

"Let's talk about you," Livvie says, stabbing her fork into her chicken and hummus. "How are things with Owen?"

I cock my head to the side and poke at a crumble of feta cheese. "Well…"

"You rode a one-way train to pound town, didn't you?"

My face scrunches and I nod.

"I want details. Oh, Lord, please give me details. I need them." She hammers the table with one fist. "*Need* them."

I laugh. "We went to dinner last night at my favorite place. A place that I would call 'our' place. Then we went back to his house—"

"Yeah you did," Livvie interrupts, eyebrows wiggling. "How many times?"

I'm quiet for a second before a full-on grin lights up my face.

"Three," I admit.

"Ahhhh," she whisper-yells. "Are you sore?"

"A little." As I say it, a small ache starts between my legs. "Why are you so curious? You've been married forever. This stuff is old news for you."

"Oh, girl. Just you wait. Married sex is boring. In five or ten years, other people's sexcapades will be interesting to you, too." She takes a bite, then asks, "Do you have real feelings for each other or was this just a physical thing?"

"Yeah," I say around a bite of food. "He told me this morning that it meant something to him."

"Hot damn," Livvie says, her voice awed. "Owen the oncologist is in love."

I spear a bite and lift it to my mouth. "Nobody said the L word."

Slow your roll, Livvie.

She gives me a withering look. "Nobody has to. You loved each other before, right? First time love is big stuff. It packs a punch." She grows quiet after she says it, and I know her mind has gone to her husband, her own first-time love.

We finish eating, and I wish Livvie safe travels on her way to pick up her husband from the Phoenix airport. *Safe travels* really means, *I hope he gives you what you want.*

And I'm certain Livvie understands that.

THAT NIGHT, I meet Owen at my front door. He looks

tired from the day, but handsome as ever. I peek over my shoulder to be certain my mother isn't nearby, then wrap my hand around his neck and plant a fleeting kiss on his lips.

"I was hoping to catch you at my mom's chemo appointment," I murmur, stepping back and letting him in the house.

"Me too," he says, voice low. "All my appointments ran late today."

My mom walks in just in time to hear the last part. "Just one of those days, huh?" she asks.

"Yep," Owen agrees, stuffing his hands in the pockets of his navy-blue slacks. She turns her back and he sends me a meaningful glance.

I purse my lips and look down at my toes, painted a bright red.

"Owen, I'm surprised my hard-ass daughter let you come for dinner on a day that doesn't start with an *M*." Mom looks at me and laughs. "You must've worn her down on your date last night."

Boy, did he wear me down. Heat creeps up my cheeks as I fantasize about him wearing me down again and again.

Owen cocks his head toward me, amusement dancing in his eyes. "She took some convincing, but I was able to show her I'm worthy of friendship."

"Good," she says, patting his cheek as she passes him. "Come on into the kitchen and help with dinner."

We both walk behind her, and Owen reaches down,

grabbing a handful of my backside and squeezing. I send him a coy look and shimmy out of his grasp with a grin.

Vegetable and chicken enchiladas are on the menu tonight. Owen chops onions, pretending to cry, and says, "I don't cook much. It's not very fun to prepare dinner for one."

"Tell me about it," my mom says, acknowledging his plight.

"I didn't cook much until I came here," I say, dicing zucchini. "I was a sandwich pro."

"Now you're little miss healthy chef," my mom says, her tone good-natured. She bumps my hip with her own.

"It's fun," I concede, watching Owen use his knife to push the onions from the cutting board into the pan. They sizzle on their way in.

"I'm pretty happy to have you here," Mom says to Owen.

Owen eyes me. "Me too."

I make it a point not to look at him, but my insides heat up at his words.

We finish assembling the enchiladas, sliding the pan into the oven and setting the timer.

"I think I'll take a short siesta while those are cooking," my mom says, yawning for emphasis. She twirls her fingers at us and leaves the kitchen.

I glance at Owen. His eyes are already on me.

"Well?" I ask.

"Well?" he counters.

"We could sit in the back yard and have a glass of wine? Or a beer? I bought beer." I'd stopped by the store on the way home from Mom's chemo and picked up a few items for dinner, grabbing beer for Owen in case he wanted one.

"A beer sounds great, actually."

I pull two from the fridge and open them, handing one to Owen. He leads the way outdoors, to the covered seating area.

We settle in, close but not too close. A safe distance, a *friendly* distance. Because, I have no idea if last night was a fluke, or something we will be repeating anytime soon.

"How was your day?" I ask, toying with one of the dangly earrings I'd threaded through my ears before he arrived.

"Good, actually." He nods happily, running a thumb across the skin between his nose and upper lip. "I got to tell a patient they're officially in remission."

His eyes light up as he says it, and he has this look on his face, almost a reluctant pride. Because he doesn't think he deserves praise or because he knows a relapse is possible?

"Congratulations, Owen. You deserve a win."

He smiles sheepishly. "Now let's get a homerun for your mom too. For the third time. She looks good. I'm hopeful."

"Why do you think it keeps coming back?" I've not

yet crossed this boundary with Owen, the one where I ask him doctorly things, but I can't help it since he's brought up my mother's case.

"There's no way to tell. It's not like she's been a smoker all her life and now she has lung cancer. This was random, as most cancers are. It's not as if cancer looks at your moral constitution and decides if you're a good or bad enough person to multiply within. Sometimes I wonder if it's an arrow being shot into the dark."

"And a little drunk demon has the bow."

Owen chuckles. "But the demon lives inside you. That's the thing about cancer. It's a cell gone rogue. Simple as that." Owen's posture changes, his happiness evaporating like spilled water on a hot sidewalk. "You know I'm doing my very best to save her, right?" Desperation outlines the fervor in his tone.

"I know, Owen. I know." It's all I can say to reassure him. Until now I hadn't considered the pressure on him, the pressure he feels to save the life of not just someone he loves, but someone I love too.

Silence sets in, and it's a good break from the macabre tone that overtook us.

We sip from our beers, until Owen breaks the silence. "You were, uh ... something else last night. And this morning." His gaze flashes up to me. "Different than before."

A grin breaks out on my lips. Now it's my turn to

feel reluctant pride. "We were young. Still figuring things out. And I wasn't confident in my body."

One side of Owen's mouth pulls up into a grin. "Do you remember our first time?"

My head shakes and I laugh quietly. "Yes," I say reluctantly.

Owen pretends to be offended. "Was it that bad?"

"No," I hurry to say, "but it wasn't amazing either."

Owen's head moves back and forth as his chin drops to his chest. "Poor sixteen-year-old Owen. I wish I could go back in time and teach him what to do."

I reach over, patting his thigh. "Honestly, I'm just happy it was with someone I loved. I've heard some horror stories."

Owen grows serious. "Loved?"

My eyebrows draw together in confusion. "We were in love, Owen. You know that."

"I guess it's the past tense part that I'm talking about." His cheeks grow red and I shift uncomfortably.

Oh. Got it.

Before I can reply, Owen's hand snakes over the cushion between us, his fingers starting at the ankle I have propped up on the seat. He charts a course up my leg, and I understand what he's doing. I'm grateful he's letting me off the hook for now, not expecting a response when I don't have one to give.

"You wore this skirt to torture me, didn't you?" He eyes my outfit, causing a grin to pull at my lips.

"My mom could be at the window," I murmur,

keeping my eyes on his fingers as they trail up to my knee, cascading higher up my thigh.

He looks at the house. "She's sleeping."

Goosebumps rise on my legs at his touch. My breathing gets shallow, causing my heartbeat to pick up pace. "The food will be ready in fifteen minutes."

Everything about Owen's touch turns me on, and it's been that way since we were teenagers. After Owen and I went off to college and broke up, I dated a few guys, but none of them I was so passionately attracted to.

"Sounds to me like we have approximately fourteen minutes." His fingers brush between my legs and I'm already sold on whatever he's offering.

"For what?" I ask, pretending my mind hasn't traveled to the carnal place alongside his.

"Let me show you," he answers, standing and pulling me up with him.

We hurry through the house to my bedroom, quiet as we can be, and I thank the heavens when we don't encounter my mom along the way.

I close my bedroom door as quietly as this morning when I snuck in, and Owen stops me before I can turn to face him, pinning me against the wall beside my door, pressing kisses against the heated skin of my upper back.

"You taste so good, Autumn," he mumbles against me.

I can't make a noise for fear of being caught by my

mom, so I arch my back, pushing against his length. Behind me, I hear the inimitable sound of a zipper, the soft noise of pants falling; the anticipation of what is about to happen pools wetness between my legs. I wore a skirt today. If last night I made it difficult for him, today I've made it all too easy.

Owen spins me around, taking me by surprise. He bends, winding a hand around the back of my knee and hoisting it up onto his hip. Reaching his fingers between my legs, he parts my underwear and I'm already biting my cheek to cover my moan. He lines himself up with me, and in one swift movement he's inside me. Warm, tight pleasure bursts between my legs as he pulls my other leg around him and supports my weight so that I'm fully riding him. He goes slowly, so slowly, eyes locked on mine the entire time.

He leans in, nibbling along my jaw, and sets a slow, steady rhythm. Pulses of pleasure start to radiate between my legs and I clench, suppressing a moan.

Owen's forehead presses against mine, and we share breath, heat, and desire. Owen lets out a gruff grunt and I reach up, slapping my hand over his mouth. He bites my finger and shudders against me. The waves of pleasure that rock through us both are delicious and hypnotic.

Somewhere in it all, our past melts into the present and I realize something startling.

I never stopped loving Owen. In fact, I think I care for

him more deeply this time around, and that scares the shit out of me.

"Autumn?" my mom yells from deep in the house, and we both burst out laughing.

"Shit, go!" I hiss, laughing, as Owen pulls away from me and sets me on the ground, pulling up his pants and running into my attached bathroom to clean up.

I fix my underwear and smooth down my hair as I slip out into the hallway and prepare to pretend like nothing just happened.

Just like high school.

Chapter 17

Owen

*S*HIT. *Shit. Shit.*

I stare down at the broken condom in my hands and realize that what Autumn and I have started again is about to come to a crashing halt. I knew it was too good to be true. Something had to come along and shatter our perfect second chance. Was I too quick to put the condom on and that's why it broke?

I stare at my reflection in Autumn's mirror. My own haunted gaze looks back at me.

Not again.

The first time it was Autumn forgetting her birth control. Now it's a torn condom. Here we are again. Albeit both of us are more mature and financially well off, but a child … we've only recently apologized to each other for the last time we fucked things up. I thought we were trying to explore each other again and see where this could lead, not jump right into starting a family.

I quickly wrap the evidence in a wad of toilet paper and clean up before grabbing my phone and pulling it to my ear with a shaky hand.

I need to get out of here.

Now.

I can't think straight, I can't tell Autumn what happened, not yet. I need a plan or we will be reliving our biggest mistake again and I'll lose her forever. The panic inside me feels just like it did ten years ago. How can that even be? I'm a fucking adult now.

I step out into the kitchen, sweat beading my brow, and start to have a fake conversation in my phone. "Push ten milligrams of Zofran, I'm on my way," I say into the phone as Autumn and Faith both turn to face me. I pull the phone an inch from my cheek for a moment. "Emergency at the hospital. I'm sorry. I gotta run."

Faith and Autumn wear matching frowns but both nod. "Come by later? I'll save you some?" Autumn reaches for me to kiss my cheek and I freeze up.

"Sure." I step away from her and hightail it out of there as fast as I can.

I don't know what to do, so I start to drive to Ace's house. My fingers tap a nervous rhythm on the wheel as I weave in and out of the streets.

You Home? I shoot him a text.

Yeah. What's up?

I think I just got Autumn pregnant. Typing those words makes me want to throw up. I mean I could totally be overreacting. She'd have to be within a few days of her ovulation window, and what are the odds of that? Except I'm a doctor and I know way too much about sperm and how well they can thrive in the viscous fluid of a woman's vagina for days on end. This is something her body was made to do, and clearly Autumn has no issues getting pregnant.

Again? I'm getting out the good whiskey, he texts back just as I turn on his street.

The moment I step into Ace's condo, he greets me with a bro-hug.

"What happened?" he asks, handing me a whiskey on the rocks. I'm not a huge fan of hard liquor, especially in light of what's going on with my dad, but I need to calm my nerves, so I drain the glass and pace his hardwood floors.

"The condom broke," I say aloud for the first time.

Ace nods. "Been there. Fucking Trojan needs to up their quality control."

I set the glass down on his coffee table and collapse into his sofa, placing my head in my hands. "How is this happening again?" I mutter.

"Is she freaking out?" I feel the couch dip as Ace sits beside me. He's the only friend who knows that Autumn had an abortion before.

I look up at him. "I haven't told her. I ... it just happened, and her mom was home and ... I ran out."

Ace grins. "You had sex with her mom home?"

"Focus, man!" I shout, and he reaches out to place a hand on my shoulder.

"Bro, you got this. Just go down to the pharmacy and grab her a Plan B pill."

Plan B.

Why the hell didn't I think about Plan B? Relief crashes through me for a split second before it's over-shadowed with disappointment. I don't want her to take a Plan B pill. Just like deep down I didn't want her to get the abortion. We're two consenting adults and the condom broke ... whatever comes of it should be left alone ... right?

But it's Autumn's choice too, and as much as I may be ready for the adult consequence of our actions, she is not. Her mother is sick and she is in a career crisis. This will stress her out. I can already see the look on her face when I tell her. She'll close back down, never touch me again. But still, I owe it to her to tell her and give her the options.

"Plan B," I say, turning it over in my mind.

"Tonya at CVS is really discreet." He winks at me.

I roll my eyes. "How many times have you done this?"

He puts a finger to his lips. "You don't want to know."

I TAP the packet of Plan B in my pocket nervously before knocking softly on Autumn's front door. After picking it up from the CVS, I got Taco Bell and ate in my car while I went over fifteen different versions of whatever I would say to her. Then I texted her telling her that we needed to talk. I'm pretty sure I freaked her out.

She opens the door in her pajamas, hair tied in a top knot, and frowns at me. "Everything okay?"

I nod, motioning to the porch swing. She shuts the front door and follows me outside, the frown still in place. She sits next to me wringing her hands together, and I feel awful that she must be worrying about what I have to say.

"I don't know how to say this so I'm just going to blurt it out," I mumble.

"Owen, what's going on?" Her voice cracks.

"Tonight … before … in your room … the condom broke."

Her mouth forms a little "Oh" and her eyes grow wide. "I see." She shifts nervously, and just like that I can see every awful memory of what happened before flood her face. Post-traumatic stress is a very real thing, and it has a long memory.

I press on with my speech, pulling the Plan B out of my pocket and laying it in her lap. "I don't know where you are in your cycle, but I wanted you to have this and to know that I support whatever you want to do."

Out of all fifteen versions I ran through in the Taco Bell parking lot, this was what I settled on. It didn't make her feel guilty; it was supportive; and it didn't press my opinions on her.

She frowns, her eyebrows drawing together. "So, this is where you were tonight?"

I nod, swallowing hard, praying she won't close up and leave me.

"It happened again..." she breathes.

I nod, a little relieved that she's talking to me, processing things.

"Maybe we're just destined to have a baby together." I laugh nervously, and then regret it the moment her face falls.

"Is that what you want?" Her face is a mask of flat emotion. I can't tell what she wants me to say. This feels like a trap. If I say yes, she feels like it's all on her again to make the hard choice. If I say no, I'm an unsupportive asshole.

"I want what you want," I hedge.

She crosses her arms and glares at me. "Owen, don't do this again. Tell me what you want, not what you think I want to hear."

She's right.

I clear my throat. "I'd love to have a baby with you. No matter what our relationship turns out to be, I'd always be there to support you and the child."

Her eyes widen like she's shocked at my answer and I suddenly feel self-conscious. "But I mean, if you take the pill that would be fine too. Whatever you decide."

She's quiet for a moment, staring down at the package. "You're a sweet man, Owen Miller. I'm not sure I deserve you."

Her words crush me. What have I done wrong that she doesn't realize her worth? That she docsn't see how lucky I am to have her?

"Autumn, look at me." I hold her gaze and she swallows hard.

"I stood drunk in your dorm room and called you a murderer in front of your entire floor. And you forgave me. It's me who doesn't deserve you."

Tears well in her eyes, before she chuckles. "Making friends was a bit of a challenge after that. Not gonna lie."

She's trying to joke but guilt threads through me as I reach out and take her hands in mine, pulling them up to my lips so that I can kiss her fingers. "This isn't like last time. You have seventy-four hours to decide which path you want to take."

She nods, and I can see the terrified deer-in-headlights look in her eyes.

"Want me to leave you some time alone? Or..." I want to be supportive of whatever she needs without smothering her.

She shakes her head. "Stay the night?"

Relief crashes through me. This time is different.

It's going to be okay, we're going to be okay. But I don't like the way she's looking at the cardboard pill box. Like she can't wait until she's alone so she can take it. Maybe that's why she asked me to stay, so she can put off the irreparable decision for just a little longer.

I'm too scared to ask her what she wants to do about the situation ... so I don't.

Chapter 18

Autumn

I COULDN'T SLEEP last night, even in Owen's arms. I just kept thinking about that fucking pill in my purse.

Plan B.

More like *Plan WTF*.

How did I get myself into this situation AGAIN? It's like Owen looks at me and *boom*, I'm pregnant. One session of wall sex in my childhood bedroom and a broken condom later and now I can't sleep.

Owen's chest rises and falls at my back in a hypnotic rhythm, but I can't lie here any longer. Instead I'm thinking of sore breasts, swollen feet, and an adorable baby with Owen's eyes and my smile.

Do I want a baby?

After the abortion so long ago, I hadn't allowed myself to dream of having a baby one day, in the way most women I know dream of it. It felt so out of reach, maybe even something not allowed to a person who'd made the kind of choice I had. *You didn't want a baby back then? Then you don't get one ever.*

That's not how the universe works, and I know that, but guilt is a multi-pronged weapon.

Instead of thinking of Owen and I in domestic bliss with a baby, I can't stop thinking about everything going wrong in my life.

My mother is battling cancer for the third time.

I am jobless and in a small town that doesn't exactly have a lot of opportunity for someone with my qualifications.

I just started hooking up with my high school sweetheart who ruined me for every other guy and...

I should throw a baby in there?

No. That would be crazy. Right? Maybe if my shit were more together ... but at this point Owen would have to financially support me and the baby and I never wanted that kind of life.

A kept woman.

I pull open my period predictor app for the fiftieth time and check the day in my cycle again.

Ovulating.

Fuck. Fuck. Fuck.

I feel like I can't breathe. I need to go for a drive. The sunlight is just peeking through the curtains in my room and I know I have to get out of here before Owen wakes up. I can't face him right now.

Stepping into my bathroom, I brush my teeth and pull my purse over my shoulder. Reaching into my bag, I pull out the Plan B and flip over the package.

When using this product you may have…

Nausea

Vomiting

Dizziness

Lower stomach pain

My eyes blur at the rest of the words. I poke my thumb through the package and pull out the tiny white pill, holding it between my fingers.

So small, yet this has the power to ensure I will not have a baby with Owen right now.

Or ever.

I have this inner knowing that if I take this pill, Owen and I won't make it through.

I toss the cardboard into my trashcan and stuff the pill into the tiny zipper portion of my purse. Then I slip out of my bathroom, tiptoe through my room, and out of my house.

By the time I get to the open road, window down with crisp air whipping through my hair, I already feel better.

I shoot Owen a text in case he wakes and worries.

Couldn't sleep, went for a drive. See you tonight for dinner? Your place?

I'm desperate to keep what he and I have going. It's like I finally realized what it's like to be happy. Happy New York City Autumn isn't the same at Happy Sedona with Owen Autumn. He ... makes me feel the most myself.

I don't even know where I'm going until I pull into the church parking lot. The grounds of the church my mom goes to are so beautiful. They cut right into the red rock, and last Sunday I even saw an outdoor labyrinth.

Stepping out of my mom's car, I lock the door and pull my hood up around my hair. The morning air is chilly but it feels good against my warm skin. I debate texting Livvie to see if she's awake, but I'm not sure I want to bother her with this. This is heavy, and I don't want to be the new friend who always brings the heavy conversation.

Instead I pop around to the back of the church and spot the small spiral of stones. The labyrinth. It's just what I need, a meditative walk to clear my head. I heard once that if you bring a problem to the labyrinth, by the time you reach the middle you will have your answer or something helpful to guide you.

I start off at a slow pace, the entire time chanting one thing.

Should I take the pill?
Should I take the pill?
Should I take the pill?
Should I take the pill?

I get close to the center, only to wind back outward, and I realize this fucking labyrinth is a metaphor for my life. Get close to having Owen, then pull back from him. Close to having my mom healed, then she gets cancer again. Get job, lose job. As I near the center, I've picked up the pace and I'm no closer to having an answer to my question than I was when I came here.

"Autumn, is that you?" a familiar voice pulls me from my manic thoughts just as I reach the center of the labyrinth. I look up to see Pastor Greg standing in a jogging suit, holding a rake and tree trimmers.

My eyes widen. "Oh no. Am I trespassing? I'm so sorry."

It was barely six A.M. and I hadn't really thought about whether I was allowed to be here or not.

Pastor Greg smiles. "Trespassing? Goodness no. It looks like you're trying to unravel a problem in your mind."

My shoulders slump. "Is it that obvious?"

He sets down the rake and tree trimmers and motions to a bench.

I suddenly wonder if the labyrinth brought me Pastor Greg. You could talk to these people and they wouldn't judge you, right? Wouldn't tell on you either? They were like a lawyer and a shrink had a baby. With some God power thrown in.

I step over the rocks that make up the labyrinth and sit on the bench next to him.

"Lovely morning," he says, looking out at the red rocks.

I gulp. Why of all places had I come to a church?

And why of all people was the pastor out here during my mental breakdown?

"Really pretty," I agree.

I'm not going to cave. I'm not telling him anything. I'm going to wish him a good day and then text Livvie.

"Do you think God forgives abortion?" I blurt out.

To his credit, he doesn't stiffen, doesn't even flinch. He just slowly nods his head.

"Of course. Our Heavenly Father forgives everything if you ask for it with an open heart."

I'm still not even sure I believe in God, but hearing him say that I could be forgiven for something that has caused me so much guilt and grief ... it lifts the burden from me in that moment. Maybe that's what I need, to forgive myself. I was young, I made a choice I didn't really think through, and I need to forgive myself for it. I did the best that I could at the time given my circumstances and what I thought I could handle.

"It's something I did years ago..." I feel like I need to explain. "But now I'm in a similar situation."

A tear slips from my eye and down my cheek and Pastor Greg turns to me. "Maybe try just letting things be what they will be."

Be what they will be.

There was something comforting in that. Not trying to control every outcome, not trying to overthink the next twenty years of my life and see what they would look like with and without a baby.

Just be what they will be.

I nod, swallowing hard. "Sorry for unloading on you like that…"

He chuckles, deep and rich. "Nature of the job."

As I walk away from my little chat with Pastor Greg, I know two things for certain.

One, I want this baby if a baby should come of it.

Two, I'm still in love with Owen and don't ever want to lose him again.

Chapter 19

Owen

TWO WEEKS.

Nearly two weeks of bliss with Autumn.

After finding the empty Plan B pill box in Autumn's trashcan the morning after I gave it to her, my heart tore in two. I thought she'd taken it, thought she'd made her choice and I was going to have to live with the aftermath.

Again.

But then she came back from her drive and pulled the tiny white pill from her bag, handing it to me.

"What will be will be," she'd said, and that was that.

We didn't say another word.

Now it's like I'm riding on fluffy clouds of cotton candy and living my best life. The energy Autumn put into hating me when she showed back up, she now puts into being with me.

It's not just the sex, which is mind-blowing and constant, it's the conversation, the quiet time we spend together. It's like our relationship from ten years ago, before we fucked it up. I'm so comfortable in her presence; she feels like home and I keep waiting for something bad to happen and it all to be taken away.

Comparing now to before isn't even enough to capture it. It's us, Owen, and Autumn, but on steroids. Adults. Playing for real in the game of life. Before, we were just starting out on roads leading away from one another. We're seasoned now, we've traveled those roads. We've both had wins and losses, pain and triumph. The roads we went down eventually brought us back together.

Autumn hasn't told me her plans once her mom is in remission, and I've been too afraid to ask, but I'd be lying if I said it wasn't constantly running through the back of my mind.

Is she going back to New York? She said her stuff was in storage there and it bugs me that she hasn't had her things sent to Arizona.

As if thinking of Autumn summons her, my phone dings with the notification of a text message. We've been texting all day, but when I pick up my phone I see it's not a continuation of our earlier conversation, but a photo of a watch, along with the message: **You keep** forgetting to take this back from my mom's. I never took you for a two-tone metal watch guy.

The skin between my eyebrows forms a bewildered "v." **Very fashionable, but not mine**, I respond, adding the thinking emoji.

She writes back immediately: **What? If it's not yours, who does it belong to?**

Your mom's secret lover... I hit send and smile at my joke.

Very funny, she says, and I imagine her holding the end of the word *funny* for an extra beat to drive home her point.

Autumn doesn't say anything more, so I put my phone back on the desk and pick up my fork. I'm in between patients right now, and I'm using the time to eat lunch. The first half of my day, I usually have appointments with my patients, and the second half I do rounds on patients who were admitted to the hospital for whatever reason. I love that working at the hospital as a staff oncologist with an office affords me the ability to do both. My next patient is new to me, so I'm in my office reading his history when Ace walks in without knocking. He sits in one of the two chairs in front of my desk and pulls a foil-wrapped sandwich from a white bag.

"How's it going?" he asks, unwrapping a Cuban sandwich and takes a big bite.

"Great," I answer, chewing a piece of the grilled

chicken I brought from home. For the record, Ace's lunch looks better.

"Bet I know what's putting you in such a *great* mood these days." Ace's eyebrows pull up and begin moving in a way that can only be described as waggling.

I haven't told Ace about Autumn not taking the pill or that Autumn and I are so serious. Truth is, I don't know what exactly to call it. We've been enjoying being together so much that we haven't labeled it, but I'd be lying if I said it wasn't starting to bother me.

I haven't told my dad either. I probably should. The news would make him beyond happy, but I'm afraid he'd use it as a cause to celebrate. Which means get shitfaced. Not that he needs a reason. He's made that abundantly clear, but I'm avoiding him altogether as much as possible right now.

My dad is a puzzle I don't know how to solve. He's supposed to be a parent. Why am I the one parenting him? It's amazing how a person can get older but always expect their parent to stay in their role. I never expected my dad to lose his shit and completely give up at adulting.

He's called me four times since Autumn and I started back up. He never calls unless he's drunk, and I'm so afraid each time is going to be *the* time—the time he has crashed his car and needs help—the time he's in the hospital because he got hurt. The possibilities are endless for someone who gets as drunk as he does.

I just don't want to deal with it.

"Just in a good mood," I tell Ace, who's sitting there, waiting for me to answer.

He raises one eyebrow. "And a person whose name rhymes with *bottom* but is spelled totally different doesn't have anything to do with it?"

A smile tugs at the corner of my lips. "It's possible," I concede, pushing away my nearly empty container.

"That's what I thought." He smirks and sticks his pointer finger into a circle he's made with his hand in a crude gesture.

"Knock it off," I growl playfully.

Ace can only go so long without thinking of sex.

I don't want to keep talking about it, mostly because I don't want to have to tell him that I don't know what's really going on between me and Autumn. It's hard enough admitting that to myself every day.

"Grow a pair and ask her to be your girlfriend," he mumbles through his food.

I blink, surprised.

He swallows and takes a swig of seltzer water. "I've been your best friend for a long time, Owen. I don't need to know why you look all doe-eyed at the mention of Autumn, and then dopey when you think too hard." He finishes off his sandwich, sucking leftover sauce from the pad of his thumb.

"I don't want to rush her."

Ace shrugs. "Just calling it like I see it. You need to have the talk with her before she thinks this is just some temporary fling and moves back to New York to marry some rich stockbroker."

At the mention of her moving back to New York and marrying someone else, my entire body clenches.

"This advice coming from a guy whose bed is a revolving door?"

"I wouldn't say *revolving*. More like an open-door policy." He winks.

I snatch my balled-up napkin and toss it at his chest. It doesn't reach, falling ineffectually near the edge of my desk.

"You'll change your mind one day. One day, a woman will come along and tame Ace Drakos, and I hope I'm there to see it."

Ace shakes his head, a sliver of sadness creeping into his voice. "No way, man. I learned my lesson. The hard way, remember?"

Unfortunately, I do.

Ace still hasn't recovered from the lashing his heart took at the hands of his college sweetheart. His open-door policy is proof. Miranda was a cheating whore and we don't speak her name.

There's a knock and we both swivel toward my door.

"Come in," I call.

Nurse Theresa steps in, papers clutched to her chest. When I see that her eyes hold fear and anguish, my face falls.

"What is it?" I ask, my stomach knotting, the chicken threatening reentry. Theresa doesn't get affected by much and she never bothers me during my lunch.

"The lab sent over Faith Cummings' latest blood-work. I emailed them to you, but..." She hurries forward, thrusting the papers in her hand at me. "I printed them out too."

I don't look at the papers first. I look to Ace. My best friend's gaze is on me, his lips pursed, eyes wide. His chin dips slightly, urging me on, telling me I can do this.

When I read the results, something inside me breaks.

With a shaky hand, I pick up the phone and call Faith.

THIS MOMENT HAS BEEN COMING for hours, and now that it's here, I don't know if I can do it.

I don't know if I can open the door and invite Faith into my office. How can I tell her I've failed her? Failed Autumn? Myself, even?

Wooden feet carry me across the tiled floor and to my office door, where a soft, hesitant knock comes through.

Breathe, just fucking breathe.

I take a deep breath and open the door. Faith stands

there, her face arranged into a peaceful expression. She is resigned and it guts me like a fish.

She knows.

"Hello, Faith," I say, listening to my voice as if it is not my own. It's clunky, stilted.

"Owen," she greets me. Her voice is the opposite of mine. Serene, accepting.

I step back from the door, ushering her in with an open arm. She strides, head high, to the seat Ace sat in just hours ago. I choose the chair beside her, needing to be closer to her as I deliver the bad news. I haven't told her why she needs to come in, just that it's to discuss some bloodwork.

She ducks her head a fraction. "So, is it as bad as I think? You're sitting on this side of the desk."

I exhale loudly, heavily. Gathering her hand in mine, I open my mouth to speak but find there are no words. Faith started out a long time ago as my girlfriend's mom but she has become so much more than that: a friend, a mentor, an ear to listen, a giver of advice when my dad began down his destructive path—a mother of my own.

Reaching out, she cups my cheek. "It's okay, Owen. Just tell me."

Something inside me gathers, growing like a tornado, extracting all my strength from the furthest corners of my body. Faith deserves a doctor who can be strong for her. *I* should be consoling *her*.

I level my gaze on hers, throat tight. "Faith, your

most recent blood test results showed an increase in white blood cells. Chemo actually works to lower your white blood cell count in its effort to attack the cancer cells, so an increase as drastic as yours tells me we need to get you in for a CT scan. The cancer is ... growing."

Her face remains passive. I'm waiting for the break-down, but I don't think it's coming. Not yet at least.

"Alright," she says, stoic. "Just tell me when."

I grab for my appointment book and open it. Despite all the technology surrounding me, I'm old school. I like writing down my appointments. I'm booked solid tomorrow, but it doesn't matter. I'll work late to squeeze her in. Javier is the best radiologist we have and a good friend. He will squeeze her in too. That way, I can see if it's spreading to her lymph nodes or surrounding organs.

My mind calculates all of the treatments we can try if this looks bad. Bone marrow, blood transfusions, even stem cells. I know of a great clinic in Scottsdale. I will pull every fucking favor I have to save this woman.

"How is tomorrow at two?"

"That works." Faith straightens her shoulders. I can't believe it was only a few nights ago that I sat at her kitchen table, eating a meal cooked by her hands, while something new, possibly another cancer, spread and grew inside her. It was a typical Monday evening, or so we thought.

Her eyes search mine, beseeching. "Can I ask something of you, Owen?"

I nod, afraid of what it is she might request.

"Don't tell Autumn. Not until we know something concrete."

My heart falls at her request but I completely understand it. I don't want to worry Autumn unnecessarily either.

With one finger, I gesture from me to her. "Client-patient confidentiality, remember?"

She raises an eyebrow. "Do you think in the dark of night, when they are with their lovers, doctors don't break their code?"

I point back at myself. "Not this doctor."

Faith smiles, just a small one, and gently pats my cheek. "You're a good man, Owen Miller. I hope my daughter knows how lucky she is."

"I make sure to tell her every day," I say, with a wink.

Faith chuckles and stands, prompting me to follow her. At the door, she turns around. "We'll take this one day at a time. Just like we always have." Then she steps through, letting the door close behind her.

The first time I told her she had cancer, I was an intern and I said we'd take it one day at a time. And that's what we've been doing ever since. Maybe that's all we can ever do, cancer or not.

I want to be optimistic like Faith, stoic in the face of

something frightening, but I have the burden of knowledge.

I chose not to tell Faith something I'd learned only from experience, something not yet verified by testing but known by gut feeling.

What I'll see tomorrow on those scans won't be good. It will be a downhill road from here on out.

I've failed the one person who never turned her back on me.

Chapter 20

Autumn

THE NIGHT IS dark and clear. Owen has pulled his outdoor couch to the middle of his back yard. Turns out, it converts into a bed of sorts, kind of like a futon.

We're on our backs, gazing up at the charcoal sky. We are linked together, the sides of our bodies pressed so close we could be the seam of a piece of clothing. Owen, however close he may be in physical proximity, is a million miles away.

"Penny for your thoughts?" I ask, keeping my gaze trained on the sky overhead. He has been like this since he picked me up this evening. I was afraid to ask why, didn't want to pry. A part of me feels like I should ask what's wrong, we've known each other long enough that I don't need to tread lightly. The other part of me feels our newness, the parts of him I don't know as well as I used to, or at all.

Owen pinches the bridge of his nose, and though he doesn't make a sound, I see the deep rise and fall of his chest.

"Tough day at work," he says, his voice immensely sad.

I shift so I'm on my side, bringing my hand up and palming the fabric of his shirt over his heart. "Can you talk about it?"

His gaze flickers over to me, then back up. I watch his eyelashes as he blinks four times in rapid succession. Almost imperceptibly, he shakes his head.

"Is there anything I can do for you to make you feel better?"

He rolls over onto his side, facing me. He looks at me, his eyes an ocean of anguish. There is apology in his expression, sown into the squint of his eyes and the pleat of his lips. What is he sorry for?

Insecurity snakes in, starting in my heart and slithering out like spokes on a bike tire. Has Owen changed his mind about us? Is this not what he wants?

I should ask him, but I know I won't. When it comes to Owen, there is still a young girl inside me nervously biting her lip, uncertain of her place in the world. I may have grown into a woman, but Owen has a way of stripping me bare and exposing my heart. Will giving it to him again lead me straight into disaster?

"MOM?" I stick my head in her bedroom door. She's sitting on the end of her bed running her hand over her freshly shaven head.

"Oh." Seeing her without hair startles me. It's been slowly thinning, even with the use of the cold cap, but I didn't want to say anything to make her uncomfortable, and now … it's gone.

She gives me a small smile. "It's been falling out in chunks. This is easier. I think it looks kind of punk rock, no?"

I choke back the sob that wants to escape me and nod. "Totally punk rock. We should book your skull tattoo later."

That causes her to genuinely smile before nodding her head. "Okay, I'm ready to go."

It's chemo day. I can't tell if the treatment is working, and that bothers me. It's not like a skin rash that we can apply cream to and watch it disappear, or a bruise that changes color and eventually fades away. No visible progression.

Mom nods at my question, yawning as her head bobs up and down.

"How can you be tired? You slept in today. It's like you're a teenager." I smile teasingly as I grab the bracelets she always wears from her nightstand and hand them to her. "Good thing I don't do to you what you used to do to me when I slept in."

She winds her hand through the bangles. "I was tough on you, wasn't I? Probably a little tougher than I should've been." She pushes the hair back from my shoulder, her fingers brushing lightly over the skin left bare by my tank-top. "I was trying to be both mom and dad. I made mistakes."

Her admittance takes me by surprise. And as nice as it is to hear, it makes me uncomfortable. It's hard hearing your parents are faulty. It humanizes them. And I was only joking so I'm thrown by this serious admission.

"I can't imagine how difficult it was to be a single mother. You did a great job, Mom."

She nods once, acknowledging my words. "Let's go."

As she steps around me, I feel a squeeze of my hand.

On the drive to the hospital, Mom listens to the kind of music you'd hear during a spa treatment. It makes me think of white sheets and heated massage tables, aromatic body scrubs and the padded footfalls of technicians.

Oh, how I miss the spa days in Manhattan with my roommate. Now I was doing my own pedicures to try to make my savings account stretch out until I found a job.

My mom places a hand on my arm as I steer the car toward the parking lot.

"Just drop me off up front, hon."

I look in the rearview mirror and let the car slow to a crawl. "You don't want me to walk you in?"

She bats a hand in the air. "I'm perfectly capable of walking in by myself. You go do whatever it is you need to do and just pick me up after."

"Are you being a teenager? You're embarrassed of me so you want me to drop you off where your friends can't see you with me?" I crack a smile to let her know I'm joking.

She laughs. "Precisely."

I do as she asks, rounding the circular driveway and stopping the car at the entrance. "I'll pick you up here when you're done."

She gathers her bag and pauses with her hand on the door handle. "You're going to make a good mom one day."

A lump immediately forms in my throat and again I'm thrown by her random sentimental statement. Has she been talking to Pastor Greg or Owen? No. Somehow I know that they would never tell her. My mom is just in a sentimental mood for some reason.

"I learned from the best."

She gets out of the car, and I watch as the automatic doors slide open and she walks through, the hospital swallowing her.

You're going to make a good mom one day.

The words have hit home. With that one sentence, my mom has reopened the possibility that I could become a mother, and it's nearly too much for me to bear.

Instead of leaving the hospital, I pull into the parking lot, sliding into a space, and cut the engine. I lean back, melting into the seat, and prop my arm on the door.

Me, a mom one day? Do I deserve it? Do I want it?

Yes and yes. All this time, I've been punishing myself for a choice made long ago. It was a choice so huge, it eclipsed all others. But what if it's time to stop punishing myself? The bravest thing a person can do is forgive, right? I've always believed that, but I'd never extended it to me personally. Never realized just how much I was withholding it from myself.

But what if I don't have to anymore?

Owen and I have been given a second chance. Can we make it count? Will the universe, God, whoever it is pulling strings, be so kind as to give us a take two?

My mind races. Excitement takes hold in my belly, in the place where maybe a life could be growing. My fingers flutter over my flat stomach.

Owen and I are new—but not really. We've hurdled the beginning of a relationship already. We're more than ready to have the talk, the one where we figure out if we're willing to go the distance.

I know I am, and I think—

Wait. What the hell?

Thirty yards away, my mom and Owen exit the

hospital, walking out of the same door I watched her walk through five minutes ago. They stop, he points across the street, and she nods. Together they walk down the sidewalk, press the walk button at the small intersection in front of the hospital, and cross the street.

I back out of my space and drive in the direction they've gone. My mind's reeling wondering what the heck they're doing. I'm stopped by a long red light and I don't see where they've gone, but I have an idea. A line of shops sits directly across the street from the hospital. I bet they've gone into one. But *why?*

The light turns and I make my way across the intersection, taking inventory of each store as I cross the street, and pull into a spot in front of a dog groomer. To the left is a sushi restaurant. To the right, a coffee shop.

Maybe my mom's appointment was pushed back and Owen took her for a coffee while she waited. That's probably it. The bunched-up muscles in my upper back uncoil. Of course Owen would do something so kind for my mom.

I laugh softly, embarrassed at my worry. Why did I jump to the worst thoughts? They're not keeping anything from me. They're getting coffee, for heaven's sake, maybe even a danish. I know how Owen likes to indulge my mom.

Honestly, I wouldn't mind a danish right now. I grab my purse from the back seat and decide I'll join them and tell them how silly I was, acting like a detective. They'll laugh.

I pull open the door to the coffee shop. It's tiny, just enough room for the counter and machines, and seven tables with two chairs each. Mom and Owen are at the back, up against the wall. A picture of Italy hangs on the wall above them.

Owen's hand covers my mom's palm. They are so engrossed in the conversation they don't see me approach. My excitement fades as something darker, a sense of foreboding, overtakes my happy feeling. I've just read Owen's lips, and he said, *Faith, I'm so sorry*.

"Mom? Owen?"

They turn to look at me in perfect unison, like they are mirror images of one another. The same surprise in their eyes, the same wetness on their cheeks.

And I know. Somehow, in this moment, I know. The fear lurking in the back of my mind steps out from the shadows. I recognize the fear, because I saw it in Owen's eyes twelve hours ago.

"Last night," I whisper, looking between my mom and Owen, my gaze finally settling on him. "You were so upset. You knew."

My mom grabs my hand. "He couldn't tell you, honey. Legally, and because I asked him not to."

I turn to her and my heart aches at the sight. Her arms that held me when I fell, hands that made thousands of meals for me, fingers that brushed away my tears ... my beautiful mother.

"Tell me."

"The cancer has spread to my bones, Autumn. The

chemo isn't working." Her matter-of-fact tone tells me she is resigned.

Well, I'm not.

Something inside me stirs. A heat, a hope, a wave of anger. The first flickers of a fight. I can do this. Where chemo has failed her, I can make her better. I'll research until my eyes are crossed, call in every favor.

Pulling a chair from a nearby table, I sink down into it, still holding my mom's hand.

"Listen," I tell her, my tone intense. "We're not giving up. There are alternative treatments. Countries without the restrictions we have here. I have money saved, Mom, and if it's not enough I'll get a loan. We'll exhaust every option." I glance down at the table, at the chocolate croissant in front of her. "No more sugar. No more dairy or gluten. I'm going to read more about eating meat." I look at her paper coffee cup. "And about caffeine. Environmental toxins too. We should probably get a whole house water filter—"

Owen interrupts: "Autumn, she only has a few months left. Six months at the most." And all of the wind is knocked out of me. He sits back, two hands wrapped around his own coffee, pity softening the corners of his eyes.

"No." I shake my head, rubbing at my temples. "No, because we haven't even finished this round of chemo, and there is—"

"Sweetheart," Mom begins, her voice cautious. Her gaze searches mine, and before she speaks, I know what she's going to say. My head shakes, but she presses on. "I don't want to do all those things. I want to have my last few months with you and Owen and my friends. Not vomiting, or chained to a hospital bed."

My voice is a growl. "You have to fight, Mom, even when it's hard."

The world sits between us, my world and hers, wishes and desires colliding. The longer she looks at me, the more I understand what she isn't saying.

"I'm done fighting, honey. I just want to live with what time I have left."

"No." It's a whisper, strangled by anguish, but a refusal nonetheless. My gaze flits between them, between two people who've had time to sit in this information, who've settled into a choice. They watch me now, both with a mixture of tenderness and uncertainty. It strikes me that they have the matching expressions of two people who've been in battle together. This is their third fight, and their first loss.

I am not where they are.

I've never felt so alone.

"I need to go," I mumble, ripping my gaze from them.

They don't stop me.

"THOUGHT I MIGHT FIND YOU HERE."

Her voice, smooth and kind, swirls around me. She

steps into my vision. The tree I'd been looking at now looms above her.

My mom gestures to the open space on the bench beside me. "May I join you?"

"Of course," I say, moving my purse. I'd set it there on purpose. Tlaquepaque is a busy place, and I didn't want anybody sitting beside me. An uncharitable move on my part, but making small talk with a stranger seemed too much for me right now.

My mom sits down, setting her own purse on her lap. She looks up at the tree. "You always did like it here." She glances around. "It's beautiful, certainly, but for you it has a magical quality."

"Yeah," I nod, looking down at the uneven floor, the places where the tree's roots have pushed up. "Did Owen tell you where to find me?"

She gives me an admonishing look. "I knew exactly where you'd go."

The glowing feeling of being known spreads through my limbs. My mom angles her body toward me, and I follow suit, propping one bent knee on the wooden bench between us.

"You may not believe this," she starts, her speech halting, "but I was thinking of you when I made the choice to discontinue chemo."

I open my mouth to protest but stop when she shakes her head.

"This is my third fight, Autumn. It's probably hard for you to imagine how tiring that is, but believe me when I tell you it's the most exhausting thing I've ever done. Physically, mentally, emotionally. All of it. Having cancer isn't a choice. I have no control over it. The one thing I do have control over is how the end of my life goes."

A sob escapes my throat, but I swallow it down as she reaches for my hand.

"Baby girl, I don't want to spend my precious time chasing a *maybe*. Owen sent my scans to be looked at by colleagues at three of the top cancer hospitals in the country. They all said the same thing. Terminal."

The sob I swallowed earlier is back up now and I can't speak.

Terminal. That one word strikes fear into my heart like no other.

"I just want to be with you. And Owen. I want to grab coffee with Linda. Go to church on Sunday. Eat ice cream, gluten, and sugar. I want to drink wine in my back yard." Her eyes light up mischievously. "I want to take a helicopter tour of the Grand Canyon."

My mouth drops open. "Mom, you're terrified of helicopters."

She smiles. "I know. Also, I want to see a show in Vegas."

I laugh, incredulous at the notion of my mom venturing out of her comfort zone and doing things she has refused to do for so long. The laughter dies in my throat when I realize it's her bucket list. "You hate crowds."

"Right," she nods, the smile still playing on her lips. "Will you do those things with me?"

Tears prick the corners of my eyes. "Of course."

She wraps me in her arms, gathering me to her, and holds me while I cry.

Chapter 21

Owen

I CAN TELL who is at my front door by the soft and hesitant knock. I'd also know who it was if the knock were loud and insistent. After what Autumn learned today, I'm anticipating a wide array of feelings. I'm glad she walked in on her mom and I having coffee and talking about stopping treatment. Now I don't have to keep this secret from her any longer. It was killing me. I needed someone to share it with, and now that it's out I can put all my energy toward being strong for her.

"Hi," Autumn says when I open the door. She looks tiny, shrunken by the weight of her mom's choice. I don't say anything. I just pull her over the threshold and into my arms. She presses her face to my chest, and when she draws back for a breath, her eyes shine with unshed tears.

"Come here," I say softly, leading her over to the couch. We sit down, but Autumn looks uncomfortable. She's facing me, her legs tucked underneath her, but she's restless. She taps two fingers against her thigh in a quick beat, and I don't think she knows she's doing it.

After a moment, she leans in. "I need you," she whispers, her hand disappearing under my shirt and skimming over my torso.

Her request surprises me, but when I look into her eyes, I understand. The heartache I see there tells me all I need to know. She's trying her damnedest to run from the pain, and as nice as it would be to sweep her up and run away from it with her, it won't make a difference. Pain doesn't disappear because you choose not to acknowledge it. Pain is a patient sonofabitch.

I take her hand out from under my shirt. "Autumn." My voice and my touch are gentle.

As if her name was the key to the gates holding back her grief, they open and everything she was avoiding spills out. At first it's her tears, followed closely by an anguished sob. I pull her onto my lap and wrap my arms around her quaking shoulders. She buries her face in my neck, and the saddest sounds I've ever heard are cried against my skin.

Autumn's ache unlocks my own. My eyes burn, and salty tears slip down my cheeks, some spilling onto my lap and others soaking into her hair.

Autumn's sobbing comes and goes, and I hold her

through each wave. Time passes, I can't tell how much because it feels insignificant in this moment. Eventually Autumn sits up, sniffling, and runs a forearm under her nose. Without a word she climbs off me and walks to the bathroom. The sink turns on and she blows her nose over and over.

While she's gone, I take my phone from my pocket and order pizza. There isn't anything I can do to fix what is breaking her heart right now, but at least I can feed her.

When she returns a few minutes later, she sits down, letting the cushions support her. Her restlessness has evaporated.

"I ordered pizza," I tell her, tossing my phone on the couch beside me and placing one arm over her shoulders.

"Good," she says, shifting so she's pressed against my side. "I'm starving."

"Do you want to talk about your mom?" My question is partially muffled by the top of her head.

"No," she answers. "Not yet."

I nod my understanding. We sit quietly, but inside my head it's loud, and I wonder if it's the same in hers.

"HERE." I hold out a beer. Autumn takes it from me, eyes grateful.

She twists off the cap and tosses it. It lands on the

dining room table and spins twice before it falls over. She takes a deep pull, her throat bobbing when she swallows.

"I needed that," she says, placing the beer on the table and opening the box of pizza that I set down a couple minutes ago. "Oh," she gasps softly, covering her mouth with her hand.

"What?" I ask, concerned. "Did I get the order wrong? Do you hate it?"

"You remembered my favorite."

Chicken and mushrooms with garlic and fresh basil. That order has been imprinted on me for over a decade. And not just because it's delicious, but because it's Autumn's order. I'd never heard of such a pizza until our second date, when we'd walked to a nearby place after school and I heard the girl who stole my heart order something that seemed so advanced for our fifteen years. It only made me like her more.

"Onion rings with barbecue sauce. Spaghetti with olive oil and garlic. The word *moist* makes you shudder, scabs on elbows gross you out, and you absolutely detest olives, which doesn't make much sense because you love pickles and they're not that different." I could go on. And on and on and on...

"Owen ... I..."

Whatever it is she's trying to say, the words just won't come out. She gets up from her chair and comes to me, sitting down on my lap.

My hands wind into her long hair, cradling her head.

"I haven't forgotten a second of you, Autumn. Not a damn second."

"Me neither, Owen. I remember all of us, every moment, every laugh, every pain."

I swallow down all my fear of losing her a second time. "What do you think about giving us another chance?"

She presses the tip of her nose to mine. I smell beer on her breath, mixed with the sweet smell of Autumn. "What do you think I've been doing these past few weeks?" she giggles.

"You're gonna make me say it, aren't you?"

She nods.

"Autumn Cummings, will you be my girlfriend?" I say in a nerdy voice that resembles my fifteen-year-old self.

Laughter peals out of her and I'm thrown by how insanely beautiful she is.

"Yes," she answers, and kisses me quickly before pulling away. "So, we're really doing this?" she asks, and I know it's not a direct question but a statement of wonder and disbelief.

"We really are," I confirm. "And this time we're going to do it a hundred times better."

"Yes," she murmurs, her velvety lips on mine. "So much better."

Autumn reaches for a slice of pizza, but she doesn't go back to her seat. She eats pizza on my lap, alternating bites and kisses. I can almost see her high fading as thoughts of her mom creep back in.

"Are you certain she can't fight, Owen?" Autumn wipes her mouth with a napkin and grabs another slice.

I've had more time to process it all, and still the thought is sharp, jabbing at me as I contemplate Autumn's question. As much as I want to sugarcoat it, I know Autumn would prefer a straight answer. "It's too advanced. There is literally nothing modern medicine can do for her now but ease her suffering. No stem cell, no bone marrow transplant or transfusion has ever medically brought someone back from how far along she is. I ... I failed her. I failed you."

I keep thinking of how I didn't catch its progression sooner. I followed every protocol and it still snuck past me.

I hear Autumn's sharp intake of breath, see it in the rise of her chest. It remains puffed up for five full seconds before she releases it. "You didn't fail anyone." She reaches out and runs her fingers through my hair, raking them along my neck. "Do you think I could change her mind?" Rueful hope lives in her question.

"Yes," I nod slowly, my answer as honest as my previous one. "But that doesn't mean you should. She has given tremendous consideration to her choice. Knowing what I know, seeing what I've seen, if I were terminal, I'd want my last days to be living life with my family."

Autumn traces lines in the wood grain of my table.

"In a way, it reminds me of the abortion. The choice, I mean. It was my body and I made the choice." Her lips twist, and I sense she's not done talking. "Do I regret it? Yes. Do I wish the circumstances had been different? With my whole heart. Did I feel I had to do it? Also yes. I made a choice for my body, using the information I had at the time. She's doing the same."

I nod, pulling her closer into me. "I know it's not easy, Autumn, but I'm going to go through this with you, if you'll let me. Okay?"

Tears line her eyes as she nods. "I want you there through every step. Including flying in a helicopter and seeing a show in Vegas."

I shake my head, confused. "How did we get from your mom to Vegas?"

"She told me some things she wants to do before … before she…" The word sticks in her throat.

"Helicopter, Vegas, what else?" I'm trying to rescue her from saying the word she so clearly cannot express.

"Time with us. Me. And you. Coffee with Linda. Basic stuff."

"We'll do it all," I assure her, brushing a kiss over the back of her neck. I don't tell her how soon we'll need to do it. Making sure it happens in a timely manner will be my job.

Autumn takes a bite of her pizza, eyebrows raising like she has just realized something.

"What?" I ask, taking a bite too.

"My period is due any day now … so I guess we'll

see..."

The broken condom. It's not that I forgot it, only that it was pushed to the back of my mind when Theresa showed up in my office with Faith's scans.

Autumn mistakes my lack of response for worry. Her eyes crease in concern. "Do you regret that I didn't take the Plan B?"

How do I tell her that I don't really care if we use protection again anytime soon? I should tread lightly, go slow, but *fuck* I don't want to. I want to snatch her up and make her mine, and if I've learned anything through all this with Faith, it's that life isn't guaranteed.

Tracing the lines on the inside of her palm, I ask, "What do you think about forgetting birth control altogether?"

She blinks in surprise. She doesn't look like she hates my question. In fact, she looks intrigued, giving me the courage I need to push on. "I'm not looking to spend years dating you," I tell her. "I don't need to get married tomorrow, but I know you're who I'm meant to be with." I run my hand up and down her arm. "So, my love, you just say the word. You tell me how all this is going to go. Because you have me. All of me. Forever."

Autumn tosses the rest of her pizza in the open box and wraps her arms around me. "How is this the saddest and happiest day of my life at the same time? Owen Miller, you are the person all the rest of my days belong to, and I don't care that our past is muddy because all the days ahead of us are bright." Leaning forward, she kisses me before pulling back and staring at me with her big brown-eyed gaze. "I love you, Owen."

My stomach warms at her declaration.

"Are you sure?" I ask, teasing her, trying to ease some of the seriousness. "You loved teenage me, but what if you don't like adult me? What if I've developed some terrible habits?"

"Too." *Kiss.* "Late." *Kiss.*

"Well, good, because I love you too, Autumn Cummings. And I never stopped."

She pulls back and eyes me. "Are you trying to one-up me?"

My nose presses against the hollow of her throat. "How about I take you back to my bedroom and show you?"

I cup her backside and lift as she wraps her legs around my waist. Carrying her to my bedroom, our lips are locked the entire time. Her hands are in my hair, dragging strokes that shoot straight down to the center of my body, the effect of them immediate.

We undress in a hurry, needing so badly to be skin-to-skin. She lies back on my bed, watching me as I crawl up her body.

I line myself up with her, easing in, my gaze steady on hers, watching her face. I need to see her, need to capture every moment.

This is heaven on Earth. All of Autumn. Nothing

held back.

Breath hisses between my teeth as I fill her completely. She wraps her hands around my neck, pulling me down, kissing me. We go slowly, relishing the closeness, reveling in the feeling of being bare. The closeness makes it difficult to hold back, but I focus my willpower and wait until I feel her muscles clench around me. The middle of her back lifts off the bed and I hold her, kissing her neck, letting go with her.

After a moment, I roll off her, trying to take her with me so I can pull her into my chest, but she resists.

"I need to clean up," she reminds me, kissing the tip of my nose and getting off the bed. I smile at her naked backside as she walks into the bathroom.

Being bare with Autumn not only felt amazing, it felt defiant. Sticking it to the man, so to speak. *Fuck you, cancer.* You can't stop us from living. You can't stop us from creating a new life.

Perhaps it was an attempt to gain control when we feel we have none in the matter. Maybe it was redemption for the choice we made so long ago. Whatever it is, I know we both feel it. We are throwing a middle finger to the powers that be, the ones who saddled Faith with something strong enough to finally take her down.

Autumn comes back to bed, snuggling into me, and we ride on a euphoric high. It remains in place alongside our reluctant acceptance of Faith's choice. This is our mood for the next few days, until Autumn gets her period.

Chapter 22

Autumn

THE ONLY THING more shocking than the arrival of my period was the disappointment I felt at the sight of the blood.

For a moment I thought that maybe, just *maybe*...

It's over now, though. I've gotten my period and the universe has given me a clear sign that I am not to be a mother, not yet anyway. I've decided to go on birth control until I can figure out my life and plan things in order like a proper adult. Still, a deep ache I never thought I'd have has opened up inside of me.

I want to be a mother.

I want to be Owen's wife.

I want more time with my mom.

I have more wants than I care to admit.

And I wasn't the only person who was disappointed.

JENNIFER MILLIKIN & LEIA STONE

Owen's gaze fell down to my kitchen table when I'd told him.

"Is it weird that I feel a little sad?" he'd asked.

"I think it's a testament to how serious we are about each other."

Then he'd pulled me onto his lap and kissed me.

Now I need to add *find a lady doctor* to my list. It can go right below *find a job*. At least I have a place to live.

Thankfully, I can push those tasks off for another day. In an hour, we're leaving for Vegas. I'm packed but my mom is not. She went to take a nap, but that was two hours ago. Her naps are becoming more frequent, and when I asked Owen about it, he said that was normal.

Normal for what?

I didn't ask, because I didn't want to know the answer. And because I can guess what he meant.

Using two knuckles, I knock lightly on my mom's bedroom door.

"Come in," she calls.

She's standing in front of her closet, her back to me. Her frame that was already thin is now gaunt. Her robe hangs off her, her peach fuzz hair peeks out of a pretty silk floral wrap I bought her.

"Mom?" I walk to her, peering at her in the mirrored closet door. Stress pulls at her face. "What's wrong?"

She flings an angry arm at her bed.

Dress after dress lie haphazardly on her comforter.

A wave of sadness rolls through me. "You don't know what to wear?"

"No." Her voice pricks with frustration. "Because everything falls off me. I don't have a single dress appropriate for a show in Vegas."

I eye the selection on her bed. I don't need to see them on her to know they don't fit. But I do have an idea.

"I'll be right back," I tell her. I go across the hall to my closet and pull it open. I've done some shopping since I came home. Not a lot, but there is one dress that might work. It's tight and stretchy, meant to hug the curves. I pull it from the hanger and return to my mom's room.

"This," I say, thrusting it into her hands. "Try this. It's a little casual, but you have that cardigan with the silvery sheen. Between that and some jewelry, we can dress it up and make it appropriate for a show."

Mom eyes the fabric in her hand. "Are you sure?"

"Absolutely, Mom. Try it on."

I turn away while she changes, pretending to sift through the jewelry box on her dresser. The sight of her body, changed as it has been by the disease ravaging her on the inside, would send me to my knees. I can't let her see me like that. She needs me to be strong.

When I hear the sound of a zipper, I turn back around. "That's perfect," I tell her, and I mean it. The silvery cardigan makes the mint green dress a little fancier. "Here." I hand her a pair of dangly earrings.

She takes them and turns away quickly. She wasn't fast enough though. I saw the shininess in her eyes.

The sight of her upset makes my own eyes burn with tears. "Mom..." I place a hand on her shoulder. "It's okay to cry. I cry all the time."

Every night, I wonder how much time I have left with my mom.

She swipes at her eyes. "What's the use in crying? I don't want to spend what precious time I have left moping around. It's such a waste, except I can't seem to stop."

She sounds like the mom I remember when I was younger. She may have relaxed a lot since then, but her pragmatism still exists.

I have an idea. "Do you want to make up a word? Every time you feel like crying, say the word instead. It will release the emotion without having to burst into tears."

She nods. "I like that idea. What's the word?"

I think about it, but it's a lot harder to make up a word when you're focused on making up a word. Instead, I say a word that I never say in everyday language. It's a little weird on its own, and doesn't have any strong connotation. "Marzipan."

Mom makes a face. "Marzipan?" She says it a second time, then a third. She nods. "I like it."

I help her finish packing her overnight bag and carry

it to the front door. I try not to pay too much attention to the fact that we're fulfilling last wishes.

Marzipan.

Marzipan.

Marzipan.

"JUST THROW it on the ground, Mom." I point down at the concrete and back to the small card she holds in her hand. We'd barely made it twenty feet from the entrance of our hotel before a man on the Las Vegas strip shoved the card at her. It's reflexive to take something being handed to you, and this happened to be an advertisement for an all-nude strip club. Not sure why, of the three of us walking together, the man chose to give it to my mom.

Mom looks down at the blond girl with the pouty lips and the bondage-style lingerie. "I feel bad throwing it on the ground. She doesn't deserve to be stepped on. And besides, it's littering." She sips from the straw of her hot pink yard cup. It's hard to take her seriously when she's drinking a daiquiri nearly as big as her. It's taking three times as long to walk the strip because we keep having to take breaks for my mom to catch her breath, but she's refused a wheelchair.

Owen and I share a grin. "Mom, look." I point at all the other cards on the ground. "It's okay."

Mom frowns, and holds the mostly-naked girl in her

hand until she finds a trashcan and tosses her in. Headed to the casino at the hotel where the show is, it's slow going at this rate, but that's why we left early. When Owen asked my mom what she wanted to see, she told him she didn't care what it was, she just wanted the experience. With only a few days' notice, there weren't a ton of choices, and we went with Cirque du Soleil. Honestly, I think she will love it.

Owen and I stop at a bar beside a row of slots and order drinks. The bartender takes our picture after I make a joke to her that I need footage of my mom with a drink meant for a twenty-one-year old.

Mom declares she wants to learn roulette, and of the two of us Owen is the only one who has played. With a grin on my face, I sit back and listen while he teaches her the basics. It sounds like gibberish to me. I've never been much of a gambler. I prefer to keep my money.

Once she thinks she's gotten it down, we find a table with two seats open beside each other. Mom and Owen take the seats, and I stand behind them.

Owen removes two one hundred-dollar bills from his pocket and sets them down separately on the felt, one in front of my mom and the other in front of him. The dealer changes the money in for chips, sliding one color to my mom and a different color to Owen.

Owen holds up his yellow chip to my mom. "Each of these is worth five dollars."

Mom nods, a determined look on her face. "Got it."

She starts tentatively, sliding one chip out to a square. Owen slides a second one out for her. "Ten-dollar minimum bet," he tells her, smiling sheepishly. "Your teacher forgot to mention that."

We watch the little ball spin around and around, slowing and then finally dropping into a slot.

"Sixteen," the dealer announces, no emotion to be found in his voice. Makes sense, I guess. It's not like he can cheer for the winners. He gets to work paying out those who won and taking the chips of those who lost. He matches Mom's two chips with two more, and she lifts her hand to high-five Owen.

They play and play, until I remind them both it's time to go or we'll miss the show. Owen is down to his last few chips, and Mom only has six left. He glances at his watch and pushes his three chips to my mom.

"Here," he nods, urging her to add them to her tiny stack. "Last bet. Whatever you want, and then we'll leave."

Mom looks up at me, winks, then turns back to the table. She slides all the chips to the number nine. *My birthday. 9/9.*

I hold my breath when the dealer releases the ball, hoping against all reason that the universe will make the ball slide into the nine slot. My mom deserves a big win.

It slows, until it loses momentum and drops, bumping along. I strain my neck to see where it stopped.

"Twenty-eight," the dealer declares.

Damn. The number right next to nine.

Mom and Owen stand up and she shrugs and sips from that ridiculous drink.

We leave for the show, and on the way, Mom tosses the yard cup in the trash.

OWEN CHOSE THE SHOW WELL; my mom absolutely loves it. I watch her more than I watch the entertainment taking place in front of me. Her eyes widen when the acrobatics shock her; she places a palm over her heart when she thinks they are dangerous, and claps heartily when they perform tricks that appear to defy possibility.

After it's over, she grabs Owen's arm and hugs him. "Thank you," she gushes. "It was amazing. Everything I wanted a show in Vegas to be. Why did I wait so long to come here?"

We leave the area and agree to get one more drink and late-night food. I've heard it said that nothing good happens after ten p.m., but I don't think that counts in this zip code.

By the time our bellies are full, Mom is exhausted. We walk her back to her room and say goodnight, making sure she gets in safely. When Owen told us he'd booked two rooms, I'd offered to stay with my mom, but she said no. To say she's supportive of my reunion with Owen would be the understatement of the century. I've never seen her so happy.

As soon as her door is closed, Owen's hand wraps around my waist and pulls me in so my back is pressed to his front. "Are you ready to turn into a pumpkin, Cinderella?" his husky voice tickles my ear. "Or can I interest you in more Vegas-style debauchery?"

I rest the back of my head on his shoulder. "How debaucherous are we talking? And yes, I know that's probably not a word."

His chuckle rolls through me. "Not small-cards-thrust-into-hands type of debauchery."

I laugh as I picture my mom carrying that blond girl around in her hand.

"More drinks. More gambling. Some gratuitous public displays of affection." He pushes against me as he says it, pressing his length against my ass.

My breath catches in my throat. "I think I could handle a little more of all three of those things."

We're stepping onto the elevator when I pull my phone from my purse. I haven't looked at it once since we left the hotel room hours and hours ago.

I'm taken aback when I see my previous boss' name listed as a missed call. Owen notices my surprise.

"Who's that?" he asks, fingertip bumping against my phone screen.

Jeanne Chapman. "My boss in New York. Old boss, I mean." A weird feeling is sneaking out from behind hidden places inside me. The feeling of waking in the morning and getting ready, of doing my hair and donning professional clothes. The energetic air of the city in the morning, the scent of coffee, the smells of food and gas and a million different perfumes. The six-figure salary I once garnered. I miss being a part of something. I can't deny that.

Owen takes my free hand, lifting it in the air between us and running a feather-light touch across the top. "Penny for your thoughts?"

The elevator descends and my stomach drops. It stops a few floors below and three people get on. Two guys, one girl. They have accents, something European that I can't place accurately.

"I have no idea why she'd be calling me," I murmur, turning into him.

"She left a voicemail. Listen to it."

The elevator deposits us on the ground floor, right into the casino. I step to the side, trying to find a quieter space, which is as futile as it should be considering my current location. Throngs of people excitedly talk over one another, slot machines whistle and ring their bells. I stick a finger in one ear to drown out the din and click on Jeanne's voicemail. Owen stands beside me, surveying the happenings of the casino, hands tucked in the pockets of his navy-blue dress pants. These slacks are not like the ones he wears for work. These are tighter, more modern, and they make him look sexy as sin.

"Autumn, hello," Jeanne's voice breaks through my carnal thoughts. It's been a mere two months since I heard her voice, but I'd already forgotten it. "Jeanne here. I'm sure you were quite surprised to see my call. I'll cut to the chase. Bill is out. He bought a ranch in Montana and moved his entire family there." I may have forgotten the sound of Jeanne's voice, but I can still pick up her emotions from her tone, and right now I hear disbelief mixed with disgust. "We'd like for you to take his place. VP of Product Marketing. I know you're spending some time in"—she pauses, and it hits me that she's trying to remember where I told her I was going —"out west." A blanket term. That's like telling someone I went *back east*. "Call me. We'd love to have you back. We're willing to work with you on a start date, and I have been authorized to double your previous pay."

The voicemail ends, and goosebumps break out onto my arms.

I slide the phone back into my purse as Jeanne's voice goes round and round my head.

Go back to New York?

Double my pay?

FUCKING VP before thirty! It's everything I've wanted as far as career goals go.

"Everything okay?" Owen asks.

I look at Owen, at his honest, open face. I know what he would say if I told him what Jeanne said. Which is why I can't.

"She was just checking in to see how things are going out here." The fib slides out smoothly.

Owen nods. I can't tell if he believes me, or if he just wants to.

"Let's go." I take his hand and pull him into the belly of the beast.

We spend the next few hours in our version of debauchery. Owen teaches me roulette and craps. I win and lose, then win again. We drink too much and stay up too late.

For a few hours, we pretend we're not here for the saddest reason ever.

Chapter 23

Owen

THERE ARE a lot of things I never thought I'd do in my life.

Getting back together with Autumn is first on that list. I mean, yeah, I prayed for it until my mouth turned dry, but I never thought it would actually happen. The chasm between us seemed too large to cross.

Second on that list? Writing a prescription for medical marijuana for Autumn's mom.

Check, and check.

It's starting to get painful for Faith, not that she lets it show. Autumn doesn't notice, and for that I'm grateful. Me, on the other hand? It's my job to notice the slightest wince, the longer blinks, the slower movements.

The first two times Faith had cancer, I offered to

write her a prescription. She declined my offer, telling me she'd escaped her teenage years without having done it and she didn't plan to start. This time?

Well, she's at the dispensary right now.

I'm sitting in Faith's living room, waiting for her to arrive. I came straight here after work, knowing Autumn was out at dinner with her new friend Livvie. Faith called me earlier in the day, and with a voice that betrayed her exhaustion and embarrassment, she asked me for the last thing I expected.

As I sit on Faith's couch, my phone dings with a text message from Autumn.

Livvie's running late, I'm waiting at the table. What are you up to?

I stare down at the phone, uncertain how to respond. I don't want to lie, but I want to respect Faith's privacy. If she wants Autumn to know about the prescription, she'll have to be the one to tell her.

I write her back. **Relaxing. When do you think you'll be done? Dessert with me?**

I could meet her somewhere. Or maybe have her meet me at my place and I'll have her for dessert. She's sweet like sugar, and she tastes divine. Our sex life pretty much picked up where we left it at age eighteen, except this time around both of us have more experience and confidence.

A twinge of guilt sneaks in at my roundabout lie. Sure, I'm relaxing. I just didn't tell her *where*. If we're keeping track, the score is now one to one. I know

Autumn didn't tell me whatever her old boss said on that voicemail. The look on her face could not have come from someone just checking in to see how she's doing. There was surprise in her arched eyebrows, then a curve of a pleased smile. Whatever made her feel that way, Autumn didn't want me to know about it.

I decided to let it go that night. We were in Vegas; it wasn't the time or place to push. A small part of me doesn't want to know. My imagination has supplied the answer already anyhow. Something along the lines of big promotion, corner office, and whatever else could be said to lure Autumn back to Manhattan.

The thought fucking shatters me. I've been pushing it away for an entire week, ever since we came back from Vegas. Without her mother, Autumn doesn't have a reason to stay. What will keep her in Sedona after Faith is gone?

The front door opens wide and Faith steps in. She holds a basic white paper bag, the name of the store she visited nowhere to be found on the sack. The hush-hush, nondescript nature of it makes me smile.

Faith blushes when she catches my gaze. "That was awkward. The girl who helped me called it 'medicating.' I asked her questions, and she kept saying 'When I medicate...' and then answering me. I felt like telling her to give up the charade, we both know she's recreational." Faith laughs. "What a fucking ordeal."

Her words leave me dumbfounded. Or, more accurately, her use of one word in particular is what has momentarily stunned my brain. I don't think I've ever heard Faith swear. Cancer has changed her; being terminal has changed her; she's much more carefree.

I stand, reaching into my pocket for my car keys. Faith is so embarrassed I imagine she'll want to be alone for the next part. I just wanted to be here in case she wanted me to go with her to the shop, but she didn't want someone to see me with a patient and get in trouble. I'm not sure that I would, but it was a good call, I guess. "Well, I'm glad you got what you needed. I'll head out now."

Her arm shoots out. "Wait. Please don't go." She looks down at the bag, her fingers tightening around it. "I don't know what I'm doing. Could you help me?"

I wish I could swipe off the cherry red color in her cheeks as if it were washable marker. Teach my girl-friend's mom how to smoke weed? Sure … no big deal, and not awkward for either of us.

"Of course, Faith. No worries." I hold out my hand and Faith gives me the bag. It crinkles in my grip as I lead her through the house and out the back door.

"You'll want to be outside," I inform her, holding open the door to allow her to step out. "It's pungent."

"Right," she nods. "I smelled it in college."

She gets settled into her favorite seat underneath the canopy, and I reach into the bag. *Pre-rolls*. Good. She got something easy. I had my fair share of experience in college, before I got super serious the last two years of undergrad and beyond, but I was terrible at packing the bowl. Ace always did it for me, and teased me mercilessly.

"Didn't want any gummies or brownies? A vape perhaps?" I grin at her.

She shoos me off with a hand. "The girl tried to give me the gummy bears. I told her I wasn't a child."

I grin. "Smoking is good. It helps a lot of my patients with pain and appetite. But the gummies are good too, I hear. Eating it feels different than smoking it."

She raises an eyebrow. "Is that right, Dr. Miller? You seem to know a lot about this."

Now it's my turn for my cheeks to flame red.

"Lighter?" I ask, holding out my palm like I'm in surgery.

Faith mouths the word *oops* and I chuckle, running inside to the junk drawer in the kitchen and grab a lighter.

"Okay," I tell her when I've returned, "you're going to hold it between your lips, and when I light it, you're going to take a drag. A lot like a cigarette."

Faith eyes me appreciatively. "Is it safe to bet you haven't done this with many of your patients?"

I pinch the pre-rolled joint between two fingers and hold it out to her. "You are definitely the first. And you don't need to feel embarrassed. You're in pain and you don't need to be. There are no prizes for enduring pain, Faith."

Even the morphine patch doesn't seem to do much,

because she won't wear it in the day around Autumn. She wants to be mobile and coherent in her last days with her only child. I don't blame her.

She sighs deeply, psyching herself up, then takes it from me. Tucking it between pursed lips, she leans closer to me. I flick the lighter and watch the flame singe the ends of the small joint.

"Inhale," I instruct.

Faith listens, and as soon as she breathes it in, she begins to cough. I run back into the house for a glass of water, cursing myself for not thinking of it ahead of time.

"Here," I thrust the plastic cup at her. She's mostly recovered now, just clearing her throat every few seconds.

She drinks deeply, finishing it in one go. "Thank you," she says, setting the empty cup on the table. "Is it always like that?" She glances at the joint on the table as if it offends her.

I shake my head. "It takes practice. Maybe get some gummies on your next run." I wink.

She bends over and grabs it from the table, lifting it up between us. "Won't you join me?"

I put up a hand in protest, but the look she gives me stops me in mid-air.

She accompanies the look by saying, "You aren't going to make me do this alone, are you?"

I cock an eyebrow. "What was it you used to say to

Autumn in high school? Something about never succumbing to peer pressure?"

Faith makes a sound, something like a *psh*, and brushes her hand back and forth in front of her, as if sweeping away my words. She raises her eyebrows and says, "Are you telling me you're going to deny the wishes of a person facing imminent death?"

I groan playfully, hiding the painful pinch of her words. "Don't tell me you're going to use the dying card."

Faith laughs and pushes the joint into my hand. "Gotta play dirty while I have the chance."

It feels like college again, minus the presence of Ace and cheap beer. Luckily the hospital doesn't drug test, so I'll have this one memory with Faith and never speak of it again. Pulling the joint to my lips, I inhale the way I showed Faith, and she nods like she's impressed. Imagine that, my girlfriend's mother is dazzled by my weed smoking prowess.

A small cough racks my body just as I see Faith's eyes go wide. She's looking at something behind me.

"What the hell is going on here?"

My head swivels to the sound of Autumn's voice. She's standing halfway across the yard, hands fisted and propped on her hips, mouth agape.

"It's Owen's fault," Faith says, and I shoot her a dirty look.

She laughs, not a normal laugh, a stoned laugh, and I can't help but feel my lips curl into a smile.

"It's not really Owen's fault," she explains as Autumn walks closer, her eyes screwed up as she absorbs what she's just walked in on. "He wrote me a prescription for medical marijuana."

Autumn sends a shocked look my way. "You what?"

Is marijuana gluten free? Seems like it should be.

"I'm in pain, Autumn," Faith adds, knowing this will help Autumn understand, and my heart aches when I see my girlfriend's face fall.

"Mom," Autumn whispers, her eyes filling with tears automatically.

"Marzipan," Faith declares.

Did I hear that right? *Marzipan?* Is this weed laced with something?

Autumn nods, wiping away the moisture stuck in her lower lashes. "Marzipan," she repeats.

I still don't get it, but I don't think I need to. Either I'm stoned as hell or they have a code word.

"Why are you home so soon?" Faith asks Autumn. "Aren't you supposed to be eating dinner with Livvie?"

Autumn settles into a chair across from the couch where Faith and I sit, tucking her feet underneath herself. "She ended up canceling. A situation with her husband."

"Uh oh," Faith says, making a bare-teeth face.

"Actually, I think it was good. She sounded happy when I talked to her."

"That's nice." Faith holds out the joint. "Want some?"

Autumns head jolts back slightly. "Mom? For real?"

Faith shrugs. "Why the hell not? Owen reminded me that I taught you not to give in to peer pressure, but I also taught you to share, so this is me sharing..." She pushes her arm a little further out in Autumn's direction.

Autumn laughs, but it's honestly more like a disbelieving giggle, and it's about the cutest damn thing I've ever heard.

"Why not?" She takes it from Faith and inhales the way I did.

Faith's eyebrows shoot up. "You do that a little too well."

"College," Autumn answers.

Ten minutes later, it's apparent Faith is high. She wants to order pizza, then changes her mind and asks for Chinese food instead. She then asks if Baskin Robbins can deliver a birthday ice cream cake.

It's not even her birthday.

I get out my phone and call Faith's favorite spot, just glad she has an appetite again. I'll do anything to get her weight up.

"Egg rolls," Faith calls out, even though I'm only two feet away. "Beef and broccoli. Black bean chicken. Lo Mein."

She keeps calling out dishes and I keep ordering. I pull my credit card from my wallet while Autumn clutches her waist and laughs so hard no sound comes out. I think now I can officially add spending one hundred and fifty dollars on a single order of Chinese food to the list of things I never thought I'd do in my life.

Right after that, I call Baskin Robbins and give them a sob story about Faith and that this ice cream birthday cake is her dying wish. They agree to have it delivered.

Once I've ordered all the food, and lectured Faith on pacing herself, I leave her and Autumn talking while I run into the house to use the bathroom. Is it really my fault that at the exact second when I pass by the kitchen, Autumn's phone that had been lying on the counter lights up with a message? I grab it with the intention of taking it to her, but when I glance down, I see it's a text from Jeanne Chapman, the old boss.

Have you given more thought to what we discussed?

My heart flipflops in my chest. There has been a discussion? The woman left a voicemail in Vegas, but clearly now there's been a discussion.

A knock on the front door startles me and I drop the phone.

Shit.

Picking it up, I toss it on the counter and answer the door. It's the Chinese food.

I set it on the counter and run to the bathroom like I'd originally intended. On my way back into the kitchen, there is a knock at the door again.

It's the ice cream birthday cake, with a get-well-soon balloon. Clearly they didn't understand my message that Faith is terminal, but it's the thought that counts.

I bring all the food to the kitchen, feeling more sober than I wish to be right now.

Reaching up, I pull plates from the cabinet, open boxes of steaming, fragrant food, and get out utensils. All the while, Autumn's phone lies there on the countertop, holding a secret.

I'm not going to listen to Autumn's voicemail, so I'm left with no choice. I have to ask her what the hell is going on.

I pull open the sliding glass door and stick my head out. "Food," I yell to Faith and Autumn.

We sit around the small table in the adjoining dining room, barely speaking as we shovel the food into our mouths. Autumn catches my eye and smiles at me, and though I manage to return the smile, my heart isn't really in it.

My heart is terrified Autumn's going to leave me behind a second time, and this time ... I'm scared I won't survive it.

Chapter 24

Autumn

I CAN'T BELIEVE yesterday I smoked weed with my mom and Owen, and tonight she smoked again and ordered a bunch more food. It's amazing. She's laughing, her appetite is up, and I think she might actually gain some weight, which Owen said could prolong her life.

I skip to the kitchen after asking my mom to pause the movie so I can make popcorn. Owen is working a late night, doing rounds at the hospital, and I'm getting just what I need. Quality time with my mom.

As I toss the popcorn in the microwave, my phone buzzes in my pocket. When I see it's from Jeanne, I hightail it to my bedroom to talk in private.

"Hi," I say quietly, the phone pressed to my cheek. I

close my bedroom door softly so I don't draw attention to what I'm doing.

"Autumn, hello. Is this a bad time?"

"No, no, it's fine," I answer, even though it's really not fine. I've already told Jeanne I don't plan to return to the city. I have no idea what I'm doing here in Sedona, but I know I can't live without Owen. I need to tell him about Jeanne and the job offer, but I know what he will say. He'll tell me to go for it, that we can figure out logistics, that I can't pass up an offer like this. He'll tell me to follow my dreams—the same shit my mother did when I left for college. Well, look where that got me...

Fucking *marzipan*. No way. Not leaving again.

"I talked with a couple other members of the team and, despite what you've already said, we're hoping if we were to sweeten the comp package you might look differently at the offer."

"Jeanne, I—"

"Autumn," I hear my mother's voice through my closed door. Her tone doesn't sound like an inquiry as to why I'm taking so long with the popcorn. It sounds more like worry. Panic rises in my throat, filling the space, and I wrench open the door. My mom stands there, her expression blank.

"Mom?" The panic I feel saturates the word.

Her knees begin to buckle and, in the doorway to the room she painted lavender after I'd begged her to when I was twelve, she wilts like a flower.

"Mom," I scream, catching her under the arms before she hits the ground. Somewhere in the back of my mind I hear my phone clatter to the floor.

"Autumn?" Jeanne's voice floats into the air. "Autumn?"

Holding my limp mother in one arm, I grab the phone. I hang up on Jeanne and dial 9-1-1. It's a sequence of numbers I've never dialed, and hoped to never need to.

The woman who answers is kind, efficient, and knowledgeable. She stays on the phone with me until the ambulance arrives.

My mom doesn't wake up, not when she's lifted onto a stretcher, not when I sob over her in the back of the ambulance, not even when Owen runs into the emergency room and tells the doctor about her current condition.

I've never seen him so in command and confident. At least that's how he appears on the outside. But I know Owen. That authoritative exterior? A facade.

On the inside, he's got to be as terrified as I am.

I HEAR Owen before I see him. He's speaking to someone else, someone beyond the white and blue patterned curtain that gives my mother a bit of privacy in the emergency room.

Owen's face appears around the curtain. He looks at

my mom first, then at me, and straightens, pulling the curtain aside.

"Good to see you awake, Faith." He smiles the easy smile of a man being handed a cocktail on a tropical beach. As if he doesn't have a care in the world, as if he isn't in a place that smells like cleaning products and sounds like scuffed shoes and beeping.

I forget for a minute that he works here day in and day out among the dying.

My mom returns his smile, but it's not like Owen's. Hers is weak. Tired. Much more appropriate given the situation. It occurs to me that Owen uses that smile to cut through worry. Maybe it works. When he smiles like that, it certainly doesn't seem like anything bad could truly be happening. He's the doctor with the news, the keeper of her fate. If he doesn't smile, then the world is ending.

It only takes two steps before he stops at the side of her bed, his gaze on the monitors. "You gave Autumn a scare," he says, his tone playfully chiding. When my mom doesn't respond, Owen glances at her. Their eyes meet and a crack forms in his cheerful demeanor. I see inside, to the place where his anguish lives.

"Just say it, Owen." Her resolute tone breaks my heart in two.

Owen looks over to me, worry in his eyes.

I nod at him, telling him I'm okay. I'm not, of course. I never will be. This is a cruel, slow torture.

Marzi-fucking-pan goddammit.

"You experienced something we call 'syncope.' Basically, you fainted. But your encounter lasted longer than typical. A lot longer." Owen pauses, takes a deep breath, and folds my mom's hand into his. "I've been spending a lot of time around you recently, Faith. So I don't need to ask either of you the questions I would normally ask a patient and their family. I know how little you've been sleeping; I've seen how hard it is for you to walk … how much pain you're in. You try hard to hide it from Autumn"—his gaze skirts over my face before returning to my mom—"but I know it's harder for you to do what you did even two weeks ago."

Mom nods, her teeth sinking into her bottom lip. I want her to look at me, will it in my mind, but she doesn't. "How much time?" Her voice is soft like a caress.

"At most, three months. But I don't think it will be that long." His answer is a knife, slicing into me swiftly. He said six months just a few weeks ago. Now it's three at most? The thought of only a few months left with my mother guts me.

I scrunch my eyes against his words. The urge to be a child overtakes me, to stuff my fingers in my ears and tuck my knees to my chest.

My mother.

There is a touch on my shoulder and I open my eyes. Owen is bent down in front of me. His eyes are glassy, unshed tears dangerously close to spilling out. He pulls me in and my arms wrap around his neck. As quietly as I can, I cry. My mom watches from her bed, tears running down her face. She's cried more lately than I've seen her cry in my entire life.

I gather myself as best as I can. "What do we do now?"

Owen stands at the sound of my voice, using the heels of his hands to wipe at his eyes. He opens his mouth to speak but my mom beats him to it.

"I want to die at home." Her hands are folded in her lap, her face almost serene.

It hits me that she has thought about this, has planned for the end of her life. I should've known that she would, because it makes sense, but the realization is painful. All of this is excruciating. For my mom, it must be almost beyond belief. I hadn't really accepted it until now. We were in Vegas, laughing, then smoking weed. It didn't seem real, not in any tangible way. Sure, Owen would say the word *terminal*, but I conveniently thought of an airport terminal, not the termination of my mother's life. This is it, I have to deal with it fully now.

"How?" I ask, my own voice taking me by surprise. It's the first time I've spoken since Owen walked in. "How do we arrange for … that?"

"There's something called hospice home care. A nurse will visit your house daily. Their job is to provide pain and symptom management. This will allow you to spend as much time with your mom as possible by removing some of the burden of caring for her."

His explanation is clinical, but his expression is soft. He's doing his job right now, being Owen the oncologist.

She's not a burden, I want to say, but I know what he means. I can't watch over her every second of the day and still get all the cooking and grocery shopping done.

"Mom?" I look to her, promising myself I will be okay with whatever she chooses.

"This is what I want, Autumn."

"Then you'll have it." It feels as though the lump in my throat might choke me.

Owen arranges my mom's discharge. I take her to the cafeteria for coffee while we wait for Owen's shift to be over. He has offered to drive us home. In the chaos and grief of this trip to the emergency room, I'd forgotten we didn't drive here. And until I looked at my phone and saw two missed calls and a text message from Jeanne, I'd completely forgotten about her too.

Chapter 25

Owen

I TIPTOE from the room and close the door quietly. It's the second time I've checked on Faith since I brought her and Autumn home from the hospital.

"She's asleep, pulse is steady," I announce as I walk into the kitchen.

Autumn has poured herself a glass of white wine. A very big glass.

"Got any more of that for me?" I take a deep breath and wrap my arms around Autumn from behind. She feels like a soft place to lay my worries down. "Fuck..." I sigh the word into her hair.

"Fuck," she agrees.

I let her go so she can pour a second glass. We cheers out of habit, but even that sound is melancholy. More of a dull thud than a clink.

My lower back presses into the edge of the counter and I reach for Autumn, my free hand curling around her hip as she steps into the triangle of open space my legs create.

Autumn flicks her hair off her shoulder and fidgets with an earring. "My old boss in the city has been calling."

"Oh?" I act surprised as relief washes over me. She's finally going to tell me.

Autumn nods. "She wants me to come back. They have a new role for me. A promotion." She shakes her head slowly as if she can't believe it. She sips her wine and says, "A huge promotion. A few months ago something like this would have made my day. Hell, it would've made my year. It's my dream job. Vice president of product marketing."

VP? Damn.

I brace myself, waiting for her to tell me she's taking it.

"I said no," Autumn says, her eyes raking over my face. "I told her I'm not moving back."

I look at the fancy stainless steel juicer on the counter—the new high-speed blender Autumn bought a few weeks ago to try to save her mom. The extravagant gadgets look out of place among the outdated kitchen.

"You should take it if you want to." I hate every word as they trip from my lips. My brain nods approvingly at my maturity, my willingness to put someone else's needs before my own. My heart flips off my brain.

"You think I should take it?" There is a quiver in Autumn's voice.

I bring my gaze back to hers. Her lovely eyes. Her lush, thick lashes. That tiny, white scar next to her hairline. "Don't you want it?" I ask. "If you still lived there, would you take the job?"

"Well, yes," she says haltingly. "But things have changed, Owen…"

I trace her jaw with the tip of one finger and her eyelashes flutter closed. Palming her cheek, she leans into my touch. "Autumn, I love you too much to make you stay on just my account."

I don't give her a chance to answer. My lips fall down onto hers, consuming her mouth. She tastes like wine and sweet Autumn, the girl who wrecked my world when I was eighteen. The woman who might very well wreck my world once more.

When I pull back to look at her, I can see the confusion in her eyes. She wants that job, but she wants me too. She's lost, and scared, and her mother is dying. This is the last thing she wants to think about. I can see it in the way her gaze goes half lidded and a sly smirk creeps across her face.

She tugs at my pants. "Let's finish what we started that night at your dad's."

And just like that she's replaced any deep conversation we would have about this with sex. Sex is our distraction from the inevitable sorrow laying in the next room and the pain it causes both of us to watch her die.

Autumn crashes her mouth on mine and I go with it. As much as Faith is on borrowed time, Autumn and I could be as well. I don't know how long this bliss will last. If I had it my way: forever. But with New York, and Autumn's fondness for running across the country when shit gets hard, I can't say with one-hundred-percent certainty that she'll stay.

I lift her in the air and turn, placing her back down on the counter. Our sweeping tongues momentarily wipe away our woes. Our kisses become frantic and needy.

I rip myself away from Autumn, stepping back, and she hops down, leading the way out of the kitchen. Instead of walking to her bedroom like I expect her to, she slips out the back door. I follow her, confused, to the shadows on the side of the house. Then her earlier comment about finishing what we started at my dad's dawns on me.

My lips press against her neck as I yank down her shorts. She hitches one leg onto my hip, and in one smooth, fluid motion I'm inside her. She swallows her strangled moan, clenching tightly around me as I wrap one arm around her back and cup the back of her head with my other hand, protecting her from the wall.

"I love you, Owen," she whispers.

It's so dark I can't see her features clearly, but I hear the tremble in her words.

I press my lips to hers, an attempt to steal her sorrow and worry.

Can she feel my love? Can she feel how devoted I am, how I'm willing to make us work, no matter where we live? We aren't teenagers anymore. Physical distance doesn't have to mean the end for us.

"I love you, Autumn. I love you so fucking much."

After that, there are no more words. There are only two people hiding in the shadows, hearts broken and grasping for a respite from the pain.

When Autumn's thigh muscles clench, I kiss her deeply. She comes hard, soaring, her release as physical as it is emotional. The feel of her, the sound of her, is more than I can take. My body jerks, and I press my lips together to keep from crying out.

We stay that way for a minute, our heart rates slowing. Before I pull away, I kiss her lightly.

On her lips, there is the salty taste of tears.

"SON? YOU THERE?"

My dad's voice creeps through the thick fog in my sleepy brain as I hold the phone to my ear. I crack an eye open and lift my head from the pillow. Beside me,

Autumn sleeps soundly, her mouth parted slightly. Deep, even breaths escape her. After the emergency room visit and what happened on the side of the house, we are both exhausted.

"What's wrong?" I whisper into the receiver, rolling over and trying like hell to get up without disturbing Autumn. How many nights has my dad called me, drunk and needing help? Too many to count. The thought irritates me. Before he can answer, I add on to my question.

"Dad, you're going to have to figure your own way out of whatever it is you've landed yourself in this time."

"Uh…" Dad pauses, and then coughs. "Going to be a little difficult to get myself out of this one, son. I'm in jail."

I pinch the bridge of my nose and stifle a sigh. "What happened?"

Behind me I hear the rustle of sheets, then feel the touch of two warm hands, followed by a set of even warmer lips on the center of my back.

I turn my head to the side, and there is just enough moonlight coming in through her window to see Autumn's features. I love her bedhead. I want to wake up next to it forever.

Not if she takes that promotion you told her to take, fuckface.

Driving the thought from my mind, I force myself to

focus on the most pressing problem at this current moment. As if there aren't enough of them.

"I made a mistake, Owen. I had a little too much and didn't want to call you, so I drove home. Guess I wasn't doing all that good of a job of it, because I got pulled over."

Well, shit. This is bad. Somehow up until now my old man had avoided getting a DUI.

"Did you hurt anyone?" My heart pounds in my chest. If he ran over a kid or something, I will disown him.

"No. Just a stop sign."

I sigh.

"I'm on my way," I tell my dad, but I don't wait for his response. I don't need to hear his *thank you*. After tonight, I'd love to forget this ever happened. I push off the bed, and Autumn's warm touch melts away.

"Owen? What's going on?"

I step into my pants and pull on my shirt. It's what I wore to work today. Or yesterday, I guess. The days are beginning to run together.

"My dad was taken to jail." In the relative darkness, Autumns gasps. "DUI," I add, pouring salt into the wound.

"Oh, Owen."

"I know, but he didn't hurt anyone … so that's good."

"What can I do?"

Smack some sense into my father? Rid him of the

disease that eats away at the last shred of a bond we have left?

"Right now? Nothing."

"Lawyer? I can get a lawyer." She looks hopeful and I know the helper in her really wants to be of use.

I shake my head, then remember she probably can't see me. "Let me figure out how bad it is first." I lean down toward the mass of dark hair and kiss the top of her head. "I love you."

"I love you too, babe."

The simple, common pet name pierces my heart. *Don't go,* I almost tell her. *Don't listen to me. Stay here and spend time coming up with more unique pet names.*

I don't say anything like that, simply because I don't have the time. My dad needs me.

"HELLO, I'm here for Michael Miller." I step up to the desk in the front of the police station. The officer behind the desk looks up slowly from whatever it is he's doing on his phone. My guess is solitaire or porn. Probably solitaire. He's looks like a solitaire guy.

He glances behind himself, somewhere in the station. When his gaze arrives back on me, it travels over me with obvious contempt. "Jones wants to see you."

"Uh … okay?" I don't know who Jones is.

"Follow me." He stands. The desk hid his stature,

but now I see he's a good head shorter than me, and much wider. We walk back through a set of doors and through a room with partitioned desks. "Jones," he yells, but it sounds more like a catcall. "The Miller kid is here."

I balk. I'd bet a hundred bucks this desk guy is my age or younger.

Ten feet away, someone steps from the partitions. Hair as red as a flaming torch catches my attention first, and I know it immediately. "Jackson?" I ask, astonished. I haven't seen the guy since high school. He'd gone down to the valley for college and that was the last I'd heard from him.

He pulls himself up to his full height and sticks out a hand. The desk guy melts away into the periphery. "Owen Miller, it's been a long time."

I shake his hand, a weird sense of nostalgia and happiness coming over me. It mixes with my tiredness and creates an altogether bizarre feeling. Jackson is a cool dude. We were friends in high school.

"Too long, man. You're back?"

He nods. "Yeah, I came back a few months ago. Got a little sick of the traffic in the valley."

"I hear you," I say. The jovial greeting turns quiet.

"So, listen," Jackson runs a hand through his hair. "One of my guys pulled your dad over tonight. He was pretty drunk, Owen."

Shame fills me. "He needs help ... I'll make sure he gets it."

Jackson sits back on the corner of his desk, his hands steepled between his knees. "Slapping a DUI on your dad isn't going to help him. It might humiliate him, but it won't solve his problem. I'm thinking you and I make a deal. You get him into a treatment program, and I won't charge him with a DUI."

Gratefulness slides in, making a home for itself beside the shame warming my skin. "Thank you, Jackson. I appreciate it."

Now to convince my dad to go to rehab.

Jackson pushes aside some papers lying on the desk beside him. "I lost my dad a year ago. Heart attack."

My face falls. "I'm sorry."

"Yeah, he was a good one. Pretty healthy too. Guess you never know." He shrugs and stands up. "If you go back up front, I'll have one of my officers bring your dad out."

I extend a hand. "Thanks again, man. Really. I'm a doctor now. An oncologist. Please let me know if you ever need anything. If I can't help you, I'll find someone who can."

I owe Jackson big-time. He accepts my offer with a nod, we shake and part ways. I'm a few feet from his desk when his voice rings out behind me. "Owen, did you and Autumn Cummings ever get married? You two were inseparable."

A few months ago, my answer would've been completely different than it is tonight. I grin and say,

"We parted ways for a while, but we're back together now."

He returns the smile, genuinely happy. "That's great, man. Good for you guys."

I continue on to the front where I came in, rejoining the surly desk guy. When my dad comes out, he appears sober. Scared straight, I suppose.

"Owen," he greets me, ducking his head.

I can't handle seeing him this way. Standing in the front of a police station, ashamed and a hairsbreadth from having a DUI.

Placing a hand on his shoulder, I steer him towards the door. "Come on, Dad. I'll take you home."

We don't talk on the drive. What is there to say? I feel like yelling, but I can't, because he's not a child and I don't have the energy. As I pull into the driveway, I put it in park but keep the car running.

My dad meets my gaze in the dim outdoor lights affixed to the front of the house. Taking a deep breath, I tell him, "You're going to a treatment facility some-where. I don't know where yet."

Dad's eyes widen. "Treatment? Owen, this was a huge mistake, I'll give you that, but I don't need that kind of help. I just need to cut back a little."

My head shakes slowly back and forth. "I made a deal with the cops, Dad. They won't give you a DUI if I get professional help for you."

He frowns and looks out the windshield. The hum of the engine becomes the only sound in the car.

"You're. Going. To. Treatment." My voice is stern and it kills me that I'm the parent now, that I have no parent left to lean on.

After a full minute, he sighs. "Fine."

Reaching out, he opens the passenger door and sticks one leg out. He uses two hands to haul himself from the seat, not because he is still drunk, but because he is getting older. My heart, already shattered by what's happening to Faith, breaks just a little more.

My dad doesn't say anything more. He walks, slow and steady, to his front door and goes inside. After allowing myself a moment to grieve the loss of the dad I once knew, I drive back to Autumn's house. I undress and crawl into her bed, and it's almost as if that middle-of-the-night call never came.

I pull her sleepy, warm body in close to me and nuzzle my face into her neck.

She knows what I need. Her legs part, and I settle between them. She kisses my forehead, my cheeks, my neck, sweet and soft kisses.

Earlier tonight, she needed to fall apart to forget her mom.

Now, I need to lose myself in her to forget my dad.

Somewhere in the quiet, in the muffled sounds we're making, I think of our agreement to be honest with each other so we don't make the same mistakes we made before.

"Don't go," I whisper, sliding into her. "Don't ever

leave my side again." I look into her eyes, and in them I see my entire future.

Her nails scratch lightly down my back as she brushes a kiss on the corner of my mouth, and whispers words I will hear for the rest of my life.

"I was never going to."

Chapter 26

Autumn

MY MOM HAS GONE DOWNHILL SO QUICKLY I'm beginning to wonder if she was powering through just for my sake. If my heart weren't already smashed to bits, it would be broken by the thought of her soldiering through an outward appearance of being okay, only to collapse once she was on her own.

It has been two weeks since we were on the Strip in Vegas; now she can barely get out of bed. The helicopter ride Owen booked has been canceled. Every day I paste on a smile and go into her room, bring her meals she hardly touches, and read to her. She falls asleep by the second paragraph, and the marijuana has stopped helping with her appetite.

How did we get here so fast?

The hospice nurse comes once a day, checking her

vitals and her meds. Owen has been sleeping here every night. He wants every last second he can get with her too. Sometimes I wake up in the middle of the night and he's not beside me. He's checking her vitals, bringing her fluids, anything he can to make her comfortable.

This morning we both woke up early, the rising sun peeking into my room at an indecent time. We went for a walk, already needing to calm our minds even though we'd only been up for just enough time to have one cup of coffee each. We held hands and listened to the cacophony of birds as we strolled around my mom's neighborhood.

Owen is off today, and tomorrow and we don't have plans other than to hang out around the house and see my mom during the precious minutes when she's awake.

I'm cleaning the countertops, the same countertops I cleaned twice yesterday, when Owen walks in from outside. The kitchen light illuminates beads of sweat in his hairline.

"Hot out there?" I bend to replace the cleaner in its spot under the counter, but think twice and pull it back out. I'll find something new to clean today. Cleaning is my yoga right now. I need it.

"Yeah. I think I've tightened every screw I can find on every piece of lawn furniture your mom owns. I've taken down the window screens and washed them. The steps have been power washed."

I laugh lightly. "Would you believe it's only ten in the morning?"

He places his sun-warmed lips on mine. "Almost time for a nap."

"Do you think she'll wake up soon?" My gaze flickers back toward my mom's room.

"Maybe she's in bed reading, hoping we don't check on her and interrupt her." Owen grins to show he's joking.

My lips tremble as I attempt a smile. She's been sleeping a little more each day, and eating a little less, and sometimes I'm scared to check on her for fear she will no longer be breathing.

Owen brushes a knuckle over my lips. "Why don't you give Livvie a call? Go out to lunch? The only place you've gone in two weeks is the grocery store."

I start to protest, but Owen stops me. "It's not going to hurt anything if you spend one hour enjoying your-self. If your mom was awake right now, she'd tell you to go."

I know he's right. Owen's still going to work, but me? I need to get out of this house for more than just a walk down every aisle at the grocery store. As long as I know my mom won't be alone, I can manage an hour out.

I call Livvie and her voice is sleep-soaked. I've been up for so long I feel like I've already lived a whole day, and Livvie is just now waking.

"Good morning, sunshine," I say, and she groans.

"Want to get lunch? Or brunch, I guess, since you probably want breakfast."

"Yes, I'm starving," she moans.

I laugh. "I feel like that's always your response."

"I forget to eat, and then when I remember it's because my stomach is eating itself."

"Great, thanks for that visual."

She chuckles, and the sound is a little more like her normal tone, and a little less sleepy.

I tell her to meet me at Tlaquepaque. I don't know when I'll be willing to leave my house again, so I might as well make it count.

I'm standing in front of my mirrored dresser, arranging a ponytail at the crown of my head, when Owen walks in. He's freshly showered, his hair damp.

He wears only shorts, and the sight of his strong shoulders, the V-shape of his body as it narrows to his waist, makes me acutely aware of my pulse. He walks up behind me and I turn in to him. My palms run the length of his chest, up his shoulders and down his arms. "Too bad I don't have more time," I murmur.

He raises an eyebrow. "Is that a challenge, because I can be fast."

My deep throaty laugh follows me out to the hallway. "Call me if my mom wakes!" I call over my shoulder.

Turning, I see Owen frowning like a puppy dog, "So, no to the quickie?"

If sex were an Olympic sport, Owen and I would win a gold medal.

"THIS PLACE IS STUNNING," Livvie says appreciatively, looking up at the Tlaquepaque architecture. "People keep telling me I need to come here, but I never got around to it because I spend all my time sitting in that musty old bookstore. I've been missing out."

Her enthusiasm makes me happy. "It's my favorite place in Sedona."

"I can see why."

"So," I begin, "is it too early for Mexican food? I know you woke up about an hour ago, and they don't have breakfast items. There's a little cafe, too. It probably has more breakfast-type items."

"Breakfast," Livvie instructs.

I take Livvie through the village toward the cafe. She spends most of our walk looking around, stopping to point out brightly-patterned tiles when they appear on the sides of the buildings, or the ornate iron work. She's as taken with this place as I am.

We step through an ivy-covered archway and into the square where the Secret Garden Cafe sits. "There," I point.

"Of course it's adorable," she says, throwing up a hand. Her gaze moves left as we walk toward the restaurant, eyes roving over to an empty store.

"An empty space. Hmmm..." She drums her fingers against her lower lip. "Interesting."

"What about it?" I ask as we step into the cafe. We're seated at a table for two outside, under a tree. We're in direct view of the empty storefront with the *For Lease* sign.

Livvie orders a cappuccino, and I ask for water. I've had enough coffee for today. She leans forward, her hands clasped on the menu lying on the table.

"Look at how packed this place is. Way more foot traffic." Her eyes squint, one corner of her mouth stretching toward her cheek.

I'm starting to feel like she's talking in riddles. "What are you getting at, Livvie?"

"My gran's bookstore has so few customers I've considered taking off my clothes and standing naked in the window. I wouldn't have to do that if my bookstore were, gee I don't know, *here*."

"Great idea," I tell her, sipping at the ice water that's just been set in front of me. "You could get a little espresso machine and even have a live poetry reading or stand-up comedy thing."

My marketing hat is on and I have to rein in the ideas or I'll go overboard.

Livvie's eyes light up. "Yes. Yes. And Yes."

"You should call the number on the sign," I encourage her. I know how much it means to her to save her grandma's family store.

She grabs her phone and dials. I love her East Coast

get-it-done attitude. If there was anything I learned to like while I lived out there, it was their tendency to make things happen. No hemming or hawing in NYC.

Which makes me think of Jeanne. After my mom collapsed while I was talking to Jeanne, I sent her a text the next day telling her that my mom had taken a turn for the worse and I wasn't going to be available to speak. I said that I'd call *her* if I ever changed my mind. I've already told her no, but she thinks I'll capitulate, and I'm not sure how to make her see otherwise.

Livvie begins talking into her phone, and I turn my attention to her side of the conversation.

"...great, and what's the monthly rent?" The tip of her tongue slides out of her mouth, resting on the center of her upper lip as she listens. "Please send all the information to my email. I'll go through it and get back to you."

She hangs up the phone at the same time our server approaches our table. Beaming up at him, she says, "Two glasses of champagne, please."

My eyebrows narrow in confusion. "Champagne?"

Livvie nods. "We're celebrating. I can't run the bookstore anymore. You have a lot going on with your mom, and I didn't want to text you so I've been waiting to tell you everything in person."

"Tell me what? And why are we celebrating you not running the store?"

Did something bad happen?

"Jeff loves Phoenix!" she squeals. "Like, really loves it."

"Yay!" I feel her happiness soak into me as it's the first positive thing I've heard all week.

"Sedona," she makes a bare-teeth face, "not so much. Too New Age for him. I think it was all those crystal shops on Main Street. Then he heard about the vortexes and it sealed the deal."

A burst of disbelieving laughter shoots from between my pursed lips. "That's understandable. It's not for everyone."

"Oh, thank you," Livvie purrs at the server, her excitement hardly contained as she takes the champagne flute from him. I grab my own and mimic Livvie's lifted glass.

"To newly leased spaces," she declares, and I laugh because it's nowhere near a done deal and we're celebrating it anyway. I bring the glass to my lips, pausing when I realize Livvie's not finished. "And," she adds, her eyes twinkling mischievously, "to the new store manager. My best friend in Sedona ... Autumn Cummings."

I'm already taking a drink when I realize what she's said. I sputter, the bubbles burning my throat. "What did you just say?" I cough out the words.

She smiles so wide I see her molars. "You heard me. You need a job and I need you. So, what do you think?"

I shake my head slowly, the burning sensation in my

throat now just a simmering heat. "I don't understand..."

"Jeff wants to live in Phoenix. I'm thrilled he likes it here, that he's willing to move, but I'm not ready to give up my grandma's store. So..." She gestures to me with her flute. "That's where you come in. You need a job, right?"

I nod, still stunned. I'd love to run my own store, and Livvie would let me practically do anything so long as I kept everything nice and made a profit.

"And given your background, you could make this store everything it should be. And in a location like this?" She points one finger in the air, swirling it around to indicate the entire village of Tlaquepaque. "You'll kill it. Espresso machine, live poetry readings, all of it."

I capture the side of my lower lip and bite down gently. "It is my favorite place, and I do have a lot of ideas for the store."

"See?" Livvie throws down a fist on the wrought-iron table top, causing the silverware to rattle. "Imagine coming to work here. You said it yourself, it's your favorite place in Sedona."

"I can tell you used to be a salesperson," I say, and our server approaches the table again. This time we order food instead of asking for more champagne.

"So?" Livvie asks, her eyes excited. "What's it going to be?"

What's there to think about? I need a job. And

managing a bookstore sounds like a job I'd like. I can put my marketing background to work by organizing themed days. Story times. Character parties. Author visits. My mind floods with ideas and adrenaline flows through me. It's been so long since I felt this way. Since I left New York.

"I'll do it."

Livvie claps twice. "Good. Also, I didn't tell you, but I'd like to bring you in as a fifty-fifty partner. That way you don't feel like an employee. You have some skin in the game."

Tears sting the backs of my eyes.

Marzipan.

I don't want to cry. I've cried so much lately, it's exhausting.

"I'm in. Thank you." I raise my flute and toast. "I'm very happy I stumbled upon you in a bookstore and offered you wine and fudge."

"Technically, you offered me soap and olive oil."

I laugh, but this time I manage not to choke on the champagne. We finish lunch, and Livvie promises to call me as soon as she reads through the documents the leasing company is sending to her.

We part ways with a hug, and as I climb into my mom's car, her scent overtakes the happiness vibrating through me.

I hate what has been forced upon her, upon us.

The tears I didn't spill with Livvie come out now.

Chapter 27

Owen

"FAITH?" I push open her door a little further and stick my head in. When I'd first cracked the door, I saw her eyes flutter open, but they're closed again.

"I'm awake," she says, her voice so low I barely hear her.

"How are you feeling?" I stride to her bedside. The fluffy duvet shrinks her, making her look even smaller than she is.

"Just keep the drugs coming," she says, cracking a tiny smile.

I check my watch to see if we're close to her next dose. Nope. Still an hour away, but if she wants it, I'll give it to her now. It's not like it will hurt anything, and the goal right now is to keep her free of physical pain. There's nothing I can do for mental and emotional pain, but Faith seems as steady as always. I wonder if she ever breaks down when she's alone?

"What are you and Autumn up to today?" Faith asks, struggling to sit up. I lean over her bed, pulling together pillows that have spread out, creating a soft wall for her to lean against.

"Autumn's making you a smoothie right now, and—" Faith grimaces.

"Nothing green, I promise. Strawberry mango banana. Your favorite." I'm almost positive Autumn's adding a little protein powder, but I don't need to tell Faith. Taking a seat on the edge of bed, I lean my elbows on my knees, tucking steepled hands under my chin. "I think we're doing a pretty good job at managing your pain, but where are you emotionally?"

She sighs and her head rolls from side to side against the pillows. "I'm ready to go. I'm so tired and I've been fighting for so long, and … I'm done." The blender starts up in the kitchen and I feel like my heart is inside of it, being torn to bits. "She's going to need you, Owen," Faith finishes with labored breath.

An ache starts in my chest. "I know, and I'll be there for her."

She nods. "Are you going to make an honest woman out of her?" She attempts a smile, obviously making a joke.

"Actually, I wanted to talk to you about that." I tap the bulge in my right pocket. The ring I've been carrying around all week feels heavier every day. I just can't find the right time to ask Autumn to marry me. But I want Faith to know she'll be taken care of. If she says yes...

Her smile burns a little brighter. "Is that right?"

"I wanted to officially ask your blessing for me to ask Autumn to be my wife."

The pallor in Faith's skin turns into a dull glow. "You know my answer, Owen Miller. You've been like a son to me since the day Autumn brought you home when you were skinny and had the appetite of a horse. I'd always hoped the two of you would find your way back to one another." She pauses to run a palm over the duvet. "Of course, it would've been preferable if it wasn't my condition that brought you together again."

I nod. *I wish that too.*

Her eyes shimmer. "Let me see the ring."

I pull it out and let her hold it, spinning it left and right. "Owen, it's lovely."

Autumn really isn't into flashy things, but I got an expensive ring anyway. I want to spend the rest of my life spoiling her.

She hands it back to me after a moment and I open my mouth to tell her something when the doorbell cuts me off. "The nurse is two hours early," I frown, looking at my watch even though I know the time.

"It's not the nurse. I asked the pastor at my church to come by. I haven't been able to get to church, and the pastor volunteered to bring last Sunday's sermon to me."

"Mom?" Autumn appears at the bedroom door, a confused "V" pulling between her eyebrows. "Pastor Greg is here to see you."

Faith smiles at Autumn. She sits up a little straighter and looks down at herself, probably to make sure she's decent. "Send him in please, hon."

Pastor Greg, who I've met a handful of times when I've attended services with Faith, steps around Autumn and into Faith's room. His casual look of khakis and a short-sleeved collared button-up throw me off. The only times I've seen him he's been in a suit.

"Hello," he nods at me, and it occurs to me that although I remember him, he probably doesn't remember me.

"Owen Miller." I extend a hand. "I'm Faith's oncologist."

He grins at Faith. "Look at you, getting house calls. You must be special." He winks at her and she laughs. It's not her real laugh, but a ghost version of something that used to be full-bodied and alive.

The room gets quiet, and it hits me that the pastor and Faith are waiting for me to leave. "Autumn, isn't there a smoothie out there with my name on it?" I ask her.

She grips the doorframe with one hand and leans around it. "Yes. Mom, I'll put yours in the fridge."

We walk out to the kitchen and Autumn hands me the drink. Even though it's hotter than the surface of the sun outside, we take our drinks out back and sit in the shade.

Despite the heat, Autumn sits beside me, tucked into the crook of my arm. She talks about Livvie's idea of the bookstore, and how Livvie called while she was making our smoothies to tell her it's a go. I'm so damn happy that she's found something she will love to do with her career here in Sedona. Absentmindedly, I stroke her arm while she talks.

"Can you believe it?" she asks, incredulous. The question doesn't really require an answer. "What if I'd said yes to Jeanne? How would I have talked my way out of that one?"

"Good thing you said no."

"I talked to her just before Livvie called, and I told her in no uncertain terms that I am passing up the opportunity and that's final." She shakes her head, the straw resting against her lower lip. "I think she was genuinely surprised, even though I'd already told her once." She sighs and shrugs. "I guess I should appreciate the tenacity."

"That's one way to look at it."

Autumn's head turns, her gaze finding Faith's bedroom window. The drapes were open when I went in, but with the screen on the window and our angle across the yard, we can't see in.

"I know you said three months, but..."Autumn draws an invisible pattern on the outside of her cup. "Do you still think that?"

Autumn needs the truth, but I'm reluctant to give it. There is no real way to know, but there are signs … and Faith is showing them. "I can't say precisely, but it won't be much longer."

I hear the intake of her breath, I feel the movement of her shoulders. "God, Owen, this is terrible. Knowing it's coming, waiting for something horrible to happen… it's—" Her voice shakes.

I set down my cup on the table in front of us and wrap her in my arms. I'm ready for her tears, but they don't come. Maybe she is cried out, drained on the inside, nearly numb from the grief process that has already begun.

I hold her until Pastor Greg opens the back door. He stops there for a moment and opens his mouth, but something gives him pause. Perhaps it's Autumn with her head on my chest, or both of us with our feet propped up on the table. He steps outside and clears his throat.

"I'm going to get going now, Autumn, but please call me if you need anything."

Autumn pulls herself away from me and stands, going to him. "I will. Thank you, Pastor."

They gaze at each other for a few moments and I wonder how close they are. I know Faith has been taking Autumn to church but this seems like more … like they share something deeper. Maybe it's just a mutual respect and love for Faith.

"See you at church on Sunday?" He gives an encouraging grin. Without her mother going, Autumn hasn't been going either.

She laughs nervously. "Sure ... see you Sunday."

She watches him go and there's a look on her face, like she's trying to figure something out. I stand and wrap my arms around her.

"The nurse will be here soon. We can run out. Grab something to make for dinner." I brush a hand through her hair as I talk.

"That sounds good." Autumn pushes up, rubbing her eyes with the heels of her palms. "I'm going to check on my mom, then get changed. I'm sweaty." She makes a face and I pinch my nose, pretending she smells. It works. She laughs, just a small chuckle, and playfully shoves my arm.

When the nurse arrives, we step out to the grocery store. Autumn picks out what's needed to make baked ziti and gets started in on the recipe. Cooking and cleaning have been her go-to methods of dealing with stress. I'm not complaining, but I have gained a few pounds.

"My mom's favorite," she explains, and I don't remind her that I already know. Faith has ordered it dozens of times or made it for me on our Monday night dinners.

I came back to Sedona after med school, still a lost and broken boy. Broken by her daughter, by our choice. My father doesn't have an emotional bone in his body, so Faith took me in. She loved me, listened to all my worries, and made me family.

She saved me.

And I couldn't save her. It will haunt me for the rest of my life.

Chapter 28

Autumn

I MAKE the baked ziti for dinner, and my mom does her best to eat it, but she doesn't manage more than a few bites, though she raves about it as enthusiastically as she can manage. It breaks my heart so see her so weak and frail. Owen clears the plates and does the dishes, while I get some time alone with my mom.

I apply lotion to her hands and feet, read her a book and tuck her into bed. Then we sit there holding hands as I stare at the small jewelry box my mom has on her dresser. I think of my mom's life, a hard but hopefully rewarding life. She raised me on my own, went without frivolous things so that I could have whatever I needed, and never really found true love.

"I'm sorry you never had a great love," I tell her. Now feels like the time to get these thoughts out.

My mom looks over at me, pulling one of her hands from mine and strokes my face. "Oh, but honey I did. It was you."

Tears roll down my cheeks before I can say marzipan, and my mom's eyes well up as well. It seems that this time we aren't going to try to hold it in.

"I'm sorry I wasn't here all those years. I'm so sorry." I weep. How many dinners have I missed, how many mornings in the garden sipping tea? Life is so precious, and none of it is promised. She's fucking fifty-five and I'm counting the days I have left with her.

My mom cups my cheeks and I know it's hard for her to hold her hands up for so long because they tremble. "I don't resent you for doing as I told you to do. I wanted to raise a strong, independent woman who would never need to depend on a man for money, and I did."

A tear slips from the corner of her eye and rolls down her cheek. "When I didn't have you here in person for company, I had Owen. I was never alone."

I nod, swallowing the lump in my throat. I would forever be grateful to that man for being there for my mom all those years when I couldn't.

My mom's hands fall away from my face and she wipes my eyes.

Rolling onto her side, she tucks her hands under her cheeks and faces me. "I went to a cancer group therapy thing my first round," she tells me, her eyelids getting heavy. "It was Owen's idea. Everyone was going around the room and saying what they felt their life purpose was."

I nod, stroking her arm and soaking in all her words, wanting more time.

"One lady really felt her purpose was to write a book, but she was too scared to put it out there to the world. If she got better, she was going to publish it. Another man, he hated his desk job, had always wanted to work with animals. If he got better, he was going to quit his job and start an animal rescue."

That sounded nice. It made me think of anything I felt I had left to do, a burning desire. The thought came to me immediately: to have a baby with Owen, to right that wrong we made so many years ago.

"What was your big regret? Your unlived purpose?" I ask her.

She smiles, her eye lids closing for a moment. "I didn't have one. My purpose has always been to be your mother, and I got my dream the day you were born."

I can't help the sob that forms in my throat. Leaning forward, I cry as my mother holds me. I cry so hard my body shakes, and all the while she rubs my back and takes care of me in what should be her darkest hour, but is mine as well.

"I love you, Mom," I tell her when I can catch my breath.

"I love you too, baby girl."

It's the last thing she said to me. Somewhere in the night my mom found her way to heaven.

"YOU KNOW there's a celebration of life going on back there, right?"

It's Livvie's voice, coming up behind me. I'm sitting on a bench in the shade outside the church. She comes into my view, backlit by the sun.

My mom didn't want a funeral. She wanted a *celebration of life*. It was written in her end- of-life instructions, which Pastor Greg had in his possession. I stayed for the formal ceremony in the sanctuary, but after only a few minutes in the room where everyone moved into for lunch, I ducked out.

"I'm aware," I say wryly, toying with the gold bracelet on my wrist. It was my mom's.

Livvie sits down beside me. "I didn't go to my grandma's funeral. Couldn't stomach it. I hated watching other people grieve, people who didn't know her like I did. I felt like they shouldn't be allowed to be sad." She chuckles, the sound holding no mirth. "As if there is some competition for who is allowed to feel grief based on who knew her best."

"I guess I'm feeling a bit of the opposite. Like I didn't know her the way all those people in there knew her, and I shouldn't be allowed to feel so hollow. Like ten years gone from here has taken away my right to grieve."

Livvie frowns. "Did you go ten years without seeing her?"

"No."

"Did you go ten years without talking to her?"

"No, we talked nearly every day."

"Did you go ten years without loving her?"

I slide my gaze up to meet Livvie's. "Obviously not."

She raises her eyebrows in a look that tells me she has led me to water, now it's up to me to drink.

My shoulder bumps hers. "I get it."

I'm realizing that I do the guilt and self-punishment thing really well.

"Good." She wraps me in a one-armed hug.

Owen finds us sitting this way and approaches cautiously. I think Livvie's tough exterior, her tell-it-like-it-is attitude, sets him off-kilter. It makes sense to me. I've lived and worked with people who acted like her. Owen hasn't.

Livvie releases me and then stands, pulling me up with her. "You have to get back in there, Autumn. Don't be a chump like me." She winks at me and walks away.

Owen watches her go, his hands tucked into his dark grey dress pants. "Chump?" he asks, bewildered.

"Chump. Technical term." Despite the day I'm having, I smile a little. Livvie is a breath of fresh air for me.

Owen reaches out to me, folding me into his body and kissing the top of my head. "You disappeared."

"I couldn't stand all the finger foods and different types of salad." I'm joking, but it's not totally untrue. The smells of all the foods were meshing together, and I pictured them as different colors, mixing into something grayish-brown and hanging over the room like smog.

"The food is mostly gone now. Do you want to go back?"

I nod against him and he lets me go, only to capture my hand. We walk back into the church, and an idea strikes me. I pull my hand from his. "Owen? I need a few minutes alone. With her..."

"Of course." He brushes a kiss onto my cheek. "I love you."

"I love you too," I answer before opening the light-colored wood doors into the sanctuary. It looks different in here. The lights have been dimmed, and without the backs of people's heads to look at, it seems so lonely. I've never been alone in a place of worship before, and it's off-putting. I creep forward quietly, matching the volume of the place, which is silent.

At the very front, to the left of the pulpit, is my mom's casket. A spray of purple and white flowers lies on top of its closed hood. When I reach the gleaming dark wood, I press a hand to it.

I don't know what I was thinking would happen. Maybe a sensation. A whisper from the great beyond. A feeling in my heart telling me she's nearby. Instead I feel nothing, and it wrecks me.

Marzipan.

It doesn't work. Fat tears roll down my cheeks and I don't wipe them away. They slip off my chin, landing somewhere, soaking into the fabric of my dress, the carpet, maybe even my shoes.

Once my tears subside, my blurry vision clears, and I see the corner of a folded piece of paper sticking out from under the flowers. Using two fingers, I pinch the paper, tugging gently, and the paper clears its hiding spot.

The first thing I notice is the handwriting. It's familiar, but I can't figure out why. I begin to read.

MY BEAUTIFUL FAITH,

I've learned something new today. Nothing can prepare a man to lose a person they love.

Looking back now, I wish we'd done things differently.

I wish—

I LOOK up from the note. I can't keep reading, it feels like an invasion of privacy. And now I realize why this handwriting is familiar. It's the same as the note I found when I first moved back, the one in her pantry. It seems that the old love isn't so old.

It seems like my mom had a secret. Someone nobody knew about.

Someone who is here now at her celebration of life, or was at least here long enough to place this note on her casket. I look around, as if they could be hiding in the shadows somewhere. Of course, there is nobody here. Only me. And the body that once housed my mother. I'm still not sure what I believe, but I'd like to think her soul has moved on to heaven. It's a peaceful idea, one that helps me believe she still exists, just in another form.

I decide not to read the note, instead slipping it in with the flowers and allowing my mom's secret to lay to rest with her.

I press my lips to my fingers, then place the kiss on the top of the casket. "Bye, Mom. I love you." I still don't feel her here, but it seems like the right thing to do and I realize that nothing can make me feel better right now. I just need to live through this and take it day by day.

I find Owen out front. He is chatting with people. They have all heard he was my mom's oncologist, and it's turned him into a sought-after discussion partner. I see him talking to Linda, my mom's chemo buddy. She survived. She survived and my mom didn't. I'm happy for her, of course, but it really hits home what a beast cancer is. It doesn't care if you're rich or poor or have a family. It takes anyone it wants.

"You're like a celebrity," I murmur into his ear after

Linda gives me a small smile and walks away.

"Z list," he says, kissing my temple. "Livvie said to tell you goodbye. She had somewhere she had to be."

The sun is hot, and I'm listless. How am I supposed to walk away? Get in Owen's car and drive back to my mom's house? Wake up in the morning and do what? The person who brought me here, who drank my green juice and ate the gluten free, kale-infused food I prepared, doesn't need those things anymore. What now?

"Are you ready?" Owen squeezes my hand.

"I suppose so." My voice shakes as I gather my hair off the back of my neck and move it so it drapes over one shoulder. "We should say goodbye to Pastor Greg."

We find the pastor standing with two other men. One man speaks, his arms moving animatedly like he's telling a story.

We make our way to him, and I touch his elbow to get his attention. Turning to me, he smiles and steps away from the conversation, nodding to the two men as he goes.

His eyes are red like he's been crying, and I'm touched he would care for a member of his congregation so much.

I extend a hand to him. "Thank you for the beautiful service."

Reaching out, he shakes it. "Your mom was a very special member of our congregation. Heaven gained an angel, that's for sure."

I smile. "Yes."

"We'd love to see you around here more often. You're welcome anytime."

I blink at the invitation, not sure what to say. I promised to go next Sunday, but the Sunday after that and after that? I'm not sure. What God lets my mother get cancer and be taken from me? I'm in the anger phase of grief. "I'm a work in progress right now."

He chuckles. "Aren't we all?"

"Pastor Greg?" An old woman walks up. "Your daughter called the church phone. She says you were supposed to pick up your granddaughter for ice cream a few minutes ago."

He makes a face. "Shoot! Can you please tell her I lost track of time and I'll be there soon?" He reaches down and peels the sleeve of his jacket up, peering at a two-toned watch that makes goosebumps break out on my arms. It's the watch.

The watch.

The one from my mom's … it's his?

My eyes widen.

A brief look of panic skips across his face as he sees me looking intently at the watch and he quickly replaces it with a smile. "Don't be a stranger. You either," he adds, his eyes jumping over to Owen.

As he walks away, I stay rooted in place and I don't move until Owen pulls me along.

"Are you okay?" he asks, glancing back at me.

"The two-toned watch belongs to the pastor…"

"What watch?"

"The watch I found in the kitchen. The watch my mom said was yours. But then you said it wasn't and I forgot about it." My mom's secret lover, the man who left the note … was Pastor Greg? Did she give him back his watch when he came to the house to see her?

Now my mind spins with different scenarios of why they didn't work out and I'm tempted to run inside and read the note on her casket in its entirety. I know that the pastor has been divorced for over a decade, and my mom isn't the type to be a mistress, but I can't help but think something scandalous might have happened. Did her cancer keep them apart, his relationship with God? His family?

Owen stops me in the middle of the parking lot, pulling me from my thoughts. He looks back at the church. "Are you saying your mom and the pastor were … together?"

"I'm saying they were *something*."

In the hot summer sun, Owen tugs me to his chest. "She must have had a reason for not telling you."

I'm sure she did. People keep secrets for different reasons. I know a little something about that.

We get in Owen's car and he cranks the air conditioning.

"Can I stay at your place tonight?" I shrug out of the cardigan I wore over my dress. "I don't want to be alone in my house right now."

"Actually," Owen says, turning to face me, "what do

you think about putting your stuff into boxes and bringing them to my place, then taking the stuff out of boxes and putting them in drawers and cabinets?"

My mouth drops open. I'm still reeling from the watch, and now this? "You want me to move in with you?"

"Yes." He purses his lips nervously.

I laugh. I don't know why but I'm laughing, and then I'm crying, and Owen pulls me into a hug and wipes away my tears.

"Of course, I'll move in with you," I say, sniffling. "I don't know why I'm laughing. Or crying. It's just a lot. This day is a lot."

He nods and then a nervous look creeps over his face. "I wanted to ask you something else ... but this day is probably not the time for it."

I frown. "Is it a good something?"

He nods, his eyes piercing into me.

"Well, then today is perfect for it because I don't want to remember this heavy feeling."

He takes my hand. "You know how you told me that your mom's last words to you were how much she loved being your mom and how much she loved you?"

I nod, getting teary-eyed at the memory. Dropping my hand, Owen reaches into his pocket and pulls out a slim ring box.

My eyes widen.

"Well ... your mom's last words to me were to give

me her blessing for us to marry..." He gulps. "If you'll have me."

A sob breaks through my throat and I feel it then. A small tingle up my arm, a presence in the car with us.

My mom.

"Yes!" I cry out and we crash together, kissing as my tears fall in a seal around our lips.

It's not as perfect as some may think this should be, proposing in a car at my mother's funeral, but it's perfect for me. It gives me hope in a future with Owen, a future I will have to navigate on my own, without my mother. It gives me faith that things are going to be okay.

Hah. *Faith.* Something I had with me my entire life.

That night, after unpacking most of my things and setting them up around Owen's house and in his dresser, I snuggle in beside him to go to sleep. Staring down at the huge princess-cut stone on my left finger, I smile.

What an emotionally draining yet also fulfilling day.

Owen reaches for me, his hand landing softly on my abdomen.

My abdomen.

My eyes flutter open, then close, and as I'm slipping back into sleep, I have a final, drowsy thought.

My period is late.

With everything going on with my mom, I never did get around to going on birth control.

Chapter 29

Owen

"Do you want to grab a beer after work?" Ace rounds the nurse's station, holding on to either end of the stethoscope that's slung around his neck.

"No can do," I answer, slapping the paper files I'm holding against the desk. "Today Autumn had all of her stuff sent to my house from New York. I gotta help her unpack."

I can't help the wide grin on my face. Fifteen-year-old me is pumping a fist in the air in excitement. Hell, twenty-eight-year-old me is doing the same.

I got the girl, the girl of my dreams. My future wife is Autumn Cummings. It still feels crazy to say.

Ace wrinkles his nose like he's just smelled rotten potatoes. "You're out of your mind. A girl tries to leave a toothbrush at my place and it's *sayonara*." He whips his hand around like he's waving goodbye. I know he's joking, he was happiest of all for Autumn and I. Even offered to throw us an engagement party.

"You'll change your mind one day," I tell him.

He shakes his head and pounds a fist against his chest twice. "Bachelor for life."

"Fifty bucks says one day you'll eat those words."

He throws out a hand. "A hundred says I never will."

We shake on it. Nurse Theresa stares at us from her spot behind the computer, wearing a low-key look that says, *I don't know how you two are doctors, because you're idiots.*

Ace takes one look at her expression and says, "Well, that's my cue to leave." He goes in the opposite direction I'm headed in, which is to my office to grab my things so I can leave the hospital.

When I get to my car, I send Autumn a message asking her if she needs me to pick up anything on my way home. She responds with a picture of some casserole cooking in the oven.

I know it won't always be this way. Next week Autumn and Livvie will start moving inventory into the new space at Tlaquepaque. She'll be interviewing potential employees, and Livvie will move down to Phoenix to be with her husband, leaving Autumn in charge of it all. But for right now, it feels like the domesticity I always wanted with her.

After pulling my car into the garage, I walk inside. The

place smells good, and it's not just the mouthwatering smells wafting in from the kitchen. There's a candle burning on a table, something that definitely wasn't there before. There are also new throw pillows on the couch, and a blanket draped artfully on the back of a chair.

"Welcome home," she says, her arms sliding around my waist from behind. She presses her nose into my back as she hugs me.

"Music to my ears." I loosen her grip so I can turn around to face her. Placing a finger under her chin, I tip up her face to kiss her. "You're beautiful." Her hair is piled messily on her head. She wears yoga pants, a tank top, and not an ounce of makeup.

She rolls her eyes as if she doesn't believe me.

"I have something to show you," she tells me, and her eyes sparkle like a clear night sky. "Follow me."

I do as I'm told, trying to guess what it is she has to show me. What if it's a floral comforter for our bed? I make a face, and I'm glad she's in front of me and can't see it. How am I going to tell her I don't want a floral comforter without hurting her feelings? I've never lived with a girl, and I'm kind of freaking out she'll want pink and flowers everywhere now.

Oh shit. What if this is our first big fight while living together? What if—?

Instead of going right into our bedroom, Autumn takes a left into an empty bedroom I have across the hall. My stress evaporates. She's probably making the room into an office for herself. That I can totally handle; she can floral the crap out of it for all I care.

I walk in and pause, trying to understand. Pieces of furniture are strewn around the middle of the room. In the corner by the window is a rocking chair. Beside it is a ridiculously huge stuffed hippo.

Hmm, not exactly the office décor I would imagine for her. I suck in a sharp intake of breath when my eyes land on one of the furniture boxes in the middle of the room.

It's a crib.

"I was trying to finish the crib before you got home, but they are way harder to assemble than you'd think." Autumn bites the side of her lower lip and watches me like a hawk.

My brain trips over my jumbled thoughts. All the weight leaves my limbs and I'm floating, except I'm not because I'm still here, standing in this ... *nursery?*

For a baby.

A *baby*.

Our baby?

The smile starts slow, somewhere down below my knees, then flies up, overtaking me like a flame to tinder. Head to toe, I'm beaming. "You're pregnant?"

She nods. Her teeth release her lip and she smiles the biggest smile I've ever seen on her face. Like me, her whole body is glowing.

"Holy shit. I'm going to be a dad." My hands run through my hair. "I'm going to be a dad!" I yell this time, for good measure. In my mind I see a small base-ball mitt, a gentle toss, a smiling boy or girl in awe as they've just caught their first baseball.

Autumn's palms are pressed together in front of her mouth and her shoulders are quaking with joy. I lift her in my arms, spin her around, then quickly put her back down.

"I'm sorry, did that hurt? Are you okay?" My eyes fall to her belly, looking for any sign that I've harmed her or the baby.

She laughs and puts her hand on my shoulders. "I'm not made of glass, Owen. I'm just pregnant."

"Say it again."

"I'm pregnant."

I kiss her, hoping the action shows her just how damn much I love her. She kisses me back, the kind of kiss that asks for more, but the timer in the kitchen interrupts us.

I hold the door open for her, but just as Autumn is about to step from the room she stalls. Her mouth widens in shock and my first thought is that it's the baby.

"What's wrong?" I ask, my hand going to her flat stomach.

She shakes her head, smiling. "Everything is fine. It's just ... I've been waiting to feel my mom again. Her spirit, you know? I felt her when you proposed, but then not again. But I think..." She glances back into the room. "I think I just felt her." Tears line her eyes and goosebumps run the length of my arms.

"She's telling you she's happy for you. For us." Most people think that doctors don't believe in God, that we are strictly scientific beings who can't conceive of a higher power.

Not me.

I've been in operating rooms, losing a patient on the table, only to have them miraculously come back after all medical options failed. I've even had a few patients who were riddled with cancer go into spontaneous remission without any chemo at all. I have no doubt Faith is looking over us with happiness right now.

Autumn nods happily, and seeing her so well adjusted, and content—and pregnant—makes my cheeks hurt from smiling so much.

That night, when dinner is finished and the sun has dipped below the horizon, we sit outside and stare up at the sky. I've pulled the outdoor couch to the middle of the yard and adjusted it so we can both lie down. I've got one arm wrapped around Autumn, and her head rests on my chest.

"Sometimes I think about what I'd be doing now if my mom had never called and asked me to come back here." She laughs dryly. "Probably the same exact thing I'd been doing for the past few years."

"Then I thank God your mom called you." I give her a small squeeze.

Autumn shifts, propping herself on an elbow and looking at me. "Do you think she knew?"

I'm confused. "Knew what?"

"Knew she was going to die? That this time would be the last time?"

"There's no way she could've known it for certain, but each repeated fight with cancer gets a little harder. She knew that, because I told her."

"I was so shocked the day she called me and asked me to come out here. I said yes immediately, without any hesitation. I knew it was going to require me to leave my job, my apartment, my life. And I knew it was going to land me squarely in your path."

I push a wayward strand of hair out of her eyes. "I'm surprised you didn't run screaming in the opposite direction."

She chuckles. "I think I always knew you were my eventuality. I just had to figure out how to move past everything that happened when we were young and find my way back to you."

"I know what you mean. I never could let you go either. I held on to it all, including the anger, until even that disappeared and all I had was an Autumn-sized hole in my heart. The moment I saw you in the kitchen at your mom's house, I wanted to grab you and kiss you until all your breath was mine."

"You can do that now." She lowers her face until the tips of our noses brush. "You can do that all you want."

"I can't take all your breath. The baby needs it," I remind her, lightly dragging my lips across hers.

Autumn laughs and it's the best damn sound in the world. "She doesn't need all of it."

"She?"

Autumn grins. "Just a hunch."

I kiss her then, but I hold back a little. Autumn knows I'm holding back, so she takes over. She takes off her clothes, lies beneath me, and asks me to make love to her in the dark, with only the stars as witnesses.

Loving Autumn is something I've been doing since I was fifteen. It's engrained into my thoughts, burned into my soul. It's what I'll be doing every day for the rest of my life.

Chapter 30

Autumn

NINE MONTHS later

Oh, the pain. The pain, the pain, the *pain*.

Waves of pain, starting at the top of my stomach and rolling down—like the worst period cramp, multiplied by seven thousand.

"Drugs," I demand, slamming a fist on the bed. The soft blanket absorbs the force. Definitely not the effect I intended to have.

Owen gives me a look I think is meant to be soothing, but it just angers me. "The anesthesiologist is with another patient right now. She'll be here as soon as possible."

I look around wildly for something to throw at him. There is nothing within my reach, and that's probably something the hospital has done on purpose. I settle for shooting daggers with my eyes. "You went to medical school—can't you do it?"

Owen smirks. "Not unless you want to be paralyzed."

I frown. If I'm paralyzed, I won't be able to feel pain, so maybe that would be okay.

The anesthesiologist sails into the room and I moan with relief. She gives me drugs and I tell her she's my favorite person in the world, which causes her to smile.

After that, the rough waters become smooth. I almost don't mind when Ace struts into the room with some chick traipsing along behind him. *Almost.*

"Who is that?" I ask rudely. I might be unable to feel the lower half of my body, but that doesn't mean I need someone I don't know witnessing me in this state.

Ace looks at the blonde in tow. "This is Felicia. My date."

I cross my arms. On a normal day, I like Ace. But this is not a normal day. I'm in labor. I do not need a crowd. When Owen asked if it was okay that Ace stop by after his shift in oncology was over, I said yes. I did not say okay to the blond girl who still hasn't spoken a word.

"Ace, are you planning on setting up a red and white checkered blanket on the floor in here? Maybe some wine and cheese?" I growl at him, glad to have a new target for my anger.

Owen snickers at my questions.

Ace's lips move like he's holding back laughter.

"You're the one who's having a baby on the same night I have a date."

Oh, I'm going to kill him. I already regret asking him to be the baby's godfather. I point to the door. "Just go."

The girl, whose lips I now believe to be sewn shut, blinks in surprise.

"Call me when the baby comes," Ace says to Owen. They shake hands, and even though I'm annoyed at Ace's single-man idiocy, I accept the gentle hug he offers.

He pats my huge belly. "Give her hell, kiddo."

"Out!" I roar, and Ace laughs, shuffling back through the door with his date. I meet Owen's eyes.

"Bye, Felicia," we say at the same time, then I laugh until I nearly cry. Maybe it helps spur the baby into action, because pretty soon after that the doctor checks me and declares me ready to push.

An hour later, Hudson Michael Miller comes into the world and a euphoric feeling comes over me. The moment my eyes land on him, an explosion of love blooms in my chest and it's like my heart has just grown a new compartment, this one made entirely for him. He is perfect, absolutely perfect, and I love him in a way I never knew possible.

When Hudson has been cleaned and checked by the doctor, he is given back to me. Owen hovers over us, alternating kisses between my forehead and the baby's. "We'll try for a girl next time," he says with a wink.

At my sixteen-week appointment, I'd spent all of ten seconds disappointed to hear my hunch had been wrong. Now, looking at the tiny face Owen and I created, I decide I don't care what gender is next in line for us. The longer I stare at Hudson, the more I think of the baby who never was.

"Are you thinking about it?" Owen asks, his voice low.

As hard as it is, I tear my gaze away from the baby who is here now. "Yes."

"Me too. And that's okay." Owen kisses my mouth, telling me he loves me, he loves us, he loves our story, as flawed as it may be.

It was a bumpy road filled with potholes and pitstops, but we got our happily ever after.

Epilogue

Autumn

TWO YEARS later

"TODAY, everyone, we have a very special guest for story time." I smile out to the small crowd of young children and their parents. Every Saturday morning, the back of the bookstore I co-own with Livvie transforms for story hour. We bring out chairs and trays of sliced apples and carrot sticks. And coffee for the parents. Can't forget the caffeine.

I bounce two-year-old Hudson on my hip. "Hudson's daddy is going to read to you!" I tell the small crowd. Hudson claps his hands and squeezes his chubby thighs in his excitement.

Owen joins me at the back of the room and kisses

my temple as I step away, settling onto a chair. Hudson climbs off me and runs back to Owen, who scoops him up and sets him down on his lap.

"Okay, everyone, remember how we show Mr. Owen we're ready to listen?" I call out, looking at all the toddlers, preschoolers, and young children. I snap my fingers, and the older ones do too. The younger kids follow suit, practicing the skill.

Owen is our most popular reader, and the discovery of his hidden talent was a happy accident. A parent who was supposed to read had the flu, so Owen filled in. That was eight months ago, and Owen has been on the regular rotation ever since. He does all the voices, ranging in pitch from a high shrieking princes in a castle to a low growling dinosaur.

Things with the store couldn't be better. Livvie is pregnant and enjoys running a financial advisor firm with her husband in Phoenix. She called me just yesterday to ask if I could give her little sister Luna a job. Apparently she married a German guy she met in Amsterdam after knowing him only a week. Then the second he got his green card, he split. Now she's twenty-two, divorced, and looking for a fresh start. I know about those all too well, and told Livvie I'd be happy to help. She arrives in Sedona next week.

As I sit back, listening to Owen, I absentmindedly rub my growing stomach. It'll only be a few more months until we meet our baby girl. This time, my hunch was right.

Owen reads, and Hudson sits still, enraptured by the story and helping turn the pages. Funny how when I returned home three years ago, I checked the weather before boarding my plane and thought about how nice it would be to have a similar, personal radar to tell me what was in store for me.

Would I have believed the radar if I saw all this? Probably not.

I wish every day that my mom were here to be a grandma to my kids. That will never happen, and it's up to me to tell them all about her. How she was a fierce mama bear, how she raised me as a single mother, how she fought cancer three times like a warrior.

Our daughter Makenzie Faith Miller will know why she carries that middle name.

Owen closes the book when the story is done, catching my eye, and winks. I smile back at him.

This is the life we always wanted together, and even though it took us longer than we thought it would to get there, we made it, and that is what counts.

We found our way home to each other. Thank God for second chances.

The End

TO STAY in touch with Jennifer Millikin join her newsletter and check out her other books here. www. jennifermillikinwrites.com

To stay in touch with Leia Stone join her newsletter and check out her other books here.

www.LeiaStone.com

THANK YOU!

A big thank you to our editor Lee, beta reader Megan and proofer Melissa. It takes a village to get these books in tip top shape, so thank you to our village! Special thanks to our ARC teams and amazing readers for letting our words occupy your heart. Biggest thank you of all to our families for being our biggest superfans.

Printed in Great Britain
by Amazon